PAINTBRUSH

Hannah Bucchin

PAINTBRUSH

ISBN print: 978-1-945519-10-9
ISBN ebook: 978-1-945519-09-3

Library of Congress: 2016954225

Cover design by
https://www.facebook.com/BlueSkyOverBoston/?fref=ts

Blaze Publishing, LLC
64 Melvin Drive
Fredericksburg, VA 22406
Visit us at www.blazepub.com

First Edition: July 2017

To Bop, who always knew I could do it.

CHAPTER ONE
JOSIE

Sometimes I close my eyes and imagine what a normal school morning looks like. The type of weekday morning routine seen on TV. Mom and Dad eating breakfast, teenagers rushing down the steps to grab some food off the table before skipping out the door to meet the bus. Parents watching their children go with an affectionate shake of the head—*those crazy kids*. A normal morning routine. A normal family. A normal life.

These are the thoughts that flit through my head as I watch an old woman doing topless yoga on my front lawn.

Well, not so much *my* front lawn as *our* front lawn. The collective front lawn of everyone who lives here. And not so much *watch* as *try to avoid* watching. But it's hard to avoid the spectacle when I'm sitting in the passenger seat of Mitchell's truck, which is parked in the gravel lot facing directly out over the lawn, the cabins, the community hall, and all the people in between.

People watching is a prime activity at the Indian Paintbrush Community Village for Sustainable Living. Especially early morning people watching. Paintbrush is a commune, a safe haven for mountain folk and hippies and eco-freaks and spiritualists and . . . anyone, really. Any lost soul Myra Gilligan, our founder, takes in. As a result, things are pretty bizarre around here. Julie, the naked old lady yogi, is just the beginning.

Which is why I can't focus on the battered copy of *The Princess Bride* lying open in my lap. People watching is so much more interesting. It's not even 7:00 a.m. yet, but already I see Myra crossing the huge expanse of green lawn from her cabin to the community hall. While everyone else at Paintbrush is just now stirring awake with the sun, Myra is already fully dressed and determined, a long gray braid bouncing down her back as she marches to the vegetable garden and begins yanking rhubarb plants from the ground. Who knows how long she's been up already. I'm not actually sure that woman ever sleeps.

At the far corner of the lawn, Ned emerges from his cabin. He shuffles out of his house, looks around discreetly, and hobbles his way off into the woods. He's almost eighty, and yet he still lights up a joint every morning like a teenage stoner. And he still thinks none of us can tell. Bernie, our other resident grumpy old man, cleans his rifle on his porch next door, a tobacco pipe hanging out of his mouth.

Joe, our newest member, paces back and forth in front of Mitchell's family's cabin until Carrie, Mitchell's mom, rushes out. They walk across the lawn, heads bent together. They're working on a project to bring a working garden to the local elementary school. Their latest obstacle involved the principal denying their proposal to bring twenty chickens to live in the schoolyard. Go figure.

I'm about to open the door and yell over to ask Carrie if Mitchell is ready, but the words die on my lips and I sigh as Libby ducks out the front door of my family's cabin.

Libby. She's dressed in all black—ripped black stockings, black combat boots, and a very tight, very short black dress. Appropriate for a rock concert, or a funeral, or maybe a funeral for a rock star. Not appropriate for eighth grade.

She dashes across the grass, dark hair flying behind her, gaze darting around the mostly empty lawn, probably to see if anyone notices her. They don't.

But *I* do. Libby doesn't see me until she's right in front of Mitchell's truck. She stops short and blinks at me. I blink back. But before I can open the door to ask her where, exactly, she's going this early in the morning, she squares her shoulders, grips her backpack, and runs right on by.

I crane my neck and watch as she clambers into a car idling at the other end of the parking lot. Before Libby's even fully inside, the car zips out of the lot and down the mountain road, out of sight.

I close my eyes and lean back against my seat. I'm graduating high school in a month. I'm the one who's supposed to be off getting into shenanigans, hopping into strange cars, and living it up. Not my little sister.

At least I have one sister who is nice and quiet. I gaze over at my cabin. Mae, Libby's twin, is probably still safe and asleep in bed like a normal fourteen-year-old. And I'm sure my mom is in there too, cleaning the kitchen and making breakfast, purposefully and cheerfully oblivious to the early morning disappearance of one of her middle schoolers.

I take a deep breath and shake off the annoyance with my mother, with Libby, with the perpetually late, still-not-here Mitchell. I may not have a normal morning. Or normal mornings, ever. But this place is home. And I wouldn't trade it for anything.

I go back to my copy of *The Princess Bride*. I'm rereading the first page when the driver's door bangs open.

"I'm late. I know I'm late." Mitchell grins at me as he launches himself behind the wheel. He chucks his backpack into the backseat.

"Cutting it kind of close this morning, aren't we?" I don't really mind it that much. It's a crisp May morning, the beautiful blue-green mountains stretch into the distance under the dusting of early morning sunlight, and I have my feet propped up on the truck's sticker-covered dashboard. It's kind of a nice morning to sit and wait and take it all in.

But I can't let Mitchell know that.

"Nah. We still got, what, twenty minutes till the bell rings?" He stuffs the key in the ignition, turns it once. Nothing. Then again. Still nothing.

"Yeah, and the drive takes thirty." I raise my eyebrows as he turns the key for a third time.

Silence.

He groans.

"Come on, baby." Mitchell closes his eyes and leans forward, gingerly placing his hands on the dashboard. "Don't do this to me. Just one more month. That's all I need."

I glance at the time on my phone. "Mitchell . . ."

He opens one eye and glares at me. "Josie." He gestures to the dashboard.

I sigh. "Fine."

I close my eyes and place my hands in front of me. My left hand rests on a sticker that reads *Hugs not Drugs*. My right hand rests on one that proclaims *My Scottish Terrier is Smarter than your Honors Student.*

We sit in reverent silence for a few seconds. After a long and dramatic sigh, Mitchell opens his eyes.

"Okay. I think she's ready." Slowly, he places his hand back on the ignition, and holding his breath, he turns the key.

With a sputter, the engine coughs to life. Mitchell pumps his fist in the air and smacks the steering wheel, and a loud *beep* echoes throughout the group of wooden cabins in front of us.

"Are you kidding me?" I say. "You'll wake everyone up!"

He throws the truck in reverse and backs out of his space, gravel crunching underneath his wheels. "It's almost seven. They're already up."

With a screech, he peels onto the road, and we are finally on our way to school. He happily pats the steering wheel as we speed along the deserted backcountry road, weaving our way down the mountain. "I knew she had it in her."

"You say that every morning."

He shrugs, and I shake my head.

Mitchell is kind of my best friend but also kind of not. When you're the only two kids growing up in a commune full of hippies and mountain folk, bonding for life just sort of comes naturally. My family joined Paintbrush almost thirteen years ago, when I was five and the twins had just turned two. My mom was only twenty-two then, basically a kid herself.

We were lost, and Myra found us—literally found us huddled together and asleep in our ancient minivan in a drugstore parking lot. Her wrinkled face was framed by crazy wisps of gray hair, she was draped in brightly colored scarves, her round eyes were a startling icy blue, and I remember thinking she looked like a witch. But when she talked to my mom, Myra's voice was low and warm and soothing, so when we followed her muddy truck up a winding mountain road, I wasn't scared. At the top of the road was a battered wooden sign painted in a deep forest green with the words: Indian Paintbrush Community Village. We unpacked our stuff into a tiny wooden cabin, and we never left.

The commune contained neither Indians nor paintbrushes. Myra named it after her favorite plant: a small red-orange wildflower that spreads over the mountains in the early summer. At that point, Paintbrush had been up and running for only two years, and there were only ten other members: two couples, two older men, and a family with one kid. That family was the Morrisons, and the little kid was Mitchell.

I glance sideways at Mitchell now. His flannel-covered arms tense as he grips the steering wheel, and his dark hair flops on his forehead as he mouths the words to the classic rock pumping through the radio. He's tall—a little over six foot— and even though he's kind of skinny, his arms and shoulders are broad from his time on the swim team. He's doesn't look anything like the little kid he used to be. The goofy little boy I met when I was six years old.

But then again, I don't look like that six-year-old girl anymore. We're eighteen now. Practically real adults. And high school is almost over.

I brace myself as we turn the corner, as the gray walls of North Mountain High come looming into sight. I steel myself for another long day of classes, another day crammed in those gray walls with hundreds of other kids. Lots of kids I know really love high school. Not the actual school part, but the part where they get to do something they love, like playing trombone in the band or sprinting for the track team or reading to little kids for community service club. High school is where people can find their place, when they can find out how to fit into the puzzle.

But I don't have a place, and I don't have a thing. All I know is that when I'm inside the school walls, the only place I really want to be is outside in the sunshine, gardening with my hands in the dirt, breathing in the fresh air.

Graduation is only a few weeks away. I repeat this in my head like a mantra. *Graduation is only a few weeks away. Graduation is only a few weeks away.*

Let's hope I can make it that long.

CHAPTER TWO
MITCHELL

The bell rings as I pull into a parking space outside school. "Just on time."

Josie shakes her head as she gathers her stuff. "Actually, you're supposed to be inside by the time the bell rings. Not standing outside in the parking lot."

I grab my backpack out of the backseat and slam the door. "Same difference. Plus, we're seniors. No one's going to give us a hard time when we're graduating in a month."

Josie makes a face at me as she weaves her long dark hair into a braid. "You mean no one's going to give *you* a hard time, Mr. Golden Boy. Not all of us are Advanced Placement, student council, swimmer stars."

"Yeah, but as long as you're with me, you're fine." I gesture to the empty parking lot. "I cast my golden shadow over everyone around me."

She shoves me as we hurry toward the school, but her mouth tugs up in a smile. "Whatever."

We step inside the front door and turn to separate. The hallways are almost empty; everyone's in homeroom by now. Josie hurries to the right, and I make a sharp left.

As she walks away, I call out over my shoulder. "Meet in

the parking lot at 4:30?"

"I'll be there." Her voice echoes down the hall. "Oh! I almost forgot."

I turn. "What?"

"Catch." She tosses a book to me, and I snatch it out of the air. "Finished it yesterday."

She jogs toward her classroom, her boots echoing on the hard, shiny floors.

I glance down at the book in my hand. *The Princess Bride.*

I smooth my hand over the worn, familiar cover and smile.

And then I look around to make sure no one's watching as I stuff it into my backpack as quickly as possible.

It's not that I'm embarrassed I like to read books. Or that I'm embarrassed to be seen with Josie. It's just that I've spent my entire life working so hard to be normal. I'm captain of the swim team, I plan pep rallies and dances, and I take as many advanced classes as my schedule will allow. So that one, I can spend less time at Paintbrush. Two, so people will know I'm a normal guy. And three, so one day soon I can get out of here—way, way out of here—and finally live a normal life. One that doesn't involve so much *spiritual sharing* and *communal energy*, or any other of Myra's scary catchphrases.

And an eighteen-year-old dude reading *The Princess Bride* for fun? It doesn't exactly fit with the whole Cool-Normal-Guy-image I'm trying to uphold.

And not to be a jerk, but neither does Josie. Which is probably why we don't hang out much at school. Or at all, really. I mean, people know that we know each other. They know we live in the same *weird hippie place.* But Josie looks the part. She has long brown hair that's always in a messy braid, and she either wears hiking boots and faded jeans and big flannels—real outdoor work clothes—or long flowing skirts and tie-dye shirts and ribbons in her hair. She has buttons on her backpack and she doesn't eat meat and she listens to the Grateful Dead. She looks like she stepped straight out of Woodstock.

And that's all cool and fine and whatever. It's just not me.

I stifle a yawn as I turn the corner down the hallway. I swear, every morning I'm already exhausted by the time I get to school. Trying to get ready in the morning and get out the door and on the road is like running the gauntlet. The insanity starts in my cabin, with my parents, who are so completely and blissfully in love with each other it's gross. No one should have to worry about walking in on their own parents making out. Or worse.

Then outside there's wrinkly old Julie doing her naked yoga thing on the front lawn. Every. Single. Morning. And I know the human body is a beautiful thing or whatever, but seriously. It's the last thing I want to see first thing in the morning.

Then I have to make sure to avoid Ned because he comes back from his early morning "nature walks" with a cloud of pot smoke hanging over him. I don't need any teachers eyeing me suspiciously, thinking I'm a stoner.

And those are just the usuals. There are always other people milling around too, smiley, huggy, chatty people who don't seem to understand I have school to attend. And that the start time is not really a suggestion so much as a hard and fast rule. Today it was Joe Jagger creeping around my house. Again. I'm not kidding—Joe Jagger. That's really his name. Joe arrived here six months ago, straight from the coast of California to "try the natural life, man." He's in his thirties, but his long blond hair and baggy shorts and tank tops scream teenage surfer dude. He's nice enough, but he tries way too hard. Like, the first time he met me, he got way too close to my face, looked right into my eyes, and told me I had a *righteous vibe*. He's like a caricature of a real person. And since he and my mom got paired together to work on some organic food initiative in town a few months ago, he's been following her around like a puppy dog. I can't wait for their project to be over. I've had enough of his *good vibes* to last me for a long, long time.

I know I sound whiny when I talk about Paintbrush. And that in the grand scheme of the universe, considering all the terrible and horrible lives I could be forced to live, mine is really not that bad. But still. I've lived with the same group of people, the same way, doing the same farming and work and community dinners since I was four years old. Since before I can even remember.

Which is why I can't wait for college. I accepted my offer of admission back in March, and I already mailed in my deposit, picked my dorm, and signed up for a meal plan. But last week, I decided that fall seemed too far away, so I sent out eight other applications for summer jobs in national parks. Now, being here at school, walking through the dim hallways and by the banged-up lockers is even more torturous than before, because I know I'm so close to a way out.

Mrs. Martinez has already started class by the time I walk

through the door. She raises her eyebrows as I slide into my seat, but she doesn't say anything. *Told you, Josie*, I think to myself. I glance across the room and make eye contact with Cord Cofax, my best friend, maybe my only real friend, from school. He crosses his eyes at me and sticks out his tongue, flopping his head to the side and playing dead. Mrs. Martinez clears her throat, glaring at him, and I press my lips together to keep from laughing out loud.

I flip open my textbook as I fight back my laughter. *I know the feeling, Cord.* Twelve years of schooling, almost completed. But it seems like these last few weeks are destined to drag on forever. And while our classmates are getting all sentimental and emotional, Cord and I are so over it. I'm ready to be done. I'm ready for a change.

I'm ready to move on.

CHAPTER THREE
JOSIE

I feel like I spend more time in the bed of Mitchell's truck than in the actual seat inside. Most days, I spend the hour or two after school lets out sitting in the back of the truck, reading or napping or listening to music and waiting for Mitchell to be done with swim practice or club meetings or whatever. It's either this or walk home, which takes two full hours and is basically all uphill. Or if we're being precise, up-mountain. So I almost always sit and wait.

Today the sun is shining, and it smells so good outside. Like pine needles and flowers and that delicious, warm, summer-is-almost-here kind of smell. I brought *Pride and Prejudice* with me to give to Mitchell. We trade books back and forth because there are no TVs at Paintbrush. We have to occupy our time somehow. I've been trying to read the first page for the past hour, but even one of my favorite books can't keep me from getting distracted by the chirping birds and blue skies.

I'm just getting back into the book when I hear the clatter of heels on cement moving toward me. I don't even have to look up to know what's coming next.

"Hi, Leah." I close my book just in time to see my best friend collapse in a heap on the pavement next to the truck.

"I'm dead," she announces from the ground.

I scoot myself over until I'm perched on the very edge of the truck, my feet swinging above the ground. I peer down at the jumbled mass of blond hair and textbooks and arms and legs below me. "No, you're not."

"Fine." Leah sits up and smooths down her dress, pushing her long hair out of her face. "But, I swear, Mr. Johanssen is trying to kill me." She reaches down and scoops her pile of books into her arms. "Do you see these? He assigned us reading from four different books tonight. Four. I tried to stuff them into my backpack, and it literally *ripped* at the *seams*."

I glance down at her backpack. It looks fine to me. Leah likes to use a lot of creative license with her use of the word literally.

"Think of how toned your arms are getting, though." I swing my feet by her head, and she bats them away.

"Do you always have to be so practical?" She sticks out her tongue at me, and I laugh.

My laugh falters as Emma Harris walks by, dark glossy hair blowing in the breeze like she's some kind of supermodel. Or at least she thinks she is. She narrows her eyes at me in a bona fide death glare—not even casual or subtle, but blatantly obvious and totally scary.

Leah follows my gaze. Her brow creases when she sees Emma. "What's her problem?"

I know exactly what her problem is: She's got a thing for Mitchell. Probably half the girls at school do. And of course, it might seem like there's something going on between us, with me spending all my free time in his truck and all, especially to people who don't know about Paintbrush.

But the truth is Mitchell just doesn't date. He hangs out and goes to parties, and if the gossip that floats around school is true, he's been known to have the occasional hook-up. But he says he's waiting until he can leave this town before he gets into anything serious. Nothing to tie him down.

And anyway, I could never have a thing for Mitchell. I know too much about him. I remember the time he got his head stuck in a yellow plastic bucket when we were six, and how his mom called him Mitchie until he was in middle school, and the time in fourth grade when he had the flu and threw up all over my shoes, and a thousand other completely unsexy things. There's no mystery there.

I glance down as Emma walks by, to avoid eye contact. She makes me nervous. But Leah glares right back, holding Emma's gaze until she's forced to look away.

"*Leah.*" I nudge her with my foot as we watch Emma's retreating back. "*God.* Do you have to be so aggressive?"

"Yes, actually. I do." Leah stands up and brushes herself off. "No one stares at my best friend like that and gets away with it."

I have to grin at that. As much as I hate confrontation, I love Leah's fierce loyalty. We've been friends since the sixth grade, when Mitchell and I stopped homeschooling at Paintbrush and started at the middle school in town. Her last name is Seely, and mine is Sedgwick, so we ended up sitting next to each other in homeroom. In all the ways I'm quiet, she's loud. She's fashionable and artistic and the center of attention, and I'm outdoorsy and earthy and happy to fade into the background. We're opposites, but it works. Like two pieces of a puzzle coming together.

A car beeps across the parking lot, and Leah hauls her backpack over her shoulder and stacks her textbooks in her arms, staggering dramatically under their weight. "Well, here I go."

I wave at the truck across the parking lot. Leah's dad sticks his head out and waves back.

"Tell your dad I say hi," I say.

"I will. If I can even make it over there."

"Has anyone ever told you that you're kind of dramatic?"

"I may have heard that before. Maybe once or twice."

Leah is the star of all the school plays. A born actress. Not to mention the only girl in a family of four rough and rowdy brothers. She probably gets told she's dramatic at least five times a day.

She traipses across the parking lot, wobbling on her high-heeled boots, and then slides into the passenger seat. I can just barely see the outline of her dad as he leans over and kisses her on the head, but it's enough for that twinge of jealousy to twist my stomach into a knot. Like always.

I'm dozing off in the sun when I hear a bang on the side of the car, close to my head. I sit up to find Mitchell smirking at me.

"Wake up, sleepyhead," he says in a sing-song voice. In one easy movement, he launches himself over the side of the truck and into the bed next to me. He lands in a graceful, cross-legged heap.

I shake my head. "I wasn't asleep."

"Oh. Sure." Mitchell watches me in amusement. "You were just reading with your eyes closed."

I make a face at him. "I was resting my eyes. And also avoiding glares."

"What glares?"

"The glares of every girl in school who happens to walk by and see me in your truck."

"Oh, come on," Mitchell scoffs. He props his backpack up behind him and leans back.

"You should have seen Emma Harris. Full on death glare."

He rolls his eyes. "And why would that be?"

"Because I get to ride home with the amazing Mitchell Morrison. Smile of a movie star. Boy next door personality. Body of a Greek god."

"Oh my god. Stop." Mitchell runs a hand through his hair and gazes up at the sky, his face turning red, a pink flush creeping over his cheeks. I grin. It takes a lot to make him uncomfortable, so it's like a special victory when it finally happens.

"You should just date someone," I continue. "Get it over with. That way the girls of North Mountain High will know you're unavailable, and they can stop torturing themselves."

"Or, you could stop being a crazy person and making up ridiculous things that have no basis in truth."

I hold up my hands in defeat. "Okay, okay. Just a suggestion."

I lean back next to him, and we both stare up at the blue above us for a second.

Finally, Mitchell sits up. "So. *The Princess Bride*."

I shrug. "It was okay."

His mouth drops open. "Are you kidding me?"

"Yeah. I am." I smile. "It was so good."

Mitchell shakes his head. "That's not even funny. Don't ever talk about my favorite book like that."

"Favorite book? Really? Last week *Watership Down* was your favorite book."

He crosses his arms. "I didn't say it was my favorite book *ever*. It's my favorite book *today*."

"Well, now it's your turn." I toss my copy of *Pride and Prejudice* onto his lap.

He picks it up and squints at the cover. "This is a girly book."

I cross my arms. "Why? Because it was written by a woman? Did I say that *The Princess Bride* was a guy book because it was written by a man?"

He cuts me off, laughing. "Whoa, whoa, calm down. You know I'll read it."

"You better." I check my phone and sigh. "We gotta go. It's almost 5:00. We can't be late again."

He groans. "Shit. I forgot it was Thursday."

I stand and hoist my backpack onto my shoulder and then reach down for Mitchell's hand and pull him to his feet. "Community dinner night. Your favorite night of the week."

He shakes his head. "Myra will be pissed if we're late again. She'll make us sit next to her and listen to her ramble on about the healing properties of plants."

I hop down onto the pavement. "I know. So let's go."

Mitchell's feet hit the pavement beside mine with a resounding smack, and he sighs. "Let's go."

CHAPTER FOUR
MITCHELL

We make it into the dining room right at 5:30, and the chaos is in full swing. Josie's mom, Layla, waves to us, and Josie jogs over to help set the table. It's a long wooden table dubbed The Meeting Place by Myra when she founded Paintbrush twelve years ago. Back then, it seemed ridiculously huge. There were only ten of us, and we would all crowd around one end while the other side stretched out to the opposite end of the dining room, long and shiny and empty. Now, there are forty or so members, and the table is full. So full, in fact, that we have to squish together way too close for comfort to make everyone fit. We bump elbows and knock stuff over during every Thursday night dinner. But it's all in the name of community. Or so Myra says.

The other main community room is the Sanctuary, the room next to the dining room. It's big and open, with huge windows and skylights. There are these old braided rugs Myra made forever ago that cover the floors, battered thrift store couches that are surprisingly comfy, plus a TV—no actual channels, but there is a DVD player. The sign on the door reads *The Sanctuary: A Place to Relax and Revel in Community and in Spirit*. I mostly use it to watch movies when I'm bored.

"Welcome, Mitchell!" Myra's booming, gravelly voice echoes over the scraping of chairs and banging of pots in the kitchen.

I turn to see her beckoning to me from the kitchen doorway, her hair in its signature long gray braid, colorful scarves draped around her shoulders. Myra is almost seventy-five, but she could pass for being in her fifties, easy, and she has the energy of an excited puppy. She has so much energy that sometimes just being around her makes me exhausted.

"Hi, Myra." I trudge toward her, but I'm forced to speed up as her waves get more and more frantic.

She grabs my arm as I reach her. "Thank god you're here. We're having an apple emergency, and we need your help. Wendy is nearly at her wits' end."

"An apple emergency?" I peer into the busy kitchen behind Myra. I can't really imagine what an apple emergency would entail.

"An emergency, a crisis, a fiasco. Whatever you want to call it." She pushes me forward into the kitchen. "See if you can't help Wendy salvage the meal. Before we all have to go to bed hungry." She strides away, toward Josie and her mom. No doubt trying to correct them on the right way to place silverware or something.

I head toward Wendy, who is humming to herself as she chops fruit in the corner of the kitchen and not at all looking like a person in the throes of an emergency. She's part of one of the young couples here. She and her husband Eric had their first baby a few months ago.

"Hi, Wendy," I say as I reach her. I lean into the nearby

sink and stick my hands under the warm water, lathering them with soap. "I heard there's something up with the apples?"

"Mitchell!" she exclaims. She wraps an arm around me and gives me a quick hug, like she hasn't seen me in forever. Even though I just saw her yesterday. A lot of people here are very touchy. "I'm making a fruit salad here. Want to peel and cut some apples for me?"

I grab a knife and the nearest apple and sink the blade into the top. The skin comes off in shiny, red peels. "Myra said it was an emergency."

"Well, I was originally going to make it without apples, but Myra thought that was a bad idea. And then I was going to put the apples in with the skins still on, but Myra said that's not a proper fruit salad. You know Myra. She thinks everything's an emergency."

I nod. "How's Lucy?"

Predictably, Wendy breaks into a huge smile. "She's beautiful, of course. So happy all the time. And I know it sounds crazy, but I think she might be starting to recognize letters already."

I don't know much about babies, but it sounds unlikely that Lucy, at five months old, is already learning how to read.

Still, I smile. "That's great, Wendy. I'll have to stop by and see her this week."

Wendy nods. "You sure do, Mitchell. Your mom was over playing with her just this afternoon."

Mom. I look around to find her. Usually she'd be here in the kitchen by now, humming with energy and activity and helping everyone with every little thing. But not today. I see

Dad, though, washing dishes at the far end of the kitchen. He catches my eye and gives me a grin, one of his classic, easy-going, ain't-life-grand type of smiles. I try to be annoyed by his constant enthusiasm for life, but it's too contagious. I wave.

My dad is actually pretty old for a dad, though he definitely doesn't look it. He hikes around and fishes and canoes and does woodworking and gardening and builds furniture, and basically anything else even remotely outdoorsy. Just last month, we celebrated his sixtieth birthday. He's toned and tanned, though, so he looks way younger. Maybe that's why my mom fell for him. They got married in their twenties, when they were both young corporate lawyers at this fancy firm in New York City. Then, they had me, and shortly after that they had some kind of big epiphany about right and wrong and the meaning of life and purposeful living or whatever. Moral of the story: They sold their big apartment and fancy car and basically all their belongings, gave all their money to charity, then moved down to the North Carolina mountains and joined Myra's new communal village. Now they spend all their time farming and working at Paintbrush and occasionally teaching business classes at the local community college for a few extra bucks. And being blissfully, annoyingly happy.

People are finishing the preparations and starting to move plates out to the dining room. I finish the last few apples and toss them in the bowl, and Wendy whisks it away. As I'm making my way out behind her, my mom breezes into the kitchen, looking a little disheveled. Her usually sleek ponytail has stray hairs falling out, and she's biting her lip.

"Mom?" I tap her on the shoulder, and she jumps, like I

yelled in her ear.

"Oh, Mitchell. Hi, honey. How was school?" She kisses the top of my head while scanning the kitchen.

"It was fine." I follow her gaze in time to see my dad bustling into the kitchen from the dining room, whistling. When he sees my mom, his face breaks into its usual giant grin. He loves her so much. Gross.

"There you are, sweetie. I was wondering where you'd got to." He strides over and wraps his arm around her, surreptitiously grabbing her butt in the process. I pretend not to see. Mostly because I wish I *hadn't* seen.

My mom pulls away as my dad leans in for a kiss. "John. Wait."

He pulls back. "What's wrong?"

She sighs and slips out of his grip. She opens her mouth to say something and then glances at me.

"What?" I ask.

She pauses and shakes her head. "Nothing. I just . . . Can we all talk? After dinner? Just the three of us?"

My dad nods. "Of course."

She looks at me. "Mitchell?"

"Uh, yeah." I roll my eyes. "Considering we do that every night."

My dad furrows his brow and places his hand on my mom's arm, but we're interrupted by the dinner bell before he can say anything.

Out at the Meeting Place, most of the seats are already taken. I grab an empty chair a few seats down from Josie and across the table, sandwiched between Ned and Maddie

Macpherson. Maddie is around eight years old, one of the younger kids here at Paintbrush, and she's part of the enormous Macpherson family—one of seven kids. She wears glasses and has very severe bangs and is overall very studious. She's like a mini-adult. Last week, she beat me at a game of chess in an embarrassingly short amount of time.

My dad is across the table from me, and my mom is all the way down at the other end. Families are supposed to split up during community dinners, for the sake of *bonding with the community* and *making connections with those you might not know as well.* Myra's words. My mom is sitting next to Joe Jagger, deep in conversation, her brow creased, her mouth moving a mile a minute. Joe nods slowly as he listens, his floppy blond hair swinging into his eyes. *God.* Dude needs a haircut.

"That sheep needs to be sheared," comes Ned's grumbling voice from beside me. I turn and find that he's looking at Joe, too.

"Hi, Ned," I say.

Ned jabs his fork in Joe's direction. "When I was his age, we always figured that boys with hair like that were playing for the other team. If you know what I mean."

Maddie leans around me to look at Ned, pushing her glasses up on her nose. "Like in a game of baseball?"

"Yep," I say quickly, at the same time that Ned says, "Not like a game of baseball. Like the game of love."

Maddie frowns. "I don't get it."

"Not that there's anything wrong with that," Ned continues. "People do what they like, and that's the way it should be. No one telling you what to do or what not to do with your own life. Especially not the government."

"What about the government?" shouts Bernie, a few spots down. I swear he can't hear a thing when I'm talking to him a foot in front of his face, but he'll hear the word government from a mile away.

"A bunch of dirty thieves, the whole lot of them," Ned shouts back. "Goddamn criminals, stealing people's guns and money and rights. Stealing our freedom right out from under us!"

"That's not a very nice word." Maddie frowns at Ned.

Ned leans over me to look at her. "I'm sorry, sweetheart. But sometimes, you have to use bad words when bad words are due. If the situation calls for a goddamn, you've got to say goddamn. If it calls for shit, well, you just gotta grit your teeth and say shit. If it calls for—"

"How was school today, Maddie?" I interrupt before things get too graphic. Who knows what Ned was about to say to this poor eight-year-old girl.

Before she can answer, a *ding ding ding* rings from the head of the table. Myra stands at her spot and taps her glass, and the chatter dies away. This is a part of the Thursday night Community Dinner ritual: Myra's toast. It's the same damn toast every Thursday night. I glance a few seats down the table and meet Josie's eyes and then pick up my butter knife and pretend to stab myself in the chest. She gives me a slow head shake, like she's disappointed in me. I place my fork back in its place and properly fold my hands, and she gives me a thumbs up.

Myra raises her glass with a very dramatic flourish and a typically solemn face. "This Thursday evening, as every Thursday evening, we give thanks—to each other, for the time and loving care that went into the preparation of this meal; to the earth, for doing such fine work in growing the food in front of us; and to whatever god or spirit or energy that gives each and every one of us this miraculous gift we call life."

There are a few mumbles of "hear, hear" around the table, and then everyone starts in on their food. It's the same speech every week, with a few words altered here and there. I like to pretend that it annoys me, but really, it's kind of comforting. I'm pretty sure I've never missed a community dinner my whole life, except maybe once or twice when I was sick. I could probably recite Myra's speech for her, word for word. Sometimes, there's something kind of comforting about that. And sometimes I want to cover my ears and hum loudly so I never have to hear it again.

There's a bustle of activity around the table as people start talking and laughing and filling their plates. I'm about to scoop a heaping spoonful of quinoa-beet salad onto my plate—a specialty of Layla, Josie's mom—when I hear my mom's voice from the end of the table.

"Actually, I have an announcement. Well, *we* have an announcement." She stands, pulling Joe up with her.

I shovel a huge spoonful of quinoa into my mouth. It's not a cheeseburger, but it'll do.

"I know that announcements are normally made after dinner, but I've been thinking about this one for a while, and it just couldn't wait." Her hands are shaking, and she opens and closes her mouth like she can't remember what she was going to say. But just when it looks like she might sit back down, Joe slips his arm around her shoulders.

And it doesn't look so much like friendly support as . . . weird. Just weird.

I put my fork down and glance at my father in the seat across from me. He's watching her with his usual look of total adoration. Hanging on to her every word.

"I know this is slightly unorthodox—well, very unorthodox, actually—I don't think it's ever been done before here, but what I'm trying to say is . . ." She closes her eyes. "Joe and I have fallen in love. We've fallen in love, and we'd like your blessing to continue to live here, together." She takes a deep, shaky breath and looks directly at my dad. "We hope that you—that *all* of you—can understand."

CHAPTER FIVE
JOSIE

The Meeting Place is dead silent for a moment. Forks paused in midair, blank stares, the air buzzing with nervous tension. After a few seconds, Lucy, the baby, breaks the silence with a happy shriek as she cheerfully smashes her tiny baby fists into a banana on the table in front of her. And after this comes a sound much worse—John, Mitchell's dad, still wearing a bemused smile on his face, asking in a heartbreakingly quiet voice: "Carrie?"

A tear slides down Carrie's face, Joe's arm around her shoulder tightens, and chaos lets loose as everyone around the table begins to chatter and ask questions. Everyone is looking at John, who is looking at Carrie helplessly. Who is looking down at her plate.

Across the table, Libby and Mae start whispering to each other, but my mom shoots them a look that quiets them right back down. They may be polar opposites, but my twin sisters are still fourteen-year-old girls, and they can't resist discussing gossip like this.

I glance down the table at Mitchell. He's staring at his mom, his mouth set in a hard line, his expression blank. I try to catch his gaze, but he won't look at me.

"Okay, people. Okay!" Myra stands, banging on her glass with a fork. "Everyone settle down."

Everyone falls silent. Carrie is full on crying now, tears falling down her cheeks, shoulders shaking. Joe is rubbing her back. And John is watching this happen with a crestfallen look on his face. Not even angry. Just devastatingly, horribly sad.

Myra clears her throat and takes a breath, like she's not quite sure how to proceed. "Well. This is . . . hmm." She clears her throat again. "This is something, I think, that calls for a community meeting. Not just dinner talk." A few people murmur their agreement. "So, I propose that everyone take tonight to think about . . . this. And what this means for our community." Her voice gets stronger as she gains momentum. "And tomorrow evening, after dinner, we'll have a community meeting to discuss and vote on whether we find this situation acceptable. Agreed?" Around the table, people nod. "Anyone opposed, say so now."

The silence in the room is thick and heavy until Mitchell stands up suddenly, his chair scraping the floor with an angry screech. He makes eye contact with his mom, his lip quivering, and then turns and strides out the door.

The door swings shut behind him. Without thinking, I stand and follow him.

But I'm too late. By the time I get outside, Mitchell has started running. I slow to a stop as he reaches his truck and hurls himself into the driver's seat. The lights flash on, the engine sputters, and Mitchell peels out of the gravel lot and down the road, out of sight.

CHAPTER SIX
MITCHELL

I'm driving too fast, but I don't really care at this point. I know I should pull over, stop, and take a few deep breaths. But right now it feels so good to be hurtling along these empty mountain highways, my lights illuminating the dark trees lining the road, the yellow lines speeding by under my wheels. I focus all my energy and thoughts on driving and try not to think about what just happened.

I was sitting there at the Meeting Place; I watched my mom talk and heard her words and saw her cry, but it still feels like something I made up in my head. And I know it was Joe standing next to her—fucking *Joe Jagger*, of all people—but in my head he keeps turning into my dad as I play the night over and over again. It's like my brain just can't help it, because it's always been my dad standing next to my mom. It's always been them standing there together, my whole life. Other people's parents fight or argue or whatever. Like Cord's parents, who've been sleeping in separate bedrooms for the past ten years. But that was never my parents. My dad would kiss my mom's neck as she cooked dinner, so gently that I'd have to look away. My mom would massage my dad's shoulders after he came in from gardening. They spent nights reading together and going over lesson plans for their community college business classes. Which they taught *together*. Just last month, I walked into the house after school to find them making out in the kitchen. My dad grinned at me apologetically and called out a "Sorry, kiddo," as I walked right back out the door, but they made no move to stop me. They loved me, but not enough to give up some alone time together. The way they are together—perfectly matched, in tune with each other, happy and comfortable and in love— that's the way I've always imagined myself being with some girl, someday. They're soul mates.

So this can't be real. It just can't be. I zoom around a sharp corner, and my grip on the steering wheel tightens as I picture my dad's face—helpless, confused—and my mom's tears. My knuckles go white, and my face burns with anger. She had no right to cry. She's the one doing this to us. She has no right to make it about her.

I press a little harder on the gas pedal, urging my mind to stop thinking and just drive. I whip around another corner when, all of a sudden, I'm face to face with a deer in the road.

I slam on my brakes and skid, hard. The truck makes an ear-splitting squeal as it slides to a stop just a few feet from the deer.

I lean on the wheel and gasp for air. *Holy shit*. When I look up, the deer is still in the road, blinking her deep brown eyes at me. And when I look closer, I see another set of four legs, spindly and small, peeking out from behind her. Her baby. He—or she, I guess, but a childhood spent watching *Bambi* has me always thinking all baby deer are boys—peers at me from behind his mother. After a gentle nudge, he skitters away on his scrawny legs and disappears into the dark tree line. The mother watches him until he is safe in the forest, blinks at me one more time, and then disappears after him.

I lean back against my seat and close my eyes for a second. That was close. Way too close. I take a deep breath. *Jesus, Mitchell. Calm the fuck down.* Slowly, carefully, I take my foot off the brake and ease myself down the road. At a legally acceptable pace this time. I can't let this get to me. I need to be okay, for my dad.

And to show my mom that she can't hurt us like this.

The blinking green clock on my dashboard reads 1:30 by the time I pull into the Paintbrush lot. The gravel crunches under my wheels, and my truck wheezes to a stop and falls silent as I pull the key out of the ignition.

I slump in my seat and examine the cluster of cabins in front of me. Most are dark, of course. Almost everyone at Paintbrush gets up by 7:00 a.m. to farm or work or go to school or whatever, so bedtime is generally early. But one cabin is still lit up, awake and waiting. Mine, of course. It could just be my dad. I can picture him sitting alone at our kitchen table, drinking his free trade coffee and crying, probably. But my mom might be there too, hashing out details or divorce plans or god knows what with him.

Either way, I definitely don't want to be there right now.

I reach into the backseat and feel around in the dark before yanking out an old blanket I use for sitting outside sometimes. The blanket is an ugly neon orange and smells kind of like dirt, but it's just worn enough to be super soft. I tuck it under my arm, hop out of the truck, and then make my way to the community building. I'll sleep in the Sanctuary tonight.

I'm halfway there when I hear a voice in the darkness that scares me so bad I almost trip.

"Mitchell?"

I turn around. There's Josie sitting on a wooden chair on her front porch. She's wearing flannel pants and a huge oversized sweatshirt decorated with coffee mugs that reads *I Love You a Latte*—a sweatshirt that a grandma on vacation would wear. She nervously twists her hair with her fingers.

"Josie?" I take a step closer. "Why are you awake?"

She stands. "I wanted to see if—" She pauses and shakes her head. "Couldn't sleep."

"Oh. Okay." I gesture behind me to the Sanctuary. "I'm gonna try and grab some sleep. Since we have to be at school in"—I check my phone—"six hours and all."

She nods. "Right."

But she doesn't move.

I shift from one foot to the other in the awkward silence. "So . . . see you tomorrow morning?"

"Sure. Of course." She flicks her gaze down at the ground and then right at me. "Mitchell? Are you okay?"

I open my mouth to say yeah, sure, that automatic *yes-of-course-I'm-fine*, but something stops me. Specifically, that something is a lump in my throat that's rising dangerously close to my mouth. I take a deep breath.

She reaches out and squeezes my arm. For one second I'm terrified she's going to hug me, because I know that if she hugs me—if anyone hugs me—I'll totally lose it. And even though we've known each other a long time, we're definitely not at a sobbing-in-each-other's-arms level of friendship. At least not anymore. But it's just her hand, resting on my arm, and her voice, warm and soft in the chilly night. "It'll be okay."

I nod. She drops her hand. And then I'm walking away, through the door of the Sanctuary, and slipping onto the hideous green-and-white checkered couch that rests against the wall next to the fireplace. But it isn't until I'm finally settled under my blanket that I hear the far-off creak of her cabin door opening and the gentle thud as it closes behind her. It's the last thing I remember before I fall asleep.

CHAPTER SEVEN
JOSIE

I can't sleep all night. I blink at the ceiling, listening to Mae's soft, even breathing and Libby's occasional sleepy mumblings from the bunk bed on the other side of the room. My mom didn't want me to wait up for Mitchell—she insisted he'd be gone hours, probably, and that I shouldn't waste any sleep—but I finally convinced her I was fine on the porch and that she should go to bed. I just kept replaying the look on his face—hard, angry, and so un-Mitchell—and I knew I wouldn't be able to sleep until I made sure he was okay.

But of course, I couldn't think of anything useful to say. *It'll be okay.* Basically the most cliché and least helpful thing I could have thought of. I might as well have said *everything happens for a reason.* Or, *it's not your fault.* Or maybe, *sometimes people just fall out of love.*

That last one always gets me. People act like some relationships just . . . fall apart. They weren't *meant to last.* It's a *mutual* thing. The relationship *ran its course.*

But in real life, that's total bullshit. It's never totally mutual. It's never for no reason. And it's always somebody's fault.

Like with my mom and dad. Before we lived at Paintbrush, we lived in South Carolina, all five of us together in a small town in a small house that I barely remember. I don't remember much about my dad either, but I do remember his voice: gravelly and slurred and loud, scary loud, echoing off the walls when he came stumbling home every night.

The night we left, he had one two many glasses of whiskey at dinner. And when my mom quietly told him that maybe, just maybe, he shouldn't be getting behind the wheel that night, he gave her a black eye. I watched it happen from my chair at the end of the table—the way his fist flew through the air, the way she went down, hard, her head knocking on the floor with a resounding smack. The way the twins immediately started wailing, their identical toddler shrieks filling the air. How he slammed the door so hard it felt like the whole house might shatter into pieces.

The hitting and yelling wasn't that unusual. What was unusual was how my mom sprang into action as soon as she could stand back up. She scurried around the house, grabbing every piece of clothing and beat-up toy and stray shoe she could find. She packed us up in our battered minivan, stuffed our clothes in the trunk, and drove until she couldn't drive anymore. We spent the night curled up in the minivan in an empty drug store parking lot. Libby and Mae got the only blanket in the car, being toddlers and all. My mom and I huddled together under a pile of sweatshirts and shivered ourselves to sleep.

Myra found us, so our story sort of has a happy ending. But my mom never called the police, never contacted her parents, never called him or confronted him or got closure of any kind. She may have escaped, but it's clear who had the upper hand.

Leah does the same thing in all her relationships. She dates boy after boy after boy, so I've seen breakup after breakup after breakup. The last boy, Evan, a cross-country guy, said he had to break up with her to "focus on his marathon training." Before that there was Brady, from the next town over, who completely and totally stopped calling out of nowhere. Just disappeared into thin air. And then there was Jackson, who straight up cheated on her with Melissa from the swim team. Leah caught them in the act—in Jackson's car behind the football stadium, with the windows all fogged up. Literally. The windows were all steamy. Leah likes to tell the story of how she wrote *it's over* in the steam on the window, tapped on the glass to get their attention, and then cheerfully flipped them both off.

Leah is perky and positive and smart, and she doesn't let much get to her. She cries for a few hours, but she always bounces back. "Relationships end," she'll tell me with a shrug. "It's not a big deal."

It is a big deal, though. In the end, someone screws someone else over. Someone comes out winning, and someone else loses. That's what happened with John and Carrie tonight at dinner. That's what happened with my mom and dad for sure. That's what happens with Leah and all her boyfriends. It could be as messed up as my dad throwing a beer bottle at my mom's head, or as simple as Evan ditching dinner plans with Leah to go on an impromptu run. Someone has the power. Someone else doesn't. And feelings always get hurt.

My eyes fly open before the first rays of sunlight even hit the cabin window. By the time I leave the cabin, I'm jittery, like I drank six cups of coffee despite the fact that I barely slept last night. I'm nervous to drive to school with Mitchell, to see him so sad and hurt, and nervous that I won't think of the right thing to say. I'm also too nervous to eat. I stick a banana in my backpack for later.

I trudge toward the truck in the early morning sunlight, early like usual. But when I get closer, I see Mitchell already sitting in the driver's seat. He never beats me.

I open the passenger door cautiously, racking my brain for something meaningful to say, when I catch sight of Mitchell's broad grin.

"Good morning, Josephine!" he calls out cheerfully. He reaches over and grabs my bag from me, pushing it into the backseat. "Need a hand?" He waggles his fingers toward me, offering to help me into my seat.

I stare at his hand. "I'm good, thanks."

He shrugs. "Suit yourself."

Mitchell twists the key in the ignition as I pull myself into the passenger seat. The truck shudders to life before my door is even fully closed.

"Ready to go?" he asks.

"Um, sure," I say, glancing at the clock on the dashboard. "I mean, school doesn't start for, like, forty-five minutes, so we'll be a little bit early, but—"

"Early! You and me? Who ever heard of such a thing?" He grins as he throws the truck in reverse and peels out of the lot. "Mrs. Martinez might actually die from the shock." He pushes the radio on as we start down the windy mountain road. Sugary pop music fills the car with a thick bass line that makes it hard to think.

I stay quiet as Mitchell hums along to the music. Glancing at him sideways, I see he's wearing his outfit from the day before, just with a different t-shirt that I'm pretty sure I saw crumpled up in the backseat yesterday. That would explain the wrinkles. And his hair is a little damp—but more like a splashing-your-hair-with-water-to-get-it-to-lie-flat type of wet, rather than an actual shower.

If I'm being honest, he doesn't look too great.

"Mitchell?" I ask.

He doesn't hear me over the music—at least, he acts like he doesn't hear me.

"Mitchell!" I try again, louder.

He turns the music down, only slightly. "What's up?"

I take a deep breath. "I just wanted to tell you that I'm really sorry about what happened last night. I know that doesn't help things, but I wanted you to know. And if you ever want to talk, I'm, you know, here for you. Or whatever. And also if you—"

"Josie." He's smiling, but his shoulders are tense. "That's really nice and everything, but I'm fine. It is what it is. No use talking about it." He waves his hand in the air, like he's pushing it all away. All his problems. Right out of the truck's slightly cracked window.

"Are you sure?" I don't know why I keep pushing. Mitchell is not really a *feelings* guy. But somehow, this seems important. "Because I feel like tonight, at the meeting, it's going to be hard to pretend—"

"I'm not going to the meeting." His smile is fading now. Not so much a smile as bared, gritted teeth.

"What?"

"I'm not going."

"Mitchell, come on. You have to be there."

"No. I don't." He shakes his head. "It's her problem. Not mine. If she wants to run off with some asshole, fine. Whatever. But I'm not going to be the one to deal with it."

He stares straight ahead, eyes on the road. Fingers tapping away on the steering wheel.

I sigh. "Okay."

He nods. "Okay." He turns the music back up, flips on his turn signal, and we pull into the school parking lot.

A few hours later, I'm at lunch with Leah. Or Lunch with Leah, as I sometimes capitalize it in my head, because it always feels like a big event, a show. Normally Leah's stories are the ones that take over. Some crazy drama from her huge redneck family that always sounds like the plot of a reality TV show, or a story about a boy—half the time blissfully romantic, half the time tragically heartbreaking. But today it's me telling the story, and Leah is the one listening with wide eyes and a dropped jaw.

"Oh. My. God." Leah leans across the greasy cafeteria table toward me, her silky hair falling in front of her face dramatically. "Out of all the people living up there with you in hippieville. Surfer boy?"

"Keep your voice down." I glance at the tables around us, each overflowing with students, but everyone is too absorbed in their own conversation to notice us. Our high school serves two whole counties, so even with four lunch periods, the cafeteria is bursting to the brim with students. All over people are digging in brown paper bags and chomping on chicken nuggets, talking and laughing and yelling and milling around on the sticky tile floor. What I'm really worried about is Mitchell hearing our conversation. He has the same lunch period as Leah and me, but he sits so far away that most days I don't even see him.

"Sorry." Leah lowers her voice. "I just can't believe it. Poor Mitchell. Poor, beautiful Mitchell."

I roll my eyes and take a bite of my PB—all natural!— and J—locally canned, strawberry—sandwich—delicious homemade bread courtesy of Libby. Leah has always had a crush on Mitchell. Well, a pseudo-crush. She doesn't know him well enough to actually have feelings for him, but she just obsesses over how adorable he is from afar. I'm glad they don't actually know each other, though. Whenever Leah has crazy drama, I can tell Mitchell about it. Whenever something happens with Mitchell, I can confide in Leah. I trust them both not to tell other people, and this way I don't have to keep any good stories or big secrets all to myself. It's not like gossiping, really. Sometimes, I just need other people to help me carry my thoughts around.

Leah pops a potato chip into her mouth. "So, how'd he take it?" she asks between crunches.

I shake my head. "Not good. He's usually the happiest guy I know, you know? I don't think I've ever seen him mad before. And he was definitely mad."

"That's crazy." Leah swallows and nods over my shoulder. "Looks like he got over it pretty quick, though."

I follow Leah's line of vision. There's Mitchell, all the way by the far wall of the cafeteria. He's laughing and talking to a redheaded girl I don't even know—*what's her name?* Katie, or Kathleen, something with a K—and leaning against the wall.

Behind me, Leah crunches on another chip. "Look at that lean. So casual. So chill."

Mitchell leans over and plucks an apple from K-girl's hand, dangling the apple high above her head. Of course she's eating an apple—just an apple—for lunch. She squeals and jumps for the apple, hands outstretched, bumping into Mitchell and laughing.

I turn around and face Leah. She's still entranced by what's going on behind me. "Josie, you're missing it! Now she's tugging on his shirt." She furrows her brow and puts on her best movie announcer voice. "Will tiny redhead girl be successful in her quest to take back what is rightfully hers? Or will the apple be tragically lost, forever, never to be returned . . . ?" She pauses and shakes her head. "Never mind. He gave it back."

"Well. He was upset last night, at least."

Leah licks the last chip crumbs from her fingers. "He's probably still upset. You know Mitchell. He never flirts. Always friendly, always warm, but respectably distant. A perfect gentleman. The guy every girl wants but none can have. If he's flirting with some random girl, in the cafeteria, where God and everyone can see him, there's definitely something wrong."

I steal a carrot off her tray. "Says the girl who's never even had a conversation with Mitchell."

Leah shrugs. "Yeah, but you talk about him so much. At this point, I probably know him better than his own mother."

I cross my arms. "I don't talk about him that much. We're not even that close."

Leah picks up her tray and stands, raising her eyebrows at me. "Favorite food: lemon garlic chicken. Favorite band: Rolling Stones. Favorite color: blue. But like faded blue jeans, not navy. Favorite movie—"

"Okay, okay. Jesus. I get it. I'll never even speak the name Mitchell Morrison again."

She grins. "Now you know I wouldn't want that."

She turns and heads toward the garbage cans, long hair bouncing behind her. Leah has perfect, shiny, naturally blond hair, the kind of hair that makes girls hate her when they don't even know her. It's like a beacon of light in the cafeteria crowds.

Before I follow her, I glance one more time toward the back cafeteria wall and see redheaded K-girl sitting with a group of her friends. But Mitchell has disappeared.

CHAPTER EIGHT
MITCHELL

I skip my last two classes of the day and go sit in my truck. I need a nap, and I need it now. Between barely sleeping last night and working so hard all day at being Happy Fun Mitchell, I'm exhausted. My eyes kept drifting closed in English class this morning, even though we were discussing *Macbeth*, which I love—though I would never tell anyone that. Plus, Cord passed me a note in the middle of class that said *you look like shit*. He included a smiley face, but still. I decided that skipping this afternoon would probably be for the best.

I wish I could just go home and crawl into my bed. If I time it right, I bet my dad won't even be there, so I could slip under the covers and be asleep before he comes back for the day. I wouldn't have to answer any questions. But I told Josie I'd give her a ride home, like always. For the first time ever, I feel annoyed about it. It's not just the fact that I have to wait, and I'm so damn tired. But I know she's going to press me to talk about stuff I am so not in the mood to talk about.

So I paste a pleasant expression on my face as she slides into the passenger seat an hour later, even though my smile muscles have been pretty much stretched to the breaking point all day. Forcing a smile can be surprisingly painful. But maybe if I just keep grinning like an idiot, she won't ask me any questions.

"*Macbeth* is boring," Josie complains as we drive. We have the same class and same teacher, just at different times.

"How can you say that?" I shake my head. "It's about murder and ghosts and witches and shit. It's like a horror movie. Just from a long time ago. And that you read."

"Fine. Then the way Miss Martinez explains it is boring."

She's kind of right. Miss Martinez is young, like really young—twenty-three years old or something. But she's so tiny she could pass for a freshman. It's her first year, and she's so intimidated by us that she doesn't do anything all class but ask us questions she clearly found online after a *Macbeth Discussion Questions* Google search.

When I pull into the gravel Paintbrush lot and still no discussion of my feelings has come up, I think I'm home free. But then Josie opens the door, hops out of the passenger seat, gathers her stuff, and looks up to see me still in the driver's seat, truck still running.

Her long braid falls over her shoulder as she squints at me. "What are you doing?"

I shrug. "I'm going to go hang out at Cord's house for a while." Cord and I don't actually have plans to hang out, but I know if I call him up and tell him I'm coming over, he'll be fine with it. He lives up in this luxury *cottage*—which is actually a huge mansion with an incredible view of the mountains—and his parents own this fancy real estate company and are never home.

Josie eyes me suspiciously. "Okay. But you'll be back by 7:00, right? For the meeting?"

I exhale, loudly, like I've been holding my breath all day. Maybe I have. "I told you. I'm not going."

"But it's *your* family. Have you even talked to your dad yet? Or your mom?"

I roll my eyes. I can't believe she's being so pushy. It's not like her. "My mom is the last person I would have talked to. She's the last person I'll ever talk to."

"But what about your dad?" Her voice is soft but firm. "He could really use you right now."

A pang of guilt twists in my stomach at the thought of my dad sleeping all alone in the cabin last night. But then I shake my head. "I told you. Not my problem."

Josie crosses her arms. "Mitchell. Would you just think for a minute? You have to come back tonight—"

"No," I cut her off, loudly. "I don't." Josie's eyes widen, but I can't stop. She's voicing everything that's been tumbling around in my head all day, so my answer comes fast and angry. "I don't have to come back tonight. And in a month, after we graduate, I don't have to come back *ever*. I'm so sick of being in the same small place with the same people. Every single fucking day is the same. This shit with my parents is just icing on the cake." I grip the steering wheel with white knuckles, even though the truck is in park. "I'm just waiting for the day when I can get out of here."

My face flushes from everything I just said, from the anger thumping in my chest and humming through my veins. Josie takes a step back, like I pushed her away. She bites her lip, and an awkward silence hangs in the air between us.

I let go of the wheel and slump back against the seat. "I'm sorry. I'm just upset. I didn't mean it."

"Yes. You did." She looks at the ground.

I don't try to convince her.

"The truth is . . . I have a date tonight," I hear myself saying. Maybe this will distract her. "So I'm going to Cord's to get ready for it."

Her head snaps up. "Really?"

"Yes, really. But thanks for the tone of surprise."

She blushes. "No, that's not what I . . . It's just that you don't date."

"I date," I respond automatically.

She's right, though. I don't really date. I hang out with girls, whatever that means. Sometimes I kiss girls at parties. But I figured dating wasn't worth it until I was ready to have something real. Something like my parents.

Today, though, when Katrina Rossi was all over me at lunch—like she has been for the past few weeks—I figured, what the hell. I'll be leaving for college soon, so it's not like anything serious is going to happen. I might as well have fun. Plus, it's a distraction from everything shitty that's happening here.

Josie's still looking at me with her arms crossed. I sigh. "I'm being serious. I promise. I'm meeting Katrina at Bobby Jenner's party tonight. You should come," I add spontaneously.

I know she'll never come—Josie's not the partying type—but hopefully she'll see my invitation as a gesture of goodwill. A peace offering. An olive branch.

"Maybe," she replies, with a tone that says *I would never come to that in a million years.*

"You should," I say. "It starts at 9:00, but I'll probably be there around 10:00 or so."

"Fashionably late." She smirks.

"I'm nothing if not fashionable."

"Your truck's still running." She points to the dashboard. "If you're gonna go, you should probably go."

"So it is." I focus on the blinking gas light on my dashboard. Maybe if I stare hard enough at the tiny red lever hovering above Empty, Josie will focus her very intense gaze somewhere else. "Well, I should head out."

"Bye." Her tone is a little cold, like maybe she's still mad at me. She shuts the door and walks away.

As I'm pulling out, I glance over my shoulder to see if she's watching me. But she doesn't turn back.

I crash on the couch at Cord's house for a couple hours. He has a home theater in his basement, and it has this huge, circular comfy couch with about a thousand pillows and a down comforter. I only know it's down because sometimes I find these tiny little gray feathers on me after I take a nap on it. Which I often do.

I wake up to something wet on my cheek. When I open my eyes, Cord's three tiny white dogs are licking my face, and Cord is sitting by my feet, grinning at me.

"Wake up, Morrison! It's almost party time." He flicks my

leg. "And you definitely need to shower before we leave. If you know what I'm saying."

I rub the sleep out of my eyes and look at him. He raises an eyebrow.

"I'm saying you look terrible," he adds.

I throw a pillow at him. "Dude. I get it." I sit up and stretch my arms. "Can't you just shake me awake like a normal person? Do you have to set your little rats on me?"

Cord's jaw drops. "How dare you." He scoops his three dogs into his arms. They start licking his face instead. "You should consider yourself lucky to be awoken by these guys. The three most noble dogs in the world."

"When I walked into your house today, Moe was peeing on the front rug."

Cord sighs. "So he was." He puts them down and they scamper off in a little herd, tripping over one another and yipping at nothing. "But Rafiki and Julie Andrews would never do such a thing. So two out of three's not bad."

The fact that Cord's dogs are named after one of the three stooges, an animated Disney baboon, and the star of *The Sound of Music* is pretty bizarre but also totally fitting for Cord. He lives in the giant mansion but dresses like he's homeless—homeless chic, he tells me—drives a fancy sports car but volunteers as a big brother at the local elementary school, loves old musicals, smokes more weed than anyone I know, obsessively reads classic novels and comic books, and knits. And with all this weird, weird behavior, he somehow manages to attract the attention of girl after girl after girl.

I'd never think of myself as the type of guy to be friends

with some disgustingly rich kid. But when I met Cord freshman year in gym class, and he came out of the swimming locker room dressed in full on scuba gear when everyone else was wearing the required red bathing suit and white t-shirt, I knew I'd be friends with him. We hang out with the same crowd of athletes and student council and all-around involved people at school—they like me because I'm fun and easygoing, and they like him because his *fuck-it* attitude is both hilarious and contagious. But we both know that while those people are our acquaintances—people we occasionally have fun with on weekends and at lunch—our friendship is different. No bullshit, no games, no drama. It's real.

I hop in the shower while Cord gets ready. His bathroom is like a hotel bathroom, with fancy soaps lining the counter and a giant shower with three different nozzles that I can never quite figure out. When I get out, I wrap myself in this enormous fluffy towel. I like being in Cord's house, but not just because of all the fancy stuff. It's just nice to be able to escape sometimes into a world that's so totally different from Paintbrush. In every possible way.

I told Cord all the stuff that happened yesterday when I first got here. He listened to it all and nodded—and didn't say a single word. And at the end, he clapped me on the back, and all he said was, "It definitely sounds like you could use a party." Which was the perfect response, and also why he's my best friend.

We leave the house at 9:30. I'm driving, and Cord is next to me smoking a bowl to get himself "in partying mode." I'm dressed in jeans and a plain black t-shirt. Cord is dressed in cut-off jean shorts—"Jorts!" he announced happily—purple socks that go halfway up his shins, an orange tank top with a giant T-rex on the front, and a visor. He looks like a country club golfer who went off his meds. But somehow, it works.

We're walking up the front lawn when Cord nudges me. "Aww. Mitchell's first date."

I roll my eyes. "Right."

But I guess it kind of is. I've never made plans to meet a girl anywhere before. I'm really not that excited about it.

Hopefully when I see Katrina, I'll change my mind.

CHAPTER NINE
JOSIE

It's not as weird as I thought it would be, being at this party. Being in Bobby Jenner's house, of all places. Bobby is this hulking football player who wears camo shirts and keeps a rifle in his trunk. Just in case he spots a deer to kill while he's driving around, I guess. I had health class with him last year, first period. He came in late one day, and when the teacher asked what his excuse was, he pulled a squirrel skin out of his backpack—still kind of bloody—and stapled it to the wall. He's a treasure.

And, of course, exactly the kind of guy Leah would date. Which she did, for a few weeks sophomore year. Though the relationship clearly wasn't meant to last, they somehow managed to remain friends. So when I texted Leah after the big Paintbrush community meeting and asked if she knew anything about this party, I shouldn't have been surprised when she showed up on my doorstep thirty minutes later.

I've been holding this red plastic cup in a death grip for the last few minutes, but I'm starting to relax. Leah alternates between scanning the room for cute boys and babbling on about my family.

"I swear, if I tried to leave the house the way Libby was

dressed tonight, I'd be dead. Not just dead—I'd be buried already. Six feet under the ground, with my mother shoveling dirt on top of me and hollering about hell and damnation." She tosses her hair over her shoulder.

"It's been like that for the past couple months. Everything she leaves the house wearing is either tight to the point of breaking her ribs or completely see through. She might as well drape herself in plastic wrap and call it a day." I take a sip of the warm punch in my cup and immediately wrinkle my nose. Gross.

"And then when your mom asked where she was going, and she just said *out*? And your mom said *have fun*? That's the part where I would have gotten locked in my closet."

"And your mom would call up all her church friends and ask them to pray for you. Like that time she caught you looking at Cosmo in the grocery store."

"You better believe it." She sighs. "I wish I had your mom. She didn't even ask us where we were going. My mom practically interrogated me."

The party is getting louder as more people arrive. There are lots of familiar faces, but no Mitchell.

"Weirdly enough, talking about my mom and her lack of parenting skills is not what I want to do on a Friday night."

"Okay, okay." Suddenly there's a gleam in her eye. "Then we'll move on to finding a guy for you."

"Leah, no."

Leah yammers on about the merits of this boy and that one as I study the room over her shoulder. Leah's been begging me all year to come to parties with her—actually, all last year too—but parties like this aren't my thing. I'd like to pretend that it's because I'm too cool for them. But really, it's more like they intimidate me. I've never had a drink before—unless a sip of Ned's homemade moonshine once counts, which basically tasted like poison. I don't really feel cool enough for parties like this.

But weirdly enough, as I stand here in Bobby Jenner's house, holding a cup of some warm liquid that tastes like a thimbleful of fruit punch mixed with an entire barrel of vodka, I don't feel out of place. Earlier Leah and I were chatting around the keg with Janie Summers, who Leah knows from band. They both play the flute, and Janie seems really nice. And I recognize a lot of kids from my honors classes. Across the room, Ted Perkins from my calculus class waves to me and starts to make his way over. It's not just cool kids here, or even kids who think they're cool. The house is packed, but everyone's really just hanging out. I don't feel like I stick out. I might even fit in.

At least, that's how I feel until I make eye contact with Mitchell as he walks through the front door. And he doesn't exactly look happy to see me. In fact, the look on his face seems to ask me: What the hell are you doing here?

CHAPTER TEN
MITCHELL

I can't believe she's actually here. Not like it's the worst thing in the world or anything, I'm just really surprised. Josie always seems so disdainful of high school shit like this. When we kind of parted ways at the beginning of high school, I always thought she was cooler than me. Like she didn't need to validate herself by coming to parties like this, the way I need to. Seeing her here, surrounded by red plastic cups and dressed up cheerleaders and the distinct smell of cheap beer . . . it's weird, but I almost feel disappointed.

And, truthfully, I feel kind of bad. I invited her here, a place she's never been before, full of people she doesn't know, and I wasn't even here when she arrived. Like I threw her to the lions. She even looks kind of out of place somehow, in a strange way that I can't quite put my finger on.

Also, who's the guy she's talking to?

I realize I'm staring at her and then notice that she notices I'm staring at her, and that she's staring back at me. I snap out of it and wave, but she turns away. Weird.

I start to make my way over to her through the crowd, but before I even take two steps, a tiny red blur detaches from the crowd, launching at me and throwing her arms around my neck. Whoever it is has a surprisingly strong grip, and she also smells like fruity body spray. And alcohol. She really, really smells like alcohol.

"You came!" Katrina exclaims. She leans back a little bit but keeps her arms around my neck so that our faces are very, very close. Her eyes seem like they're trying to focus on my face, but apparently it's too much work, because then she just closes them and sways in place.

"Of course I came." I gently try to untangle myself, prying her arms off me and lowering them to her side. "I said we would meet at the party."

Her eyes flutter open again. "And here you are!" She reaches toward me in what looks like an attempt to run her fingers through my hair, but she ends up just poking me in the eye.

I immediately clap my hand over my eye. Shit, that hurt.

"Oh no!" Katrina gasps, horrified. "I am so, so, sorry, Mitchell."

"It's okay," I say. I try to smile at her, but I think it comes out as more of a grimace. Probably because of the throbbing pain.

"I know what'll make you feel better." She flutters her eyelashes at me, and I'm very concerned about where exactly she thinks this is going. The girl can barely stand. But then she exclaims, "A drink! I'll get it!" and stumbles away.

I watch her go and sigh. *So that's how this night is going to go.* I'll stay and keep an eye on her for a little bit, make sure one of her friends is sober and planning to drive her home. And that'll be it.

I want to be disappointed, but I'm really not. Last week at lunch I heard her tell someone that her favorite book was something called *Total Loser: Revenge of the BFF Clique Part Two*. That should have been a sign that we weren't meant to be.

It's too bad, because I could really have used a distraction tonight. And with Josie here, it's going to be hard to avoid all the things I'm trying to avoid.

I glance around. Where is Josie, anyway?

I find her in the kitchen, still talking to that same guy, Ted Perkins. He's one of the few in our class heading to an Ivy League next year. So we'll both be in New England for college. For some reason, watching him talking and laughing with Josie, this thought annoys me. Before I know it, I'm standing next to them. Like my feet have been programmed on autopilot.

"Hey, Ted," I say, smiling.

I reach out my hand and he grabs it, bro-style. Josie eyes me warily as she takes a sip from a red plastic cup.

"Mitchell!" He grins back and motions toward Josie. "Do you know Josie?"

I grin at her. "Yeah, we know each other."

She glares at me over her cup. Yep, definitely not happy with me interrupting her conversation.

"Actually, that's why I came over here." I look at Josie. "Any chance you could spare a minute? I've got a question about English homework."

"Dude!" Ted shoves my arm. "It's a Friday night. No school talk."

"Just a quick second, I promise."

"Okay, okay. I was about to go get a refill, anyway." Ted looks at Josie. "You want one?"

This guy is really annoying me now. *She is perfectly capable of getting her own drink,* I think to myself. *Not that she* should *be drinking.*

But Josie just smiles politely back. "I'm good for now, thanks."

Ted nods, tipping his red cup back and gulping down the dregs of his drink as he turns and heads toward the back porch, where I'm guessing the alcohol is. Smart move on Bobby's part, trying to minimize the mess from spills by sticking the drinks outside. Though if I know Bobby, it was probably just a fluke. He's not exactly a forward thinker.

Josie crosses her arms. "What?"

I frown. "What? I came over here to say hi."

"Then why did you make up a lie about homework?"

Good question. And I don't have a good answer. I can't exactly say *Ted Perkins was annoying me for no good reason.*

So I say the first thing that pops into my head. "How'd the meeting go tonight?"

Josie's face softens at this. And I actually feel a little bit of tension leaving my chest and shoulders as I ask the question. I've spent the whole night so far actively not thinking about what may or may not have happened tonight at Paintbrush. It's been exhausting.

Josie's voice is quiet as she speaks, so I have to duck my head to hear her over the party noise. "Myra and everyone else thought that it was really up to your dad to decide what he wanted. So they decided to give your mom and Joe a trial month of living together and staying at Paintbrush. And at the end, we'll have another special meeting and your dad can decide whether he's okay with it or whether he wants them to go."

I let this sink in. As much as I hate to admit it, it makes sense. Myra might be a crazy person, but she's a good leader. I wonder what my dad will choose. I know what I want him to choose.

Like she's reading my mind, Josie adds, "Your dad spoke, too, just something really short. He said he thanks everyone for respecting his space and his feelings, and that once he gets a chance to talk to you in person, he'll be able to make more sense of it all."

The guilt twinges in my stomach again, rising up in me like a wave. I texted him today to tell him I wouldn't be home tonight, so it's not like he doesn't know where I am. But for all his hands-off parenting approach, I bet he's still worried. My mom has texted and called me about a thousand times today. I haven't answered her at all.

I open my mouth to ask more questions when a body crashes to the floor in front of me. *Katrina.* I reach down to help her up, noticing that her knee landed right on top of Josie's toes. To her credit, Josie doesn't say anything, even as a grimace of pain spreads across her face.

"Sorry, Mitchell," Katrina says when she's upright again. Her mascara is a little smeared, and her face is all flushed. She totally ignores Josie, who backs up a few paces with an amused expression on her face. "I got you a drink. But on the way back, I drank it."

Katrina looks so genuinely ashamed. She hangs her head, like she's admitting to first-degree murder instead of drinking a cup of disgusting warm punch that I wasn't going to drink anyway. It's terrible, but I have to physically stop myself from laughing at her. I look up to see if Josie's laughing, too. But she's gone.

I was ready to leave this party before it even started. Katrina fell asleep on a couch around midnight. I didn't know a girl so tiny could snore so incredibly loud. I tucked her in with a blanket and then made sure one of her friends, Katie Everett, was looking out for her. Poor Katie. She was apparently the DD for Katrina and her whole group tonight and, as a result of being the only sober one, has already cleaned up vomit twice, broken up a catfight, and untangled an earring from a sobbing girl's hair. Katie is in for a long night.

I was looking around for Cord to tell him it was time to leave when I spotted him talking to Josie across the kitchen. I've been watching her all night, out of the corner of my eye, in case she needed saving. But she was talking and laughing with different people all night, people I didn't even realize she knew. Watching her now with Cord, I realize she doesn't really look out of place. I must have underestimated her. I actually don't see her much outside Paintbrush, so maybe I just wasn't used to her in this type of setting. To me, Josie is Paintbrush and Paintbrush is Josie. One without the other throws me off a little bit. With her long hair out of its braid and flowing around her shoulders, wearing a pink shirt that matches the pink glow of her cheeks, she actually looks really normal. Well, not normal. She still sticks out. But not in a bad way, I guess.

Something brushes my arm, and I turn to see Ted standing beside me. He's looking at Josie, too.

"She's cool, right?" He nods at Josie.

I don't know what Cord is saying to her, but he looks pretty intense. I nod, hoping Ted will drop whatever stupid thing he's about to say. This is not a conversation I want to have right now.

"I might ask her out," he continues. He takes another sip of his drink, spilling some down the front of his polo shirt.

"Really." I glance at him. It's not a question, but he takes it as one.

"I know. I never thought of her like that either. But tonight, I realized she's kind of hot."

My annoyance with Ted is back in full force. *Please stop talking*, I think.

"She's just so . . . quirky." He beams, like he's pleased with himself for coming up with the word.

"*Quirky*?" I roll my eyes. I can't help myself. This guy is such an idiot. "Next you'll be telling me she's a free spirit. A dreamer. The kind of girl who skips around barefoot and braids flowers into her hair." Incidentally, Josie does spend a lot of time barefoot, but that's not the point.

He shrugs. "Maybe she does."

"Quirky is such a cop-out. Like, 'everyone else thought this girl was just a big weirdo, but then I came along and *found* her.' Like you're the first guy to ever notice her. She's a person, not a rare species or a dinosaur bone or something. It's not like you made some kind of *discovery*."

He holds up his hands, and more drink sloshes to the ground. "Sorry, dude. I didn't realize."

I stare at him. "Realize what?"

"That you and her were a thing. Or that you have a thing for her. Or whatever."

"We don't. I just—we're friends. I just thought—" I'm sputtering. I force myself to pause, to take a breath, and then I force myself to smile. "Sorry, dude. Way too much to drink. I don't even know what I'm saying."

He laughs, a too-loud drunk laugh, and slings an arm around my neck. "We've all been there, right?" He drains his drink and then holds it up. "And speaking of."

He stumbles back outside, presumably for a refill that he certainly doesn't need. When I turn around again, I see Josie and Cord face to face. Literally. Their faces are touching. My face goes hot. They don't even know each other.

Josie must be wasted.

CHAPTER ELEVEN
JOSIE

Cord Cofax has his forehead pressed against my forehead, and I am ready to go home.

I did what I came to do, which was check on Mitchell and tell him about what happened at the meeting. Now it's past midnight, and more and more people are drunk, which means the party is getting messier and messier. Katrina is passed out on the couch, her hair in a mass of tangles around her head. Bobby and a few guys from the basketball team keep having rap battles. None of them should rap. None of them *can* rap. It was funny about an hour ago. Now it's just annoying. I would probably find it funnier if I was drunk, but I'm still holding the same cup of punch Leah handed to me when we first arrived, and it's still mostly full. She warned me not to drink much because it's so strong. She's off somewhere, deep in conversation with Diego, this super hipster guy from our class. They're probably bonding over the fact that they both bring tea, still steeping, in little mason jars to class in the morning. When most normal people bring coffee in a thermos, or a Styrofoam cup. And the way they both wear scarves in the summer and glasses with thick black rims when I suspect they both have perfect vision.

Plus, there's Ted. He keeps following me around, trying to talk to me. He's nice enough, but he keeps getting closer and closer when he talks, and a few minutes ago he put his arm around my shoulder while we were talking about our football team. I told him I had to use the bathroom just so I could get away. But as I was leaving the bathroom, I got cornered by Cord, Mitchell's best friend and the strangest guy alive. And now here we are, standing in the middle of the kitchen and talking about Mitchell.

Cord's eyes are red and a little bleary, and his overly intense stare is really freaking me out. "I'm just saying, Mitchell is my best friend," he says. For the third time. He's definitely had too much to drink. And he smells so much like weed, exactly the way Ned and Bernie smell after they go on their daily *nature walk* every afternoon at two.

"I know." I nod to get the message across, and our foreheads bump. I figure his fuzzy brain could use all the help it can get right now. It's funny how this is Mitchell's very best friend, and yet we've never actually spoken before. I always assumed that while I knew who Cord was, he didn't know much about me. Apparently, I was wrong.

"And I don't think he's doing too hot. With this thing with his mom."

So Mitchell did tell Cord. Mitchell won't talk to me, but at least he's talking to somebody. "I know."

"So we need to keep an eye on him," Cord whispers. His face is so close to mine that I have no choice but to look straight into his eyes. His very bloodshot eyes. His voice is a whisper, but the loudest whisper I've ever heard. Anyone within a ten-foot radius could hear us for sure, if they were actually paying attention. "You and me. We gotta watch out for him."

"I think Mitchell's pretty good at taking care of himself," I whisper back.

Cord shakes his head. "That's just what he wants you to think. That's what he wants everyone to think."

I lean back a little to consider this, when I feel a hand on my arm. I look up to see Mitchell. And he does not look happy.

"Come on. We're leaving."

Ten minutes later, I'm in the truck with Mitchell and Cord. Don't ask me how I got here, when I was supposed to get a ride home with Leah. But Mitchell acted like he had to leave *right then*, like there was some kind of emergency, and like I just *had* to come with him. So I went and found Leah—sitting on hipster boy's lap, of course—told her I had to leave, and made her promise to get home safe. She hadn't had a single sip of alcohol, so I figured it was fine. And then I made my way out to the truck, where Cord insisted I take the front seat so he could lie down in the back.

Now he's back there, lying face down and humming the *Pirates of the Caribbean* theme song for no apparent reason. Meanwhile, Mitchell and I are sitting in the front seat, in a silence that could be described as awkward at best and angry at worst. And I have no idea why. So I just look out the window.

"Are we there yet?" Cord mumbles from the backseat.

"No," Mitchell and I respond simultaneously. I peek over

at him, but he keeps staring ahead.

A few minutes pass in silence. Then: "Are we there yet?"

This time, just Mitchell answers. "Dude, no. You'd know if we were there yet, because I'd have dumped your drunk ass on the front lawn and driven away."

Cord laughs and then hiccups. With a groan, he pulls himself into a sitting position and leans over the driver's seat and nuzzles his head onto Mitchell's shoulder.

"You're such a good friend," Cord slurs.

I expect Mitchell to shove him off. But instead, his face softens a little, and he shakes his head. "You're damn right I am."

When we finally pull into Cord's driveway, Mitchell puts the truck in park and jumps out to help Cord inside. As he's sliding out of the backseat, Cord puts a hand on my shoulder. It would be a nice gesture, except his hand is kind of sticky, like he spilled beer on it.

"Remember what I said," he stage-whispers to me.

"I'll remember," I whisper back.

Mitchell groans. "What exactly did you say that needs to be remembered?"

"Not for your ears, young Mr. Morrison," Cord proclaims as he stumbles out of the truck and across the lawn. "Highly classified information. Me and Josie are keeping it on the down toe."

Mitchell frowns. "What?"

"I think he means down low," I say.

Cord points at me. "Agree to disagree."

Cord falls twice on his way across his enormous front yard,

and then he takes off his left shoe and throws it in the bushes because "it's itchy." Mitchell finally manages to corral Cord into the dark house by offering him a piggyback ride. The house is huge, but it looks pretty empty. Either his parents are asleep, or they're out of town. Either way, it seems like a lonely place to spend the night. But then again, Cord's probably too drunk to notice.

After a good fifteen minutes, Mitchell hops back in the truck. He throws it into drive and pulls away.

"Is he okay?" I ask.

"He'll be fine. I made him throw up and drink a glass of water. He was asleep in his bed when I left. Nothing worse than usual."

I nod. "Good."

We drive in a thick silence. I lean my forehead against the window and watch the trees rush by. Sometimes I can see little eyes blinking at me from the forest—raccoons, possums, deer. Sometimes I'll even see bears. I like to think of these forest animals, living their whole lives in the quiet nighttime while all us humans are asleep.

Finally, I turn toward Mitchell. "So, do you want to tell me what the big emergency is?"

He keeps his eyes on the road, hands at ten and two. "What are you talking about?"

"You tell me. The reason I just *had* to leave the party with you, instead of waiting for my ride with Leah."

He pauses, like he's considering his words. "Because I had to leave. To take Cord home. And I couldn't leave you there like that."

I frown. "Like what?"

"Drunk."

I snap my head around to stare at him. Is he kidding? I cross my arms. "What are you talking about? Do I seem drunk to you?"

"I saw you. You had a cup in your hand all night."

"First of all, why were you watching me?" Does he think I'm so socially incompetent that I need a babysitter? "I can handle myself. Second of all, it was the same cup all night. Which I took, like, three sips out of. That stuff was disgusting."

"Oh." His tone is genuinely surprised. But then he shakes his head. "Well, it doesn't matter. Everyone else was drunk. I didn't trust Leah to get you home."

"It doesn't matter whether or not you trust Leah. I trust Leah. She didn't have anything to drink all night."

He sighs, an exasperated sigh, like he's so done with this conversation. "Fine. But there's no use talking about it anymore. It's over. We already left."

"Oh really?" My face flushes. "Just because I'm not the golden boy of North Mountain High, just because I don't usually go to parties like this, doesn't mean I need your protection, Mitchell. I'm not some pathetic social leper who can't handle herself."

"I never said you were."

"Actually, you kind of did."

"Jesus. Fine." He pulls over suddenly, onto a big grassy patch on the side of the road. I know where we are—on the mountain road on the way to Paintbrush, about twenty minutes away. Sometimes kids from Paintbrush ride their bikes down here to play pickup soccer in the big grassy clearing surrounded by woods. They get picked up afterward, though, instead of biking home. The mountain is a bitch to walk up.

"You want me to turn around? Go back to Bobby's house so you can find Leah? Since I ruined your party and all." He glares at me, arms crossed, car in park.

I'm so tempted to make him turn around, but the truth is I really don't want to go back there. I'm ready to get to sleep in my own bed. But I hate that he's putting me in this position. My face is hot, my arms are crossed, my hands are shaky. I hate confrontation. And it's extra weird because this is so different from the normal cheerful, joking, not-a-care-in-the-world Mitchell that I've always known. This is touchy, mean, I-don't-know-what-he's-thinking Mitchell. And since our contact is usually limited to car rides and Paintbrush stuff, this whole night has felt like some kind of parallel universe. And honestly, I'm ready for it to be over.

Finally, I shake my head. "Just keep going."

He smirks, pleased with himself. But as he reaches for the gear to put the truck back in drive, the engine shudders and dies.

CHAPTER TWELVE
MITCHELL

This can't be happening. I turn the key again and again, but there's nothing, not even a sputter. I frown at the dashboard. *What the hell?*

And then I remember. Gas. My truck's been running on E since this morning. I meant to stop and get gas after the party, but in my rush to get a drunk Cord and what I thought was a drunk Josie home, I totally forgot. *Shit.* I lean back against the seat and close my eyes.

"What?" Josie asks.

I open my eyes to find her peering at me, concerned. Even after I've been such a dick to her, she's still concerned about me. It makes me feel even worse. "We ran out of gas."

"Oh."

We sit in silence. Josie fidgets in her seat, biting her lip.

"So?" she asks after the silence has stretched on long enough to make us both uncomfortable. "What are we going to do?"

"What time is it?" I sit back up.

She pulls her phone from her pocket, but the screen stays black. "I don't know. My phone's dead."

I pull mine out and glance at the screen. "It's two in the

morning."

"Well. We're, what, twenty minutes away from Paintbrush? We could call someone to come get us, I guess."

"Like who?"

"I don't know." She sighs. "My mom doesn't have a car."

"I know."

"And I'm assuming you're not really in the mood to call your parents," she continues.

It's too dark to see much of her, just the outline of her hair down around her shoulders, her pale skin that glows softly in the moonlight. I can't see her face to know what she's thinking.

"I'm sorry," I say, slowly. "But I really, really don't want to call them."

She nods. "Okay."

She doesn't push it, and for a moment I feel so grateful that I don't have to explain it to her. I know my parents would come get us. But I don't want them to feel like I need them. Not right now.

"We could walk," I suggest half-heartedly. "It would only take us . . ."

"At least an hour," Josie responds. "All uphill. In the dark. There's no way I'm doing that."

I laugh, a real and genuine laugh, for the first time since last night. "Thank god. I was trying not to be a baby about it, but I really do not want to come across a bear at night."

She nods. "Agreed."

"So." I clear my throat. I want to word this in the least awkward way possible. "I guess we're sleeping in the truck until morning?" I meant to word it as a statement, but it comes off as a question. Like we really have another option. I just don't want her to get the wrong idea.

But her response is quick and confident. "I guess we are. In here? Or in the back?"

Of course she wouldn't get the wrong idea. This is Josie. Josie, that I had mud fights with when it rained. Josie, who watched *Bambi* with me about a thousand times, when it used to be the only movie we had at Paintbrush. Josie, who taught me how to tell if a tomato is ripe enough to be picked. We might not be as close as we used to be, but she's still the same girl.

"We could spread out more in the truck bed," I tell her. "I have enough blankets to keep us warm." I blush. Why am I blushing? I'm glad she can't see my face turning red. "Not us, together. Separately. I have enough blankets for us to each have our own. So we can be warm. By ourselves." I sound like a maniac.

She looks at me like I've lost my mind. "Okay, weirdo." She reaches into my messy backseat, grabs a loose sweatshirt and an armful of old quilts, and hops out of the truck.

A few minutes later, I've laid a tarp down on the bed and a blanket on top of it, made pillows out of the old clothes I had stuffed in the backseat, and handed Josie two quilts. That only leaves one for me, but I'll be fine. My body temperature runs hot, always. It's why I sometimes wear shorts in winter and why my mom always thinks I have a fever when I don't. And besides, it's not that cold out. It feels almost like summer—a little chilly, but no wind. There are even fireflies out, their blinking lights creating patterns against the starry sky. It smells like summer, too—like pine needles and fresh air and something else, something sweet and almost salty and impossible to define.

I'm sitting in the corner of the truck bed, a ratty red quilt draped over my shoulders. Josie is across from me, curled up against the wall of the bed. I can hear her breathing, slow and steady, and I think she must be asleep. Until she talks.

"Thanks for the blankets, Mitchell." Her voice is sleepy and slow and buried under the blankets she has pulled up to her nose. "Even if they do smell like dirt."

"Yeah. Of course." I blink up at the sky. "Josie?"

"Yeah?"

"I'm sorry I took you away from the party. It was stupid, and I was mean, and I'm sorry." I swallow. "I'm not really myself tonight."

"It's okay." She pauses. "Though I'd probably be home sleeping in my warm bed if you hadn't kidnapped me."

I laugh, softly. "Probably. But then you'd be missing out on all this."

"This what? Scary darkness? Bears and coyotes prowling around, looking for fresh meat?"

I roll my eyes. Not like she can see me. "This *adventure*."

"I know." There's a hint of a smile in her voice. "Everything seems better in the fresh air. You know?"

I nod and close my eyes, taking a deep breath. One upside of growing up at Paintbrush: There was never a shortage of fresh air and the great outdoors. I fill my lungs with the soft spring air, my chest rising, until I can't take in any more. Slowly, I let it out. "I know."

I slide down into my spot, curled up against the opposite side of the truck. I don't want to make Josie feel weird or anything. But there's a good two feet of space between us, so we should be fine. I close my eyes and listen to the crickets chirping in the woods around us.

"Mitchell?" comes Josie's voice again.

"Yeah?"

"Why did you do it?"

I open my eyes and stare at the dark sky, until the stars above me start to swim. I want to pretend I don't know what she's talking about—*Why did I do what?*—but I know what she means.

"It was just . . . too much," I say, softly. "I didn't want to see you there, like that. Partying and drinking and whatever. That's what other people do. Stupid high schoolers who don't know anything about real life. But you're Josie. You're different."

I feel stupid saying it out loud.

Her voice carries back to me, across the truck. "Maybe I'm not."

I shake my head. "No. You are."

I wait for her to respond, but she stays quiet. Eventually I hear her breathing, soft and slow and even, and I know she's probably asleep. Her breathing mixes with the crickets, with the sound of rustling leaves. Like a mini symphony. A perfect forest lullaby.

I'm still listening as I drift off to sleep.

CHAPTER THIRTEEN
JOSIE

I wake up with Mitchell. Actually, that's not true. I wake up before Mitchell. Judging by the sun, I'm guessing it's around seven or so. I think about waking him up, but his face looks so peaceful, and his usually well-combed dark hair is all messy and tangled. He looks relaxed, actually relaxed, for the first time since Thursday night dinner. So I let him sleep.

I can't believe this whole debacle with his family was just on Thursday. It's only Saturday morning now, so less than two days ago. It feels like it's been an eternity. And if it feels that way to me, I can only guess how it feels for Mitchell.

I sit up and pull my blankets around my shoulders. If today is Saturday, then tomorrow is Sunday, which means that as of tomorrow, graduation will be in three weeks. My heart speeds up a little bit at the thought. Next to everyone's name in the program—at least everyone from my AP classes—there will be a college listed. Mostly the big state schools, but some fancy private schools, too. A few people are headed to California, I think. Mitchell and Ted are the only ones headed to New England, as far as I know. Leah is going to the local community college for a year or two, to save up money until she can transfer. She wants to go to school somewhere in New

York City, to study Art History. Everyone has a plan.

Everyone except me.

I don't know why I didn't apply. I went to the library after school every day for three weeks straight back in October. I sat there and stared at the applications. I filled out my name, my date of birth, my essential SAT and GPA information. I had picked five schools—three in state, two out, all with pretty green campuses and lots of different majors and good reputations. But when it came to the essays—*Why do you want to attend this school?*—I sat and stared at the blinking cursor, my fingers hovering aimlessly over the keyboard. I didn't know why I wanted to attend. And every time I pictured myself packing up my stuff, driving away from Paintbrush, leaving Mae and Libby and my mom behind, the beautiful mountains fading in my rearview mirror . . . I couldn't do it. I tried, over and over again, to picture my mom, alone in the cabin with my sisters, cooking and cleaning for them all by herself. Drinking tea in the kitchen all by herself, her thin arms holding a tattered book. I tried to picture her doing it all, all by herself. And I just couldn't.

So I didn't apply. Anywhere. I told my mom I applied to three schools, and that they all rejected me. And then I told her it didn't matter because I was just going to spend some time at Paintbrush until I figured things out. And the truth is: That doesn't seem so bad. Mitchell acts like he can't wait to get out of there, like we're living in some kind of cult instead of a community, like our lives are terrible and horrible and awful. But the people are so nice and genuine, the farm work we do is so straightforward and simple and comforting, the places and buildings and hiking trails behind the property are so familiar and warm. And I'm happy there. And if I'm happy, why shouldn't I stay?

As I'm contemplating all this in the dewy early morning sunlight, a bird lands on Mitchell. I'm not kidding. Not near him. *On* him. It's a blue jay, too, bright blue with a pointy feathered head. Totally gorgeous. I sit as still as I can, fascinated. But then I remember that blue jays can be kind of mean. Myra got some of her hair pulled out by one once when she was setting up a bird feeder outside. I guess the bird thought some of her frizzier strands would make perfect nesting material. Needless to say, she was not a happy camper.

Just as I'm opening my mouth to shoo it away, Mitchell sleepily opens his eyes and slowly focuses on the blue shape perched on his chest.

"Mitchell," I whisper, trying to warn him. But it's too late.

"Ahhh!" he screeches, his voice echoing against the nearby mountain. And with a start, the blue jay jumps forward, gives Mitchell's forehead a good solid peck, and then launches itself from the truck and flies away.

"Are you kidding me?" Mitchell throws the blankets off and sits straight up, grasping his head in pain. "Are you fucking kidding me right now? What a great wake-up call. I fucking love nature."

I press my lips together, afraid I'm going to start laughing. "Are you okay?"

"Do I *look* okay?" He squints at me. "Wait. Are you *laughing* at me?"

"No!" I exclaim. But I can't keep the grin from spreading

across my face. "I just can't believe that happened to you." I shake my head. "This has not been your week."

He just glares at me. Slowly, he takes his hand away, leaving a smear of blood on his forehead. He looks down at his hand. "Oh god. Am I *bleeding*?" There's panic in his eyes. "Is it okay? How do I look?"

His eyes are all bleary from sleep. His hair is sticking straight up. And right in the middle of his forehead, a tiny gash trickles a small but steady stream of blood.

I try to compose myself. "Good. You look good."

He throws a blanket at me. "Liar." But he's grinning as he pulls out his phone and tosses it to me. "I guess we'd better call Myra."

CHAPTER FOURTEEN
MITCHELL

Since Josie's mom doesn't have her own car, and I since I don't want to deal with my parents, we call Myra to come help us out. She brings a gas can and fills up my tank enough for me to make it to the nearest gas station. The whole time she gives us a lecture on responsibility, preparedness, and the importance of being mindful.

"Your parents must be worried sick." Her voice is loud and disapproving, and the breeze whips her wispy gray hair around in a way that's somehow a little frightening. "Don't you care about their feelings?"

Josie and I glance at each other and say, "Yes, of course, we're sorry." But the truth is that neither of our parents are very strict. Mine like to know where I am, but beyond that they have a *trusting* parenting style, which essentially means I don't have a curfew or have to check in or anything. It's kind of ridiculous, but then again, I don't do anything overly illegal or dangerous, and I have good grades and all, so I guess it's worked out so far. And from what I can tell, Josie's mom doesn't ever ask where she's going or what she's doing or anything like that. Just says bye when she leaves and hi when she comes back. Kind of weird. But again, Josie's probably a better kid than even I am. Maybe it's because Myra's stricter than any parent.

Myra insists that Josie go with her back to Paintbrush while I head into town to get gas. Myra's still lecturing as Josie slides into the passenger seat. I catch her gaze and grin; she mouths *save me* through the window as I drive away.

When I pull into the Paintbrush lot a few minutes later, I'm strangely calm. I've been dreading coming back here and facing my parents. But knowing I'm about to get it out of the way is a good feeling. There's a nervous buzz in my chest, an anxious energy in my fingertips. I'm ready.

Until I walk into the cabin and find my parents leaning against the wall, arms around each other, lips locked. I'm so not ready for that.

"What the fuck?" My words sound extra harsh in the tiny cabin.

My mom spins around and straightens her shirt, her hand flying to her mouth.

"Mitchell!" she says, her voice a relieved gasp, at the same time my father says, "Watch your language."

My mom moves to hug me, but I take a deliberate step back. She freezes, her arms still half extended. Her mouth turns down a little, like she's trying not to cry, and I instinctively want to reach out and hug her. But then I think of her and my dad, pressed together, and I just can't.

"What was that?" I ask again. "Did something change while I was gone?"

A small flutter rises in my chest, a glimmer of hope that I hate myself for having. Because as soon as I see my mom and dad exchange glances, I know nothing has changed.

"Oh, honey. No," my mom stammers. "We were just . . ."

She trails off, looking at my dad for help. But he jams his hands in his pockets and looks down at the ground.

"So you're still with Joe." My heart clenches, my throat tightening. "Does this mean you're cheating on him now, too?"

She shakes her head, and her eyes glisten, her voice wavering slightly. "No, sweetie. I mean, yes, I'm still with Joe. But he knows things are complicated right now. I love him"— at this my dad turns and walks to the sink and starts shuffling dishes around—"but I've loved your dad for so long, and some feelings don't go away." She pauses and looks up, like she's searching for the right words in the air or something. "I just . . . I needed to say goodbye."

I stare at her. *Is she kidding?* I glance at my dad, who's still moving dishes around. It's like he's trying to do the dishes, but he can't remember how. "Dad?"

"Yes, Mitchell?" He sounds exhausted, his voice emotionless.

"You're just going to let this happen?"

He sighs. "It's your mother's choice. She chose someone else."

At this my mom cringes, and a tear slides down her cheek. But I don't let up. "That's not what I meant. I mean, you're going to let her come in here and manipulate you like this?"

He crosses his arms. "It's not like that—"

"It *is* like that. She doesn't live here anymore. She's not part of this family anymore. You should be mad."

My mom is full on crying now, shoulders shaking under

her faded denim shirt, blotchy face, the whole thing. And I feel bad, but I can't give in. This is her fault. Not mine.

My dad watches her, his shoulders hunched. He looks so, so tired, and for the first time ever, he seems old to me. "I'm sorry this is confusing to you, Mitchell. It's just complicated right now."

I want to scream. Mostly at my mom, but at him too, for letting her cry here in the kitchen. For letting her see his sadness. For not screaming at her to get out like she deserves. But instead, I take a deep breath and swallow my words, along with the lump rising in my throat. I've caused enough damage for today.

"I've got work to do," I tell them both. And then I turn and walk out the door.

Everyone at Paintbrush has chores to do. Some people actually work full-time at Paintbrush, selling our produce at farmer's markets and stuff. The more each member works at Paintbrush, the less that member has to pay per year. Not that it's much of a payment, anyway. Myra uses a sliding scale, so people who don't make much money barely have to pay at all. And lots of people work in town, too. But everyone is required to at least do something. Mostly I help Bernie with the handiwork that needs to be done, like painting and sanding and fixing chairs and installing light bulbs. Today, I'm mowing the grass.

A bead of sweat slides into my eye with a sharp sting.

I've only been mowing for twenty minutes, and I'm already ridiculously sweaty. The Paintbrush lawn stretches around and between all the cabins—there are currently thirty-four—the common building, and the various gardens; and way past that, there's this huge stretch of field. It's a huge job—normally takes me about two hours with a riding mower—but I don't really mind because riding the mower is kind of badass. And also because one time I had to spend my entire Saturday sanding the floor in the Meeting Place when we put new boards in, and I practically broke my back. And then when I complained, Myra said it was a shame that "they just don't make strapping young boys like they used to." So anything is better than that.

But today, the riding mower is broken. Bernie's fiddling with it out in one of our tool sheds, but he said it might be a while. So here I am, dragging our old red push mower around the lawn in the hot beating sun and trying to avoid old stumps and hidden holes.

It's a good distraction from my parents. And it's a Saturday, which means basically everyone is out working—cleaning and gardening and everything else. I pass Ned on his front porch, ominously cleaning his rifle; he barely ever uses it anymore, but he likes to make a big show out of cleaning it so everyone will think he's tough. The Macpherson kids—all seven of them—are playing tag next to the herb patch where their parents are gardening, using baby Lucy as home base. Wendy sits in the grass holding Lucy, looking highly amused and also slightly terrified each time a Macpherson child comes tearing across the lawn. I wave as I pass. Ada Macpherson, the five-year-old, sticks out her tongue and crosses her eyes at me. Maddie gives me a very solemn nod.

By the time I reach the back field, it's already been three hours. I strip off my sweaty shirt and take another hour to finish the meadow. And I'm so exhausted from two nights of little to no sleep that I almost run over my own foot with the mower. I put it back in the shed, go back to the cabin, chug two huge glasses of water, shower, and climb into bed. It's only six when I pull the covers up to my chin. My dad's not even in from doing his work yet. But when I close my eyes, I don't open them again until almost nine the next morning.

CHAPTER FIFTEEN
JOSIE

When Myra drops me off after my night with Mitchell in the truck, I walk into my cabin to find my mom cleaning the kitchen. It's not even messy; my mom just likes to clean, to wipe every tiny smudge and speck from the green-and-blue tile, to straighten all our mason jars and plates in the cabinet until they stand in perfect lines, to neatly fold every dish towel into pressed squares. She says it relaxes her. I say she needs to find something better to do with her time.

She turns around when she hears the door open, sponge in hand, and smiles when she sees me. "Hi, honey. Did you have a good night?"

That's it. That's really all she says. I've been gone all night and she has no idea where, and all she asks me is if I had a good time.

"Yep," I say.

She starts scrubbing the tile again. "And Leah did too?"

"I think so."

"Glad to hear it." And just like that, the conversation is over. I know a lot of kids my age would kill to have parents that let them do whatever they want. But it just makes me mad. Like she doesn't care.

Mom hums a tune under her breath, no idea that I'm annoyed. I force a smile and walk into my room, willing myself not to slam the door.

In my bedroom I find both my sisters still asleep. Mae is basically where I left her last night, curled up with her book still pressed to her chest. When I peer into Libby's bed, though, I see she's still wearing clothes from the night before—a dress I know for a fact is *way* too short on her—and that she has black eyeliner smeared around her eyes. I frown. Isn't fourteen too young to be wearing eyeliner? I definitely didn't wear eyeliner when I was her age. But maybe I was weird.

I sigh and pull Libby's quilt up to her chin, covering her skimpy dress. My mom should be the one in here. She should be shaking Libby awake and making her change out of this dress, wiping the makeup off her face and asking where she went last night. Mom needs to keep tabs on Libby. But Mom's not. Just another reason why I'm glad I'll be home in the fall.

I could definitely use a couple more hours of sleep—sleeping in the back of a truck is not all that comfortable, it turns out—but it's Saturday morning. And Saturday mornings are for work. So I throw on my old jeans and head outside to do my gardening. I'm working on the tomatoes, like always—Myra says I have a gift, a sixth sense for when to plant the seeds and how to water the vines and which plant will produce the fattest, juiciest results. I don't know about that, but I do know our tomatoes always sell really big at the farmers markets in the summer. So maybe she's right.

I work on the tomatoes all day, getting the field ready to plant. I can feel the sun tanning my skin—okay, burning my skin—and I'm covered in dirt after like ten minutes, but it's a good feeling. To do something with my hands and to actually see the results in front of me.

Plus, it gets my mind off Mitchell. Ever since last night, my stomach has been twisting into knots, and I can't figure out why. Maybe because it feels like our friendship got pushed to some weird new level. But I'm torn between desperately wanting to see him and talk to him and also desperately wanting to avoid him at all costs. I see him pushing the old mower around all day, but I'm never quite close enough to actually talk to him. And later, I catch a glimpse of him mowing the back lawn. His shirt is off, and even though he's too far away to see me looking at him, it makes me blush, for some unknown reason, and then I feel stupid for blushing. Ultimately, it all just makes me want to curl up in my cabin and read for the rest of the night. So I do.

I'm getting ready to crawl under the covers when my phone pings with a text from Leah: *Diego is the cutest. Thank the Lord for an actual good guy. Let's hope it lasts!*

I roll my eyes. Classic Leah. But I text her back: *Yay! Fingers crossed.*

Leah: *You have a good night? Get home safe?*

I'm about to respond with the whole big story, the fight with Mitchell and the sleeping outside and the blue jay and all that. But as my fingers hover over the keyboard, I realize Leah will read something into all this. Something that's probably not even there. So I just reply: *All good.*

It must be late when I finally drift off because I don't wake up until nine or so in the morning, which is late for me. I think about spending today—Sunday, my one day off from school *and* from Paintbrush chores—like yesterday, stressed out from talking to Mitchell and also from not talking to Mitchell, annoyed at my mom, worried about Libby, wondering about the whole John/Carrie debacle.

I'm exhausted just thinking about it. And it's definitely not how I want to spend my day off. So I pack a sandwich, an apple, and a handful of oatmeal raisin cookies, throw a book into a backpack, and head out onto the trails up the mountain behind Paintbrush. There's one trail that's my absolute favorite. It has a waterfall with a beautiful swimming hole underneath, a rushing creek that follows the trail the whole way, and a gorgeous lookout at the end. It's a long one, at least two hours to get to the end and then two hours back again, but a long hike is exactly what I need.

CHAPTER SIXTEEN
MITCHELL

I'm pretty sure a bear is following me up the mountain. Usually I'm not paranoid about stuff like this, but with the whole blue jay incident yesterday, I kind of feel like nature is out to get me. And there's definitely something coming up behind me.

Except when I turn around to make sure I'm not about to be attacked by an angry mama bear, I spot Josie coming around the corner.

My heart kind of sputters in this nervous way when I see her, but I can't tell if it's because she scared me or if I'm anxious or disappointed that my hike is no longer solo or . . . something else. Whatever it is, I don't have time to figure it out.

I cup my hands around my mouth and call to her. "Are you following me or something?"

She stops, blinks at me, and then walks a few more paces until she's about twenty feet away. She shields her eyes with her hand as she peers at me, other hand firmly grasping the strap of the beat-up canvas backpack on her shoulders.

"I'm . . . sorry." Her voice wavers.

"For what?"

She shrugs. "Getting all up in your nature, I guess."

"Come on, Josie." I make a sweeping gesture with my arms. "This is *America*. The woods are free for everyone."

She takes a few steps closer. "You're sure you don't mind?"

I'm not sure, actually. I came up here to be alone, to think things out. And also, I can't get the whole sleeping together in my truck thing out of my head. Now that I know how she curls up on her side like a cat when she sleeps, how her breathing is deep and steady and slow, how her wispy hair curls around her face in the morning, it's like I'm not quite sure how to act around her anymore. I'm looking at her now, dressed in these flowing bright-green pants and a white tank top, with her hair tucked up under a trucker hat that reads *Eat Your Veggies* in lettering made out of carrots. But all I can see is her face scrunched up and snuggled into a blanket, and the way her mouth moves in her sleep, like she's talking to someone in her dreams.

It's weird, and I feel weird for thinking about it, and then I feel weird for thinking about how I need to stop thinking about it. I shake my head and take a deep breath. *Get it together.*

I smile at her. "I don't mind. As long as you're not stalking me."

She takes her last few steps toward me and raises her eyebrows. "I have a very busy schedule, Mitchell. If I'm going to take the time to stalk someone, it's going to be someone cooler than you."

"Ouch," I say, hand over my heart. "That hurts. I'll have you know that I'm very exciting and important. Prime stalking material."

She breezes past me, striding up the rocky mountain path at a surprisingly fast pace. "You can't lie to me, Mitchell Morrison. I know you too well."

I quicken my pace to match hers, following her dark bobbing ponytail up the mountain, and it occurs to me that she might be right.

We reach the swimming hole about an hour later. From here it's only about twenty minutes to the top and the pretty mountain views, but I almost always make a stop at the swimming hole. It's just so perfect: gushing water falls from about twenty feet up, cascading over mossy rocks into this big, beautiful clear pool below. It's only like five feet deep, but in the summer I always jump in for a quick dip. It's cold, but it feels so good.

I was definitely planning on jumping in, but now I'm not really sure what Josie wants to do. We stop at the edge, and I crouch forward and trail my hands through the water.

"Is it cold?" Josie asks from behind me.

I stand back up. "It's not too bad."

"Liar." She shakes her head at me. "It's always freezing this time of year."

I look closely at her, and that's when I notice a blue strap tied behind her neck, poking out of her tank top. I grin. "Then why do you have your bathing suit on?"

"What?" Her already rosy cheeks turn an even deeper shade of pink. She reaches behind her neck, touching the tied strap. "Well, I thought it would be hot."

"You thought right," I say. My shirt is completely soaked and plastered to my back and chest, and tiny rivulets of sweat run down my neck and face. Climbing up a mountain is no joke.

"I know. I feel . . . moist." She shudders.

"Gross word choice."

"Gross feelings call for gross words."

She's gazing at the water with this hungry look. Like she's dying to jump in but can't. Because . . . I'm here, maybe? Because there's this weird tension between us for some reason? I shake my head. I'm done with this awkwardness. It's too fucking hot.

"So let's go in," I say. I know she's looking at me as I drop my backpack and yank off my shirt. Before I can feel self-conscious—which is so stupid, I try to remind myself, because it's *just Josie*—I hoist myself up on my favorite rock and jump in.

It's a shock to my system, how the icy water slips over my skin as I plunge into the pool. And it's also a shock when I surface, sputtering, drops of water snaking down my face, to find Josie taking off her clothes on the bank.

I don't know if I expected her not to join me or what. But something about the way her dark-blue one piece makes her legs seem really long, or maybe the way her hair spills out of her cap in long waves, or even the way she carefully folds her tank top and pants and puts them in a neat pile—something about all these things makes me want to straight up stare at her and also makes me want to close my eyes, like I've been looking too long at a bright light. Instead of deciding between these two ridiculous options, I take a deep, deep breath and dive back under, letting the cool water rinse away my thoughts.

CHAPTER SEVENTEEN
JOSIE

I'm lying on my stomach on the flat rocks at the top of the mountain, gazing down at the valley below, letting the delicious warmth of the sun toast my skin and warm me up from my icy dip under the waterfall. I've done this a million times before—with my sisters and my mom when I was little, with Leah a few times, and mostly by myself—but never with Mitchell lying on the rock right next to me.

Not to say that this is the first time Mitchell and I have gone swimming together. When we were little, our moms used to put a sprinkler out in the big field behind Paintbrush, and Mitchell and I would run through it for hours on hot sunny days. Afterward, my mom and Carrie would wrap us in big towels and give us homemade orange juice popsicles to suck on. They would melt so fast that the juice would run down our chins, turning us into these big sticky messes our moms would have to clean up. I was always more careful with my popsicle. I would try to lick all around the edges evenly so I could make the smallest mess possible. But Mitchell would dive headfirst into his popsicle, licking one side repeatedly while the other melted into a steady river of orange that dripped down his hands and all over his lap. Even then, I was efficient and careful and clean, and he was messy and carefree and bold.

Next to me, Mitchell is in the process of devouring what must be his sixth oatmeal cookie. There are crumbs everywhere. His brown hair, still damp, flops on his forehead as he turns his head to look at me. Looking at him.

"What?" he asks.

"You're getting cookie everywhere," I say. "Bears can probably smell us from a mile away. I bet a whole herd is headed our way as we speak."

"Bears don't move in herds." He licks his fingers.

"Not usually," I say. "But this is a special circumstance. Since there are *so many* crumbs."

He sighs. "I can't help it. These are so good." He pushes the bag toward me, sits up, and stretches his arms above his head. "I miss the days when I used to come over to your house all the time. I've missed Layla's baking."

I shake my head. "My mom didn't bake them. Libby's the big baker now. She whips up a batch of cookies, like, every other day. Our cabin is overflowing with baked goods."

Mitchell frowns. "Really? But I thought Libby was the twin who . . ." He pauses, like he's searching for the right word. "She's more . . ."

"Crazy?" I suggest. "Shallow? Makes more questionable decisions?"

"No," he says quickly. He pauses and tilts his head. "Well. Kind of."

"Underneath all that makeup and age-inappropriate clothing, there's actually a real person. Deep, deep down.

We're talking *really* deep."

Mitchell laughs, leaning back on his hands. "She's not that bad. She looks like most of the girls at our high school."

"That's exactly my point," I say. "She's in eighth grade."

"Almost to ninth," Mitchell points out. "Then she'll actually *be* one of the girls at our high school."

I sigh. "I don't really care how old she is. No one should feel the need to wear clothing that tight. Or the need to wake up a full two hours before school just to curl her hair."

Mitchell snorts.

"I'm not kidding. The girl gets up at six every morning. *6:00 a.m.* I'd rather wear a trash bag to school and sleep in than get up that early just to look nice."

Mitchell rolls his eyes. "You always look nice."

There's a moment of awkward silence. I don't know what to say to that, so I change the subject with the first thing I can think of. "I just wish my mom cared more about Libby."

Mitchell raises his eyebrows. "Cared how?"

"I guess it's not so much that I wish she cared more." I pause, considering. "More like I wish she trusted less."

He frowns. "You wish your mom didn't trust you guys?"

"Not like that. Well, kind of like that." I sigh. I'm regretting bringing this up. I'm not making sense. But Mitchell is looking at me with his big brown eyes, with that intense stare of his, and now I feel like I have to keep going. "It's just that my mom did so much stupid stuff when she was a teenager. She partied all the time and skipped so much school, and then got pregnant at sixteen. She never even got to finish high school because of all the stupid decisions she made." I'm talking fast, trying to get all my thoughts out at once. "And then after all that—after all her firsthand experience with exactly how stupid teenagers can be—she just lets me walk in and out the door whenever I want. And Libby too, and Mae. They're only fourteen. Not even a question about where we're going or who we're with or what we're doing. She never worries about us. It's like she doesn't care at all."

There's a quiet in the air as I finish my tangent. I gaze out over the valley below us, at the bright treetops and snaking roadways and ridge of mountains stretching in the distance. I must sound insane, blurting all that out. Maybe we haven't gotten to a whole new level of friendship the past few days. Mitchell and I, we joke, and we talk about homework, and we gossip about Paintbrush. But we don't really do deep and personal.

But Mitchell's words are slow and careful when he speaks. Like he's trying hard to say the right thing. "Layla loves you guys, though. I see the way she hugs you, and the way she always pauses to look around for you three on work days or at community dinners. And then, when she finds you among the crowd, she always smiles." He shrugs. "You guys make her happy."

I turn my gaze from the view in front of me to him. "You notice that much about my family?"

He trails his fingers over the ground. "It's been twelve years since you all moved here. After twelve years, you start to notice some things."

He's really blushing now, and looking at him is making me blush too. So I sit up and pull off my hiking boots, one by one, and then slide over to dangle my feet off the ledge. My bare feet swing in the air, high above the treetops.

"So want to hear a funny story?" Mitchell asks.

Thank god for a change of subject. "Yeah."

He pulls off his boots and scoots over, swinging his legs over the ledge next to me. Our thighs are touching, the black of his athletic shorts brushing against the pale skin of my leg, and I'm finding it hard to look at anything else.

He points off to our left. "See that mountain over there?"

I lean around him and squint. "Yeah?"

"That's Mount Mitchell. That's the mountain I'm named after."

"Really?" I tilt my head, confused. "But you're not even from here. You were born in New York City."

"Yeah, but my parents were vacationing here. Nine months before I was born, if you know what I mean."

"What?" I frown. And then it clicks. "Oh. *Oh*." I pause for a second. "So wait. That mountain was where . . . ?"

"Yep. That mountain was where I was conceived. 'Out in nature, the way God intended,' if I remember correctly. Which I wish I didn't."

I laugh. "Oh god. I would probably throw up if my mom tried to tell about the moment of my conception."

He nodded. "Imagine your parents telling you about it *together*. And then following it up with a safe sex talk. It took me months to recover."

I grin. "I can imagine. My story's probably pretty boring, anyway. I bet I was conceived in a car. Or wherever teenagers have sex. I wouldn't know."

"Don't look at me," Mitchell says. "I wouldn't know, either."

I'm surprised that I said it, and even more surprised at Mitchell's response. I've always assumed, with all the girls at school who fall all over him, something probably happened at some point. But it's stupid to waste time thinking about it. It's not like Mitchell's sex life has anything to do with me.

I scoot backward from the ledge and lie down, my back warm against the sunbaked rock. The sky is bright with the summer sun, and I close my eyes.

After a few seconds, Mitchell starts moving around. I don't open my eyes, but I hear his soft breathing, and I can almost feel his warm skin radiating heat. He's lying down next to me.

I squeeze my eyes even tighter, so I won't be tempted to peek and see how close he really is. *Don't be stupid*, I tell myself. *It's Mitchell. It's just Mitchell.*

I'm still telling myself this as I drift off to sleep in the sunshine.

CHAPTER EIGHTEEN
MITCHELL

When I wake up, I find myself face to face with Josie. Again. For the second time in two days. I don't think we've slept in the same place since first or second grade, when we used to fall asleep side by side watching kid movies in the Sanctuary. So twice in two days is pretty weird. But not in a bad way.

I reach for my backpack and check my phone. My heart is thumping with that sleepy, panicked feeling I always get when I fall asleep accidentally and wake up confused. But it's only late afternoon, and we've only been asleep for half an hour. We still have plenty of time to get back down to Paintbrush before it gets dark.

Josie murmurs in her sleep and rolls over, and my heart catches. She's getting kind of close to the edge. I inch closer and shake her shoulder.

"Josie?"

She cracks opens one eye and sits up, her damp hair falling in front of her face. "Oh god. What time is it?"

"Five," I say. "We're fine."

She nods and stretches her arms way up to the sky, yawning. She's still wearing her bathing suit, and halfway through her yawn she looks down at herself and quickly folds her arms. Like she's self-conscious or something. It makes me feel like I should look away.

She stands up and gathers her clothes. "We've been up here a while," she says. She slips on her loose green pants then tugs on her hiking boots. "We should probably get going."

I nod. "Sure." But I really don't want to go back down. These past few hours, this golden afternoon in my favorite mountain paradise, have been so relaxing and quiet and perfect. Almost like I dreamed it up and exactly what I needed. Going back down means going back to real life, my real life, where things are complicated and messy and stressful. I want to just stay up here, in the sunlight and fresh air, forever.

But Josie is pulling on her shirt now and looking at me with a confused why-are-you-still-sitting-down expression. So I stand up, slowly, and reach for my backpack with a sigh.

Two hours later, we're walking onto the grounds of Paintbrush, and my desperation to avoid my problems claws at my ribcage and flutters in my throat. I'm dragging my feet, casting around in my head for ways to avoid going back to my cabin. Because if I go back and just my dad is there, it'll be sad. And if I go back and both of them are there, I'll be angry. There's nowhere for me to go.

Josie and I walk side by side in a quiet silence, arms swinging. We're almost to Josie's cabin when someone shouts from our left.

"You two! Get in here!" Ned's voice echoes from inside his

cabin. His front door is propped open, and somewhere inside, a baby wails.

I glance at Josie. She squints toward his front door.

"Ned?"

Next door, Bernie pokes his head out of his cabin. "What's all the commotion about? Some people are trying to sleep!"

"It's not even 7:30 yet, you old goat!" shouts Ned from inside. "We all know you weren't asleep. Now one of you three better get in here and help me if you know what's good for you."

"I mighta been asleep," Bernie grumbles under his breath. But he follows Josie and me into the cabin.

Inside, Ned is perched on an old rocking chair, a beautiful cedar piece that looks hand-carved—probably by him. In his lap is baby Lucy, awkwardly enfolded in Ned's flannel-clad arms and wailing with a bright-red face. Ned rocks back and forth at a frantic pace.

"What's going on in here?" I ask, carefully stepping over a whittling knife on the floor. Not exactly a kid-friendly space.

"What does it look like?" Ned growls. "Damn thing won't be quiet."

"First rule of babysitting," I say. "Don't refer to the child as 'thing.'"

Bernie snorts, but Josie gives me a you're-not-helping look. She turns back to face Ned. "Ned, why do you have Lucy?"

"Wendy and Eric went to the store. Emergency diaper run, they said." In his arms, Lucy lets out another scream, high-pitched and angry. Ned winces and continues. "But I'm starting to get real suspicious. Seems like they abandoned me here with this screaming mess just so they could get a break."

"They must have been pretty desperate," agrees Bernie. "If their best option for a babysitter was you."

Ned glares at him.

I take a step closer and peer into Ned's arms. Lucy flails her tiny baby fists as she screams, her face twisted. I smile, despite myself. Even in distress, Lucy is pretty cute. But then, without warning, Ned thrusts her into my arms.

"You're supposed to be some kind of smart guy, college boy. Give it a try."

Lucy is a tiny bundle in my arms, soft and warm. I hold her against my chest and hum softly, my favorite lullaby from when I was little: *Uncle John's Band*. Of course, I later learned that it was actually a Grateful Dead song. My parents were nuts like that. But when I was little, and I was crying or tired or scared, it always did the trick.

Lucy falls quiet, blinking at me as I hum. I glance at Josie, who is watching me with wide eyes. I raise my eyebrows triumphantly. *I am the baby whisperer*, I think. But seconds later, Lucy starts screaming again.

"Give her to me." Josie reaches out and tugs Lucy from my arms, cradling the baby in the crook of her elbow. Lucy doesn't stop crying for even one moment. Her tiny eyes scrunch up as her little screams turn into one long wail. She doesn't even pause for a breath. This kid has some serious lung capacity. It would be impressive if the sound wasn't so grating.

Josie bites her bottom lip and rocks Lucy, but it's no use. I swear Lucy's screams get even louder.

"You try," Josie says to Bernie, thrusting the baby out

toward him.

Bernie takes a step back. "No can do," he says. "I don't do babies."

"What in the world are you talking about?" demands Ned.

Bernie shrugs. "They creep me out," he calls back, his voice loud over the screams. "They're like little tiny people."

"You know, Bernie, I never thought of it that way," I say slowly. "But now that you mention it, babies are kind of like people."

"See?" Bernie points to me. "He gets it."

Josie ignores me, desperately bouncing Lucy up and down.

Ned rolls his eyes and says to Bernie, "He's making fun of you, you idiot."

"No, he's not," shouts Bernie, at the same time I say, "I would never—"

But before I can finish my thought, the cabin door swings open, revealing a small but serious Maddie Macpherson.

"What's going on in here?" Maddie steps in and pushes her glasses up on her nose.

"Damn thing won't stop crying," says Ned.

"Ned!" Josie glares at him.

"Sorry," he says. "Damn *baby* won't stop crying."

Josie rolls her eyes.

"I know," says Maddie. "I've been trying to study my multiplication problems, but I can hear her all the way from my cabin."

"I'm sorry." Josie desperately jiggles Lucy up and down. "We just got here, and I've been trying, but—"

"Here." Maddie crosses over to Josie, gently but firmly

plucks Lucy from her arms, and crosses to the kitchen table, where a pink bag is perched. Maddie rummages through it, pulls out a pacifier, and in one swift move places it in Lucy's mouth. Immediately, Lucy's face fades from an angry red to a happy pink, her tiny eyes go wide, her clenched fists unfurl, and the cabin is miraculously, blissfully quiet.

Ned, Bernie, Josie, and I stare at Maddie as she rocks Lucy back and forth. Maddie's brows knit together as she peers at the baby in her arms. Her rocking is steady and rhythmic, almost business-like. The baby squirms one more time before she stills completely. Maddie nods, apparently satisfied. She looks up at us.

"What?" she asks.

"You're like magic," I say.

Beside me, Josie nods.

Maddie rolls her eyes. "Please. When a baby is crying, you stick a pacifier in its mouth. It's not rocket science."

The door behind me creaks open, and we all turn. Wendy ducks inside, followed by Eric.

"What's not rocket science?" She smiles at all of us.

"Getting your baby to be quiet," Ned grumbles. "But I sure as hell couldn't do it."

Eric frowns. He's a tall guy, over six feet, with thick dark hair and tanned skin and big broad shoulders. He's huge, and he barely smiles, and he's pretty quiet, which makes him seem even scarier. I used to think it was so funny that he was married to Wendy, the bounciest, friendliest, happiest woman of all time. But after Lucy was born, I could see why. It's hard to shake the image of a giant manly man speaking baby talk.

Watching him coo to Lucy these last few weeks has made me see the soft side of Eric. The side Wendy probably saw all along.

"Was she a lot of trouble?" Eric asks.

"No," Josie and Maddie say in unison, at the same that Ned replies, "Yes."

"I'm sorry if she made a fuss," Wendy says nervously. "But she looks pretty happy now."

"Why does it take two people to run to the store, anyway?" asks Ned. "You two got separation anxiety or something?"

Wendy glances at Eric and then to the ground, shuffling her feet, and a distinct red floods Eric's dark cheeks. It's then that I notice Wendy's mussed hair and wrinkled shirt. And a distinct red mark on Eric's neck. I look at Josie and raise my eyebrows, and she cocks her head, confused.

"W-Well," Wendy stammers, but I cut her off.

"Don't try and change the subject, Ned," I say. "You can't distract us from the fact that you couldn't handle one tiny baby for one tiny hour."

Bernie laughs. "He's right."

Wendy and Eric both glance at each other, relieved, a look only I catch.

"Look," Josie whispers. "She's sleeping."

Everyone creeps a little closer. I shuffle off to the side to make room for Wendy and Eric. Sure enough, Lucy's eyes are closed, her soft eyelashes fluttering with every gentle breath she takes. The cabin, cozy in the now-darkness outside, is filled with a soft quiet.

I watch them all there, peering at the peaceful sleeping

bundle in Maddie's arms. Two wrinkled old men wearing faded trucker hats, a smug eight-year-old in pigtails, two blissfully happy young parents, and Josie. Josie, whose smile takes over her whole face, rounding her cheeks into apples and creasing the skin around her eyes and making her look soft and warm and beautiful.

Beautiful. I've never thought of Josie as beautiful before. I've never thought to think of Josie as beautiful before. But now here's that word, humming in my head, as I watch her watch Lucy.

They look like a family, huddled in a group, the fading sunlight from the window casting them in a dusty glow. And here I am, close enough but still a few steps back. Enjoying the moment, but not quite part of the group. It's always this way with me at Paintbrush. I hang around the fringes of every moment. Not because I'm not included or not welcome, but because, sometimes, I'm afraid I'll get in too deep here. And then I'll never be able to leave.

By the time the crowd in Ned's cabin disperses, it's almost nine. Bernie says he's going back to sleep, Ned says he's working on a whittling project, and Wendy and Eric head out to put Lucy to bed. It's Sunday night, a school night. It's time for me to go back to my cabin. And it's time for Josie to go back to hers.

Which is why I'm surprised to hear the words tumbling out of my mouth. "How about a game of chess?"

Even in the darkness outside Ned's cabin, I can see Josie squinting at me.

"You want to play a game of chess?" She sounds skeptical.

"Yeah," I say, trying to sound casual. I cast around for an excuse in my head. "You know, school's winding down for us. No homework and all that."

"We have English homework," Josie says.

"Oh. Right." I pause for a second. "I meant . . . we should sharpen our brains while we have the chance. Studies show that playing chess can really improve your concentration, your memory, your focus. All of that. Real brain food."

I'm totally babbling now, embarrassed just listening to the nonsense coming out of my mouth. Josie just looks at me.

"Brain food," she repeats. She is not making this easy for me.

I take a deep breath, and I tell the truth. "I don't want to go home yet. And I don't want to be alone." *And I don't want this day to end*, I think. But that I don't say. I don't know what's happening right now between Josie and me, what's *been* happening these last few days. All I know is that today, which should have been totally miserable and awful, was actually kind of beautiful and good. And I know that Josie is the reason why.

But I have no idea if she feels this way. Maybe she feels like all my talking ruined her solitary nature hike. Maybe she thinks that I'm totally insane for wanting to play a random game of chess on a random Sunday night.

But after a brief pause, Josie nods. "Okay," she says simply. And she follows me across the soft grass and through the dark, all the way to the Sanctuary.

CHAPTER NINETEEN
JOSIE

"No," I say.

"Yep." Mitchell grins at me.

"Are you sure?"

"One hundred percent. There was a hickey on his neck and everything. They stuck Ned with their baby so they could go fool around."

Hearing Mitchell say the phrase fool around makes my face heat up. I hope he doesn't notice. "They must have been really desperate for some alone time if they stuck Lucy with Ned."

Mitchell nods. "Agreed. You have to admit it's pretty cute, though."

I move a bishop. "What do you mean?"

"I mean, she just had a baby. Which I've heard is a pretty messy experience." I scrunch up my nose at this gross image, but he continues. "And the last few months have been full of crying and diapers and baby food. Not exactly sexy stuff. But they're still all over each other."

I consider this. "I guess you're right."

"I'm always right," he says.

I raise my eyebrows and point to the board. "Checkmate."

Mitchell groans. "Three times. Are you really gonna beat me at chess three times in a row? Couldn't you have let me win one to save face?"

"If I let you win, how will you ever learn?" I start to collect my pieces.

"Round four?" Mitchell looks at me hopefully.

I glance at the clock. It's almost midnight. *I shouldn't*, I think. But I start to set up my pieces again. He does the same, shuffling his knights and pawns and king and queen back to starting position.

"It's been a long time since I beat you at chess," I say as we work.

"That makes it sound like I usually beat you." He smirks at me.

I roll my eyes. "You know what I mean. It's been a long time since we've played chess. Period."

We learned to play chess together at this very table, back in first grade. John, Mitchell's dad, taught us; he said knowing how to play chess is an important life skill everyone should have. Learning the game was annoying at first. But once we picked it up, Mitchell and I were unstoppable. We played every chance for months and months.

"I seem to remember you beating me a lot back then, too." It's like Mitchell's reading my mind.

I shake my head. "It was pretty even."

He points at me. "Don't baby me. I can take it."

"Fine." I laugh. "I was definitely always better than you."

"Not at blackjack, though." He grins. "I was always better at blackjack."

"Very true," I say.

Another *life skill* we acquired in first grade: Ned and Bernie insisted on teaching us to play blackjack. They thought if they trained us early enough, we would be able to count cards when we grew up and hit it big at casinos. When Myra found out, she was horrified at first. And then kind of impressed when she realized we could actually play. We never got the hang of counting cards, though.

"It's amazing what first graders can do when they don't have TV to distract them," says Mitchell.

The board is all set up for another game, but neither of us makes a move to start. Mitchell collapses back against the couch he's sitting on. I lean forward on the folding table and rest my chin on my hands.

"That's definitely why I learned to read so early," I agree. "Nothing better to do."

"Nah," he says. "You were always so naturally smart."

I look down at the table. The glow from the lamp in the corner is dim; hopefully he can't see my cheeks turning pink.

"It's true." He leans forward, across the table, until our faces are only a foot or so apart. "Josie. Can I ask you a question?"

My heart pounds. The new nervous energy I've felt the past few days is definitely tangible now. "Yeah?"

"Why aren't you going to college?" he asks softly.

My heart falls a little. I don't know what I expected him to ask, but it wasn't this. My shoulders tense, and I cross my arms.

"I am going," I say. "To community college."

"You know what I mean." He sits back, running a hand through his hair. "Community college can be useful, and it saves you money, and I'm not trying to say anything bad about it. But you're smart. You take all AP classes. You could have gone to so many places."

I pick up one of my pawns, rolling it in my hand. "I don't know what I would do in college."

He frowns. "What do you mean? You would live in a dorm; you would go to class—"

"No, I mean what I would actually do. What I would study."

"Lots of people don't know what they want to study. You figure it out along the way."

"It's more than that. I don't even have the faintest idea. I don't feel pulled to anything, or passionate about anything. Everything I like is here." I laugh weakly. "The only thing I like is planting tomatoes. And you can't major in tomatoes."

"You can major in agricultural engineering, though. Or biology, or botany." He rests his forearms on the table.

I stay quiet. *He thinks I'm boring*, I think. *Or pathetic. Or maybe both*. I don't really know what to say. So I go with my standard, easy answer, the one I've been telling myself since the college application deadlines came and went back in the winter.

"I want to stay here." My voice wobbles. I do want to stay here. Right? I straighten up and square my shoulders, force my voice to even out. "My mom needs my help. And my sisters need someone who is actually going to watch out for them."

"So you never want to leave Paintbrush."

It's a statement more than a question. He's judging me.

He keeps his expression neutral and blank, but there's no way he isn't judging me. Mitchell wants to leave here so, so badly; how could he ever respect someone who wants to stay?

I don't know what to say, so I shrug again. There's an awkward silence. Mitchell leans away again.

"I didn't mean—"

"It's okay," I say quickly. "It's not a big deal."

He runs a hand through his hair. "I don't want you to think I'm judging you. I'm just curious."

I take a deep breath. "I just don't think I'm a college type of girl."

Mitchell tilts his head, like he's trying to figure me out. "Then what type of girl are you?"

So many answers tumble through my head, jostling for attention. A daughter. A sister. A Paintbrush girl. And one last answer, the most unexpected of all, and the one that sticks out the most: *a girl who might really like you.*

But none of these are good answers. They all sound stupid or boring, even in my head, and the last one is just embarrassing. So I say, "The type of girl who needs to go to bed."

Mitchell laughs. "Yeah. That's the type of guy I am right now, too."

We put the chess pieces back, working in a comfortable silence to put everything in the right place. When we walk out the front door a little later, Paintbrush is totally quiet, the cabins enveloped in darkness. Every cabin but one.

"Are you kidding me?" Mitchell mutters. He stops and squints at his cabin in the distance, the only dot of light in the dark landscape. "It's after midnight." He groans. "I bet she's in there. Trying to trap me before I go to bed."

I reach out to touch his arm, but I think better of it at the last second and just shake my head. "I'm sorry."

He slumps his shoulders and gestures back at the Sanctuary. "Maybe I should sleep in there again."

"Or maybe . . ." I glance at him out of the corner of my eye.

He sighs. "Just say it."

"Maybe you should go talk to her?" I suggest, my voice small. "I mean, it's not really my business, but . . ."

"It kind of is your business, actually," he says. "She made it everyone's business with that dramatic dinner announcement."

"It wasn't the most subtle way of doing things," I agree.

Mitchell snorts. It's not quite a laugh, but it's better than angry yelling. Or worse, crying.

"Okay." He squares his shoulders.

"Okay," I say back. But he makes no move to actually go.

"*Okay*," I say again, more forcefully, and I give him a little push in the middle of his back.

He stumbles forward and laughs. "Okay, okay. I'm going. Here I go."

He starts forward. After a few steps, he whips around.

I cross my arms. "What now?"

"Thanks, Josie." He gives me a tired smile.

I'm not entirely sure what he's thanking me for, so I just nod. He turns around and slowly starts making his way to his cabin. And I walk to mine, slipping into the dark living room and gently closing the door behind me and feeling unexpectedly, inexplicably, happy.

CHAPTER TWENTY
MITCHELL

I was right. When I walk into my cabin, letting the screen door slam behind me, my mom is sitting at the kitchen table. A book lies on the table in front of her, but it is closed. And a coffee mug sits in front of her, completely full and untouched. My dad is nowhere to be seen.

She shoots up when she sees me, her chair screeching backward.

"Hi, honey," she says. She is buzzing with a nervous, tired energy; her fingers tap a frantic beat on her thighs, she bites her lower lip, and her hair is thrown up in a sloppy ponytail.

I stand just inside the doorway, making no move to get any closer. "Where's Dad?"

She glances toward his closed bedroom door. "He went to sleep," she says. "But he let me wait up here so I could see you."

"Well, here I am." I sound sarcastic and obnoxious, and I know it.

Her hopeful expression falls at my tone, and as terrible as it sounds, her disappointment gives me a definite sense of satisfaction.

"Sweetie." She gestures toward the seat across from her. "I

know it's late. But can you please sit with me? Just for a few minutes?"

She's practically shaking, the bags under her eyes like bruises on her skin. She looks so desperate, so sad, so completely terrified that I'll say no. It's so tempting to just walk into my room and slam the door. But I look at her red, tired eyes and reluctantly slide into the seat across from her. She closes her eyes, relieved, and then slowly takes her seat.

I cross my arms. "What, Mom?"

She leans forward. "I want to explain."

"There's not much to explain, is there?"

She furrows her brow. "Don't you want to know what happened?"

"I know what happened," I say. "You got bored with us. You met a douchey teenager from California. You slept with him. You left us."

She closes her eyes. "First of all, Joe is thirty-five."

"Wow. It's amazing someone that old manages to look like he just started shaving."

"Well, he actually has very fine blond hair," my mom says. "So he really doesn't need to shave often at all."

Are you kidding me? "Mom, I don't actually give a shit about Joe."

She winces. "Mitchell. Please. Language."

I take a breath. I need to calm down. "I'm tired. It's past midnight. Are you here to tell me that you and Dad are getting divorced? Because I figured."

"No. Well, yes. We are getting divorced." She looks down at her hands. "But I was actually here to invite you to have dinner with Joe and me tomorrow. At our cabin."

Joe and me. Our cabin. Pressure builds up in my chest, the pressure of trying to hold back my biting words and my anger and to keep breathing, all at the same time.

"I think you'll really like Joe once you get to know him," she continues. "And if we're all going to live here together, it would mean a lot to me if we could all get along."

It's too much. I feel like screaming, but instead my voice comes out a steady, deadly quiet. "You have got to be kidding me."

She blinks at me. "What?"

I speak slowly, like I'm talking to a toddler. "I don't like Joe. I *never* liked him. I *will never* like him. If I live my whole life without ever speaking to him, I'll be better for it." My voice wavers a little, but I don't stop. "And I don't know who told you we're all going to live here together. You two get a trial month. That's four weeks. Four weeks until Dad gets to say whether you stay or go. Four weeks until I graduate. And I couldn't care less what Dad's answer is. Because either way, I am getting the hell out of here in four weeks. And now, thanks to you, I'm never coming back."

She's watching me with wide eyes, glassy with tears, and her lips pressed tightly together. I'm out of breath from my rant. Already, I regret my words, I regret making my mom cry, I regret acting like a spoiled brat. But it feels so good to say what I've wanted to say to her. I can't take it back. Even if I wanted to.

"Mitchell." Her voice comes out soft and strangled. The tears in her eyes spill over and run quietly down her cheeks.

"Please don't say that. I love you so much." She reaches a hand across the table toward me, palm up and outstretched. She's trembling. "Please. You have every right to be mad at me. But I'm still your mother."

My hand twitches in my lap. I know I can take her hand, soft and familiar, and she'll forgive everything I said. That we can talk it out. That we'll make it work. She's my mom, and I'm her only child. I know if I take her hand, I'll start to cry too, and she'll hug me and we'll talk and maybe, just maybe, everything that's happened these past few days will hurt just a little less.

I stare at her hand, open and waiting. I look up at her face, expectant and hopeful and scared. And then I look at the third chair at the table. My dad's chair. Empty.

I stand up, walk into my room, and close the door. I quietly slide down to the floor and lean my back against the hard wood, my head resting just below the doorknob. I listen to my mom cry on the other side, soft, steady sobs.

It isn't until the front door opens and closes a few minutes later that I finally let myself cry, too.

I wake up, my eyes tired and sore, partly from the crying and partly from the tossing and turning I did all night. Despite being exhausted, I make myself get up early so that I have enough time to have a cup of coffee with my dad.

He blinks in surprise when I come out of my room, fully dressed, a full fifteen minutes before I have to leave. But he doesn't say anything. He just pours me a cup of coffee in my favorite mug—with the handle shaped like an octopus—and slides half the morning paper across the table to me. And we sit in a comfortable silence, reading and drinking, until I have to leave. It still feels weird without my mom there. But I feel like I owe it to him after my disappearing act the last few days.

My spirits don't really lift until I glimpse Josie. She's walking out of her cabin as I'm walking to my truck. She calls a cheerful "Have a good day!" at her family as she closes the door and then scampers down the wooden porch stairs and onto the green grass. It still smells freshly mowed from my work on Saturday, the little piles of grass clippings filling the air with their fresh, damp smell. I take in her long lavender skirt and black tank top and the lacy scarf wrapped around her hair. She strides toward the truck, quickly braiding her hair as she goes, eyes on the ground. She doesn't see me until we're almost face-to-face.

"Hi!" I say, loudly.

She stumbles and lets go of her almost-finished braid. "Mitchell!" She puts a hand on her chest. "I didn't see you."

I grin. "I was going to say something, but I thought it would be more fun to scare you."

She reaches out and shoves my arm, and I stumble backward. "You suck," she snaps, but she's smiling.

My arm burns where she touched it, and my whole body feels warm all of a sudden. I open my mouth to say something, but nothing comes out.

"You okay?" She looks up at me, brow furrowed.

I take a deep breath and take a step back. It's easier to

focus when I'm not standing so close to her. "Sorry," I say. "I was just thinking . . . Is it really 7:30?"

She frowns and glances at her phone, and her eyes widen. "Shit!"

"*Someone's* running late," I say. "For *once* in her life." I laugh as she starts jogging toward the truck.

"Mitchell Morrison!" she calls over her shoulder. "Hurry! I'm not about to get my first detention three weeks before I graduate."

I jog after her. Her long hair is falling out of its braid, wild and tangled and tumbling in the breeze, and her shoulders are already a golden brown from her work in the sun this weekend.

Suddenly, my problems all seem to fade into the back corners of my mind. Suddenly, my day is getting way, way better.

CHAPTER TWENTY-ONE
JOSIE

"There's something you're not telling me." Leah eyes me suspiciously over her chicken patty.

My face reddens, and I look down at my tray.

"No, there's not," I reply automatically.

Leah puts her sandwich down and points at me with narrowed eyes. "There totally is. Something weird went on at that party, and you're not telling me." Her eyes widen. "Oh my god. Did you smoke weed?"

"Leah—"

"Because you promised me that we'd do it together for the first time. And that we could get it from Ned and Bernie so that we know what we're getting into."

"I didn't smoke anything."

Her shoulders fall, and she raises her sandwich to her mouth. But before she bites into the cafeteria chicken, her eyes light up and she drops the sandwich back to her tray. "I know! You kissed a boy."

"Leah." I glare at her.

"Josie." She glares back. "This guessing could go on all day. All week, even. Unless you tell me what you're hiding."

"I'm not hiding anything." I fiddle with my braid. "It's just not worth telling."

She just stares at me, her big blue eyes wide and expectant.

"Fine," I say. "On the way home, Mitchell and I had a fight."

Leah gasps, loud and dramatic. "A fight! About what?"

I shake my head. "He thought I was drunk, and he wanted to take me home. And I basically told him it was none of his business. That's it."

Leah leans in closer to me. "That's it? That's definitely not it. He was jealous, Josie! He was worried about you!"

"In a totally misguided and weird way."

Leah shrugs. "Still."

I exhale. "And then, on our way home, his truck ran out of gas. So we had to sleep in the truck overnight."

She shrieks. "You slept with Mitchell Morrison?"

"Jesus, Leah. Could you be any louder?"

"Sorry," she says. She leans forward and rests her chin on her hand, not looking sorry at all. "I just can't believe it. He's so dreamy."

I snort. "What are you, a Disney princess? Who uses the word dreamy?"

She ignores me. "That's hot, Josie. A night together under the stars. I bet he can't stop thinking about it."

"Oh my god. Stop." There's a crash as someone nearby drops their tray on the ground next to a group of freshman girls. I wait until the shrieking stops to continue. "We slept as far apart as possible. We didn't even bump into each other or roll over or anything. It was not hot. It was the opposite of hot."

"I don't believe you."

I sigh. "Leah, Mitchell is not pining away for me. We slept

in a truck together for a few hours. It didn't mean anything."

Leah takes a gulp of water. "Once again, my friend, you totally underestimate yourself. And your hotness. Any guy would be going crazy after a night under a blanket with you."

"Separate blankets," I point out. "And that is so not true."

Leah crosses her arms, about to respond, when a shadow falls over our table. I look up to find Mitchell towering over me.

"Hey," he says.

I open my mouth. Then close it again. Then open it again. *God.* I probably look like a fish.

I pull myself together enough to respond. "Hey."

Very smooth. Very original. I'm sure all the girls who flirt with Mitchell over on the other side of the cafeteria are full of witty repartee and hilarious anecdotes, and I'm over here with monosyllabic answers, opening and closing my mouth like a trout.

He looks at Leah. "Hi."

"Hi yourself," she says. She smirks at me, and I kick her under the table.

Mitchell focuses back on me. "I was wondering what you were doing right now."

I blink down at my lunch tray and then back up at him. "Um. Eating lunch. And then when the bell rings in two minutes, going to class."

"Good. Right. Good." He bobs his head up and down in a vigorous nod. "Well, our next classes are close, I think. So would it be okay if I walked with you?"

I'm pretty sure he has no idea what class I have next. I definitely don't know what he has next. But when I glance at Leah, she's staring at me so hard that I can practically see a blinking *Say Yes Say Yes Say Yes* sign flashing on her forehead. I glance back up at Mitchell and nod just as the bell rings.

"Okay."

I get up and gather my trash, and Leah wiggles her eyebrows at me as I leave. I cross my fingers that Mitchell doesn't notice.

The hallways are packed and loud, as usual. The swarm of students moves in a current; go with the flow, or get swept away. A tall guy with an enormous green backpack slams into Mitchell, while next to me a tiny girl with scary crooked teeth elbows me out of the way in order to catch up with a friend. Mitchell's arm bumps into mine. There's nowhere for us to go. So we keep walking in the bustling, jostling crowd, shoulder to shoulder, neither of us talking.

To our left Emma Harris leans against a locker, playing with her long dark hair. She gives me the evil eye—twice in one week! A new record—and then calls a very loud, very seductive, "Hey, Mitchell."

Mitchell keeps looking straight ahead. He doesn't even bat an eye. The hallway is noisy and all, but I know he heard her. A flash of annoyance crosses Emma's face before she quickly rearranges her features back into her perfectly styled I-couldn't-care-less expression. I concentrate on the ground and try not to smile.

We reach my classroom in less than a minute; it's right around the corner from the cafeteria. And we still haven't spoken. It's just too weird, hanging out with Mitchell at school. If seeing him at the party on Friday was strange, this is even stranger. I've always observed Mitchell from afar here:

at pep rallies, in the cafeteria, in the halls. We never exchange anything more than a friendly wave or the occasional hello. So to be walking with him, purposefully, down the hallway—and it being his idea, no less—is beyond bizarre. And as it turns out, also kind of awkward.

I turn to him at the doorway. He bounces on the heels of his feet, looking at the ground, then at me, then down the hallway, then back at me again.

"Well . . ." I say. "Thanks for the walk?"

It comes out as a question because I'm confused as to what, exactly, the point of this was.

"Right. Sure. Yeah." He shuffles his feet back and forth. "I just wanted to ask you . . ."

He's acting so weird, and it's making me nervous. My palms are sweaty, and I'm pretty sure some of my classmates are staring now. "Ask me what?"

"If . . . you were gonna need a ride after school?" he asks in a rush.

"Um. If that's okay." *What's wrong with him?* Obviously I need a ride after school. The same as every single other day in the history of forever.

"Yep!" Again with the crazed nodding. He looks like a deranged bobblehead. A cute deranged bobblehead, but still. "No problem! So I'll see you then!"

He is talking in exclamation points. Big, enthusiastic pronouncements. Like maybe he thinks I've gone deaf since we last spoke.

The bell rings again, and Mitchell winces at the sound. "Shit. I have Calc. Gotta run." And he dashes down the hall.

I watch him go, as guys reach out to slap him on the back and girls give him friendly waves. He weaves his way through the crowds with ease, the same way he navigates his life at this school. He never swaggers through the halls yelling at his friends, but he never quite blends into the crowd, either. I'm beginning to reconcile the Paintbrush version of Mitchell, the one I grew up with, and the school version of Mitchell, this calm, cool, happy-go-lucky guy. I'm finally getting to know both sides of him, and suddenly, he's a whole new person.

Mitchell zips around the corner, and a realization hits me. I have to smile.

Because the math wing is all the way across the school. Nowhere near my classroom.

English is boring. Someone who loves to read as much as I do should enjoy English class a little more. While Miss Martinez drones on and on about the upcoming final essay, I discreetly rummage in the front pocket of my backpack. In my mind I call it the trash pocket because I basically use it to dump all the shit I don't want but am too lazy to throw away: snack wrappers, pencils that need lead, old homework assignments, etc. Finally I close my fingers around what I'm looking for: the stack of wrinkled brochures at the bottom. I pull them out and smooth them over my desk.

They're college brochures. One for each of the colleges I started an application to and a few other ones as well. I agonized over these brochures for weeks before stuffing them into the dark chasm of my backpack. I knew the black hole of the trash pocket would swallow them right up so I wouldn't have to think about them anymore.

I don't know why I'm dragging them back out now. *Boredom*, I tell myself. I skim them again, just the bold-faced headlines at the top of each paragraph: Starting a New Chapter; New Life. New Experiences. New You; The Adventure of a Lifetime; The Path to Success. And one from the bottommost brochure: Your New Home Is Waiting.

The pages are shiny and silky under my fingers. The fonts are crisp, the colors are bright, every picture features a group of attractive, racially diverse friends smiling—in lab coats, on a perfectly manicured green lawn, at a stately library table. These places look too good to be true. They look fun and interesting and happy. And they look very, very different from my cozy home in the North Carolina mountains.

Suddenly, I feel anxious. Like all the cheerful college students in the pictures are staring right through me. I push the brochures back down into the trash pocket, as far as they truck go. And I push all thoughts of them out of my mind until the bell rings, and I practically race outside toward Mitchell's truck. I don't know what all his stuttering weirdness in the hallway was about, but I intend to find out.

I'm not fast enough because he still beats me there. If I raced out of school today, he must have sprinted. He's fiddling with the radio as I approach the car. But as soon as I pull the passenger door open, he sits up straight.

"Josie." He gazes at me, intense and serious. "We're going on a mission."

CHAPTER TWENTY-TWO
MITCHELL

We've been driving for forty minutes straight so far, weaving around backcountry roads and rolling through small towns. And still our mission has not been completed.

"How exactly am I supposed to help you complete this mission when I have no idea what we're looking for?" Josie's bare feet are propped on the dashboard, and the wind from the open window is tangling her hair. She sticks her hand outside as we zoom around a corner, making waves in the air. And then a fly smacks right into her fingers.

"Shit!"

She jerks up and yanks her arm inside. I crack up as she desperately shakes her hand, trying to get rid of the bug guts. She glares at me and gives me the finger.

"Told you. Nature's a bitch," I say. "And as for the mission: You'll know it when you see it."

"Whatever it is, it better be worth a bug attack," she grumbles. But she sticks her arm right back out the window anyway.

I'm feeling good. The sun is shining, the mountains are gray-blue and gleaming and beautiful, and my truck is running smoothly and quietly, for once. I'm not thinking about things

I don't want to be thinking about. All I can think about is how I hope to god Josie recognizes the place when we get to it, and how totally and completely embarrassing it will be if she doesn't.

We drive for another half hour, and the scenery gets prettier and prettier. We don't talk, but I play my favorite CD on repeat. It was made for me by Bernie when I first got my license, and on the front he scrawled *Don't crash the goddamn car* in his messy chicken scratch. It's a road trip CD, full of songs to drive to, from a time when "music wasn't so shitty," as Bernie puts it. As we near our destination, one of my favorite tracks comes on, a song from the sixties by Jim Croce. *Like the pine trees lining the winding road, I got a name.* Out of the corner of my eye I can see Josie mouthing the words. We both grew up on Ned and Bernie's music.

Two minutes away. I glance at Josie, and she sits up a little straighter. A glimmer of recognition crosses her face, but she doesn't say anything. We turn onto a tree-lined gravel road, and the tires rumble and creak on the uneven terrain. And then we take a left and then a right, and there it is.

There's no one in the lot, but I park far away anyway. I get out and slam the door, and Josie does the same. She still doesn't say anything. Together, we walk across the parking lot.

A huge battered sign reads Jimbo's Drive-Thru in peeling black letters, perched precariously atop an old school bus. The bus has been taken off its wheels and painted a bright turquoise, with a big window in the front surrounded by an even bigger menu. A field off to the side sports a handful of picnic tables, all covered in red-and-white checkered tablecloths.

Josie is still quiet. And I am getting more and more nervous.

We reach the window, but there's no one behind the counter. Josie squints at the menu. I cautiously stick my head in.

"Hello?" I call.

Almost immediately a head pops up, making Josie jump. A cheerful older woman with bright purple hair grins at me. "Mitchell Morrison!"

"Hi, Angie."

She reaches right through the window and envelops me in a hug. Josie watches, bemused.

Angie pulls back and studies Josie. "Is this your girlfriend?"

Josie's face almost immediately turns pink.

I quickly shake my head. "No. Nope. This is my Josie."

Angie's eyebrows shoot up, and Josie's face turns even redder.

"Not *my* Josie!" Now my face is red, too. "Just Josie."

"Well hi, Just Josie," says Angie warmly. "You're lucky to be hanging around this guy. Even if you are just friends."

Josie smiles faintly. "He's all right."

"He's a good kid," says Angie. "Our most loyal customer."

"Really?" asks Josie. "But we live over an hour away."

Angie leans forward and whispers, "We have really, really good fries."

I laugh, and Angie joins in. Josie looks back and forth between us.

"So." Angie picks up a spatula and gestures to the menu. "What'll it be today?"

I sneak a quick glance at Josie. "We'll have two chocolate milkshakes."

"I knew it!" Josie's eyes light up, and she grins and shoves my arm.

Internally, I let out a huge sigh of relief. She *does* remember.

Angie raises her eyebrows and turns toward the back. "Coming right up."

Josie shakes her head. "I can't believe it. This is really the same place?"

"It really is," I say. "I thought you would recognize it sooner. How many restaurants operate out of a rusty blue school bus?"

"Well, yeah," she says. "But it was a long time ago. And I didn't expect . . ."

I know what she means. The last time we were here together, we were eleven. In fifth grade. That was the last year we were homeschooled by Myra at Paintbrush, our last year before public school and other kids and the real world. When we passed our state-issued end of year exams, our moms always took us out. That year, we drove a whole hour to go to this special dinosaur-themed novelty restaurant, one of those quirky small town tourist traps my mom had read about in a travel magazine. But when we got there, it was closed. A frazzled-looking employee told us that the animatronic T-Rex was malfunctioning; we could hear it roaring from outside, fierce and loud, in a constant, unending loop. So we drove ten minutes to the next town over, and found . . . this. Jimbo's.

It looked exactly the same back then. We ordered chicken fingers and french fries and chocolate milkshakes. It was the best chocolate milkshake I'd ever had. And then later, while Josie's little sisters finished their food and our moms chatted away, we found a tree to climb. And way high up, in the tallest, thickest branches, we kissed.

It was a dare. Josie dared me eat a pine needle. I dared her to lick a piece of bark. She dared me to swing upside down on a branch . . . and I was too scared to do it. I was going to lose our game. So I dared her to do something I knew she would never do: kiss me.

"On the *lips*," I declared dramatically.

"Ew!" she answered, horrified. And I grinned smugly.

But before I knew it, she was scrunching up her face, closing her eyes, and leaning in. And she pecked me right on the lips.

"Gross!" we said at the same time. And then we said "Jinx!" at the same time. And then we laughed and climbed down.

It was a first kiss for both of us. Her lips were cool and soft and tasted like chocolate milkshake. We never talked about it again.

The next year, we both went off to middle school. We made different friends. We stopped hanging out as much. We really only saw each other during our morning and afternoon carpool, and at Paintbrush. We were still friends. We've always been friends. But it was different after that summer.

Josie is examining the giant menu when Angie returns with our milkshakes.

"Here you go," Angie says. "Extra whipped cream, three cherries. As usual."

"Thanks, Angie," I say.

"How do you make all this stuff?" Josie asks, picking her milkshake up from the counter. "Teriyaki chicken fingers? Cajun fries? Fish tacos?" She squints toward the top. "Does that say Haggis? Isn't that—?"

"Sheep's innards?" Angie asks cheerfully. "Yep. It is. A traditional Scottish delicacy." She lowers her voice to a conspiratorial whisper. "We don't really make it, though. We just like to see if anyone's brave enough to order it. If they are, we give them their food for free."

Josie laughs. "In that case, I'll have the haggis."

Angie shakes her head. "There's no point. It's already on us."

I try to slide her a ten, but it's no use. She shakes her head and shoos us away toward the grove of picnic tables.

I smile gratefully. "Thanks, Angie. See you next week. And tell Gretchen I say hi."

Josie and I wander over and take a seat at the nearest table. I slurp my milkshake and close my eyes. These milkshakes are the closest thing to heaven on earth I've ever encountered.

"Gretchen?" asks Josie. She takes a sip, and her eyes widen. "Oh my god. Even better than I remembered."

"Right?" I grin. "And Gretchen is Angie's wife. And business partner. They've run this place ever since Angie's dad died and left it to them."

Josie toys with her straw, considering this. "And you know them . . . how?"

I gesture to the bus behind us. "From here. Just from coming here so much."

She looks at me for a long moment.

"What?" I ask.

"Nothing." Her eyes twinkle, the corners of her mouth turned up. "You're just a little bit mysterious. That's all."

We sit in a companionable silence for a while, sipping our milkshakes and soaking up the late afternoon sun. I'm a little worried she's going to ask why I brought her here. Because I really don't have a good answer.

And I'm also wondering if she's remembering our tree kiss right now. Like I am. If she even remembers it at all.

I'm slurping up the last chocolaty dregs before Josie is even halfway done with hers. She stares at me.

"Seriously? Already?"

I pop the last maraschino cherry into my mouth. "I can't help it. It's like crack."

"So that's why you brought me here?" she asks. "To help you break your habit?"

"The first step," I say solemnly, "is admitting you have a problem."

She rolls her eyes and sips her shake. Her gaze roams the scenery around us. "I can see why you drive all the way here. Not just the milkshakes. It's beautiful."

She's right. Jimbo's is on the outskirts of a small mountain town, sitting smack in the center of this deep valley. All around us are mountains, rising steeply everywhere we look. It's gorgeous.

"It's my favorite place to come and think," I say.

"Chocolate milkshakes. The perfect thinking food." She hesitates and then adds, "New England will be different."

"Yeah. It will." I look at her face, framed by long hair that glows a golden-brown in the late-afternoon sun.

"Won't you miss this?" she asks.

"There are mountains in New England."

"But they're different mountains."

I shrug. "This place is beautiful." I look down at the table, trailing a finger across the sticky red-and-white checkers. "But a mountain's a mountain. No matter where it is."

"Maybe." But she doesn't sound convinced.

Another silence. I can't tell if it's comfortable or awkward. But then Josie interrupts it with a big slurp.

"Finished!" She holds up her empty cup.

"Damn it. I was hoping you'd get full so I could finish yours."

Her jaw drops. "How dare you imply that I can't handle a whole milkshake. I could eat *two* whole milkshakes and not bat an eye."

I stand and stretch. "Well, coming from someone who has done that very thing on multiple occasions, let me tell you. It's not a great idea."

"Wait. You actually did that?" She stands too, climbing out of the picnic table bench. "And you actually thought it would be a good idea?"

Together, we start toward the truck. "Hey. You could be a little nicer to the guy who just helped you relive a cherished childhood memory."

My cheeks flush as soon as the words leave my mouth. I meant the day. Not the kiss.

Josie doesn't say anything, but I swear she glances toward the tall pine towering in the corner of the field. *She remembers.*

I walk a little closer to her. I can't help it. She smells like fresh grass and a little salty, that warm summer smell of sweat. She walks with a little bounce in her step, and our shoulders brush. I chance a glance at her face, at her eyes that sparkle in the golden sunlight, at her lips curled up into a small smile.

I bet she tastes like chocolate milkshake.

"Something is going on," Cord announces as I slide across from him at the lunch table.

I pick up my banana and start to unpeel it.

"What's going on," I reply, "is that it smells like Woodstock at this table."

"Like fresh air and good times?" he asks hopefully.

"Like you smoked a bunch of weed before school today."

He waves his hand in the air, dismissing me. "Two weeks until graduation, dude. I'd be stupid if I showed up to class and I *wasn't* high. I'm getting a whole new perspective on my education."

"We still have to take finals." I shake my head. "You're going to college in a few months, man. You can't pull this kind of shit there."

"What are you talking about? It's college! It's *exactly* where I can pull this kind of shit." I open my mouth to respond, but he cuts me off. "Besides. You're avoiding the question."

I take a big bite of banana and chew as slowly as I can, just to make him mad. I take my time swallowing before I speak. "What question?"

He sighs and pulls out his phone. "Last night. I texted you the following." He clears his throat dramatically, and I roll my eyes. "Yo. Stay over here this weekend. I bought the *West Side Story* restored version on Blu-Ray with commentary, plus *Zombie Revolution Four: The Final Countdown*. Also the five pound bag of cheese balls from Wal-Mart."

He looks up and tilts his head at me, like he's waiting for an excuse. I don't say anything.

"And you texted me back saying: Sorry, dude. Plans this weekend." He drops his phone back onto the table. "*Plans this weekend*? Since when do you or I have *plans this weekend* that don't involve each other?"

I shrug. "You know I'm not a big *West Side Story* guy."

"I know. You like *Guys and Dolls* much better."

Sadly, this is true. This is what my friendship with Cord has done to me.

He continues, "But normally you'd sit with me through a viewing of *West Side* in order to get to the good stuff."

"The good stuff being fake cheese snacks and zombie killing?" I ask.

"*Five pounds* of cheese balls, Mitchell. Five. Pounds."

He's right. Not a lot could drag me away from cheese balls and *Zombie Revolution*. Except . . .

"I think I know what this is about." Cord smirks at me as he slices his greasy cafeteria pizza into small squares.

"Normal people eat their pizza with their hands, dude. You know that, right?"

He completely ignores me. "It's the same reason that you've mysteriously disappeared every day this week after school.

The same reason we've been sitting over here by ourselves, and not"—he tilts his head toward our usual lunch table, stuffed with laughing cheerleaders and burly athletes—"over there." He frowns. "The same reason you've cruelly abandoned me on a Friday night to watch Maria cry over Tony's dead body all by myself."

I eat my last bite of banana and toss the peel onto my tray. The peel hits the blue plastic with a loud smack. "Just spit it out, Cord."

He grins. "Josie Sedgwick."

He's right. Josie and I have hung out every day this week. On Tuesday, we drove out to Silver Lake and waded around in the water. On Wednesday, we went to the big used bookstore in Asheville and each bought a book for the other to read. On Thursday, we went to the local park and swung on the swings. Before community dinner, of course. Which I didn't attend.

None of these were planned things. They just sort of . . . happened. I try explaining this to Cord, but he shakes his head.

"What you're describing are dates, dude. Not hanging out."

My heart jumps a little at that word. *Date. They're not dates*, I tell myself. They're just coincidences.

Then why do I feel like I need to keep my entire weekend totally free, on the off chance that Josie will, at some point, want to hang out with me for even a few minutes?

Cord has been talking while I've been lost in thought. I don't hear a word until he says, "Like I told her to."

I focus back on him. "Told her to what?"

"At the party?" He smirks. "When you got all mad at us?

You acted like a jealous boyfriend when I was talking to her."

"No, I didn't."

"Yes, you did. Anyway, all I was telling her was to keep an eye on you. Because you could use a distraction." He smirks. "Seems like it's working."

"Shut up, Cord," I reply automatically. But my brain is turning. Are we just hanging out because Josie thinks I need help? Because she's watching out for me, after everything that happened with my mom?

Maybe this isn't anything. Maybe she just feels sorry for me.

But *maybe* isn't enough for me to stop myself from seeing her tonight.

CHAPTER TWENTY-THREE
JOSIE

I think Leah might explode. She is quivering, actually quivering, from excitement. And from what I suspect is an effort to not shriek at the top of her lungs across the parking lot.

"Date!" she shouts. "You have a date!"

A few people walking by turn their heads, and I grab her arm.

"You have got to stop," I hiss. "And you've also got to go."

I point to her car across the lot. Leah has me cornered up against Mitchell's truck. She showed up a second ago and shouted a loud and dramatic, "*Aha!*" as she spied me getting into the passenger seat. Like she had caught me committing some kind of crime. Now we're leaning against the side of the truck as I desperately try to convince her to leave.

"I always drive home with Mitchell." I look around. He's still nowhere to be seen. Thank god.

"But you're not usually so secretive." Leah is practically cackling. She adores drama and secrets, and she loves to feel like she's right. Today, she's hit the jackpot. "And you never hang out with him like you've been hanging out this week. And you get that starry-eyed look when you talk about him."

"*Starry-eyed?*" I practically spit the word out. "I don't

know what *starry-eyed* even looks like, but I can promise you, it's not a look I've ever had."

She pokes my shoulder. "And then you avoided all my questions at lunch today, and now you're looking all suspicious and sneaky." She claps her hands together. "Josie Sedgwick, you have a date."

"Leah." I stare her straight in the eyes, as seriously as I can. "I do not have a date."

And it's true. I don't have a date. I'm just hoping, in a totally desperate way, that somehow our nothing plans will evolve into something plans. The way it's been happening the past few days.

Leah's expression falls. She slumps her shoulders and sighs. "Fine. But I expect a text from you tonight telling me all about it."

"All about what? There's nothing to tell."

She looks at me knowingly. "After the way the last few days have been? You and I both know that there'll be something to tell."

I shake my head at her, but I can't deny the hope rising in my chest. It's a desperate, nervous, pathetic hope. And every time it rises, it gets pushed down by the truth: that whatever I think is happening has probably been all in my head.

"It's nothing," I say to Leah. It sounds like I'm trying to convince myself. "He needs a distraction, and I'm the distraction. That's all."

She opens her mouth to respond, but then something behind me makes her eyes widen. "Code red, code red," she mutters. "The eagle has landed. The package has been delivered. The chicken has crossed the road."

I whip around and come face to face with Mitchell. He wears a politely confused expression.

"Chicken?" he asks.

"We were just talking about you!" Leah exclaims, beaming.

"Were you?" He glances between Leah and me. "Well, I hope I'm not the chicken."

"You're not," I assure him.

Leah laughs. "He's funny," she stage-whispers to me.

I am going to kill Leah. Mitchell's face twitches, like he can't decide whether to laugh or be offended.

"We were actually talking about all the things Leah has to do this afternoon." I glare at Leah.

She gives me a blank look.

"She's incredibly busy, and she's really crunched for time." I pull out my phone and glance at it. "Oh man, Leah. Better get moving."

Realization dawns across her face. "Oh, right," she says knowingly. "*Things*. I have *things* to do. And *stuff*. I have *stuff* to do as well." She starts to move off. "Bye, guys!" But before she makes it even two steps, she turns around again. "Oh, and Josie?"

"What?"

She holds her hand up to her ear like a phone and, with Mitchell still watching, mouths *call me*. Oh my god. She is officially the worst best friend in the world.

Mitchell and I watch her walk off in silence.

"She's off to do . . . things?" Mitchell clarifies.

"Yep."

"And stuff."

"Uh-huh."

"So am I supposed to assume Leah is a drug dealer now?"

I laugh while watching her flowing blond hair and lacy white dress bounce out of sight. "Yep. She's international."

He nods seriously. "I can see that. It's her frightening looks and no-nonsense personality."

"And her worldwide connections and vast knowledge of the underground drug world," I add. "Plus, she loves cocaine."

"Who doesn't?" Mitchell grins at me, and I grin back. And for a second, I am lost. It's quite a thing, being the focus of one of Mitchell's million-watt smiles. It's beautiful and blinding and disorienting, all at once.

He breaks the spell. "Ready to go?"

Where? I want to ask. But I don't want to ruin it, whatever it is.

So I just smile back. "I'm always ready."

I do everything I can to make the time pass by as quickly as possible. I do my homework out on the porch. I clean my room. I help my mom cook dinner—veggie burgers and kale salad. I eat at our small round table, chatting with my mom and Mae and even Libby, when she stops texting long enough to actually participate in the conversation. I clear the table and wash the dishes.

And then I meet Mitchell outside with a flashlight, because that's what he told me to do.

I'm fiddling with the switch, turning it on and off and on again, when Mitchell shows up.

"Are you signaling for me or something?" He points his flashlight in my direction and flashes it on and off.

"I think it would have to be darker for me to do that." I tilt my head up to the sky. It's dimming, but it's definitely not dark enough to need flashlights.

"It's not dark enough yet," Mitchell agrees. "But it will be soon."

For some reason, this sends chills down my spine. But not in a scary way.

"Is this the part where you lure me away and murder me?"

Mitchell laughs. "If I wanted to murder you, I would have done it yesterday. Or the day before." He pauses. "Or the day before that."

"Or the day before *that,*" I add.

"Right." In the almost-darkness, his features are blurred and soft, his messy hair, his dark eyes, the sharp broad line of his shoulders. He's wearing a dark-gray flannel, and it looks soft and worn. I have this sudden urge to reach out and touch it, and I cross my arms and clamp my hands down to stop myself. *Josie, pull yourself together.*

Mitchell clears his throat. "So it takes a little while to get where we're going. And then back again. Is that okay with your mom?"

I raise my eyebrows.

"Right. I know." He holds up his hands. "Just checking."

We start walking toward his truck. "What about you?" I ask. "Is this okay with your parents?"

"It's okay with my dad," he says pointedly.

I leave it at that.

We arrive at our destination an hour and a half later. At least, I guess it's our destination because Mitchell has stopped the car. We are the only truck in a tiny dirt parking lot. The truck's dusty headlights illuminate a sign that simply reads hike at your own risk.

"This isn't creepy at all," I say.

Mitchell laughs, but he sounds a little bit nervous. "It's worth it. I promise."

"Okay." I open the door. "But next time, I'm picking the place."

Why did I say that? What if he doesn't want there to be a next time? But before I have time to be embarrassed, Mitchell responds with an eager, "Okay." He gazes over at me. "I'll hold you to that."

We clamber out of the truck, and I switch on my flashlight, sweeping the beam of light over the woods around us. Mitchell does the same.

"All clear," he says. "Okay. It's not that far from here."

He leads me to a small, winding path across from the truck. For twenty minutes, I follow him in silence as he slowly makes his way down the twisting path. Our footsteps are soft on the thick layer of pine needles, and all around us the forest is alive with noise: rustling leaves and crickets chirping and branches scratching and owls calling. It doesn't scare me. It's the same soundtrack outside my cabin window, the same soundtrack I fall asleep to every night. It sounds like home.

I don't realize that I've spoken this last thought out loud until Mitchell chuckles.

"What?" I whisper.

"I know what you mean, that's all," he says.

"Then why are you laughing?"

"Because we sound like weird forest people. 'The forest is our home.' Like we wear leaves for clothes and worship pine needles and rub sticks together for fire and shit."

I snort, the sound echoing in the dark stillness. "Like we're part of a freaky nature cult."

"Honestly, that's not far from the truth."

Our laughs mingle in the darkness. When they fade, the forest seems quieter. It's almost enough to scare me, just a little. I inch closer to Mitchell until my nose is practically touching his shoulder blades. He smells like soap and sweat and a little bit like cologne. *Cologne.* Did he put that on for me? I inhale again, until my head is swimming with the smell of Mitchell.

The smell of Mitchell. Did I really just think that? What's wrong with me? We're just friends. I repeat it to myself like a mantra in the dark. *We're just friends. I'm just a distraction. We're just friends.*

Suddenly, Mitchell comes to a total stop with no warning. And since I'm walking so creepily close behind him, I smash into his back with an alarming amount of force. I launch him right off his feet, and we both go tumbling down.

Oh god. If I were dainty and tiny and graceful, he would

barely have felt me bump into him. It would have been cute. *Oh, look how clumsy and adorable Josie is.* Instead, I plowed into him with the force of a thousand elephants. I feel like a huge battering ram. I'm lying on top of him in the dark, and I am probably totally crushing him. The more I scramble to right myself, the more I make it worse.

"I'm sorry!" My voice sounds too loud, too high-pitched. I try to stand up and knee him, hard.

"Oof."

"I'm sorry!" I tumble back down. I have no idea where I just kneed him. I have no idea where his body parts are compared to my body parts.

And oh god, just thinking of the words *body parts* has my cheeks in flames. I've somehow ended up with my face pressed to his chest, and I'm sure he can feel the heat from my face and from my total and complete embarrassment radiating right through his shirt. His flannel shirt, which, it turns out, is as soft as it looks. Maybe even softer.

"Hey, hey." His voice is amused, and I'm so glad he doesn't sound like he's in any serious pain. "Stop moving for a second."

"I'm sorry," I say again, a desperate edge to my voice. I try to make my limbs go still, try to calm the thumping of my heart.

I feel a pull in my hair and realize my braid must be caught on a button on his shirt. I yank my head up, and immediately pain shoots across my scalp. "Ow."

"Hey," Mitchell says again, softer this time. "Hold still."

He props himself up next to me and gently unravels my hair.

"Hey." His voice is low and a little raspy. He clears his throat. "Um. I might have to undo your braid."

"Yeah. That's fine. I'm sorry," I say again, automatically. I'm ruining this adventure.

"My fault," he murmurs. He pulls out my hair tie, and I close my eyes. "Don't be sorry."

I don't say anything. He weaves his fingers through my hair, and my braid falls apart. At the base of my neck, he fiddles with the knot. "There."

I don't want to move. I want to lie here in the dark with Mitchell Morrison playing with my hair forever. I think I could do this for eternity and be happy.

But lying on top of Mitchell on the forest floor is not really socially acceptable behavior. I lift my head, testing, and then sit all the way up. "Thanks."

"No problem. Sorry about that." He pushes himself to his feet. In the darkness, I can barely see his outstretched hand. "Here."

I clasp my fingers around his, and he pulls me to my feet. Our hands stay connected for a second longer than necessary. I'm a little bit stunned by my reaction to the events of the last thirty seconds. By the way my heart batters against my rib cage. By the way my whole body is hot and feverish and flushed.

It feels terrible. It feels perfect and beautiful and terrible all at the same time.

This can't be good.

CHAPTER TWENTY-FOUR
MITCHELL

I've kissed girls. Four girls, to be exact. My sophomore year, I got to second base at a party with Brandi Hillman, captain of the tennis team and collectively known as the hottest girl in school. Brandi was kind of mean and condescending and definitely only wanted to make out with me because her friends dared her to. After twenty minutes, she pulled away from me, told me that was pretty good, and then sauntered out of the room. Not my proudest moment. But it was my best sexual experience. Until now.

I don't know how touching Josie's hair could be considered a sexual experience. But it definitely, definitely was. Her whole body felt so warm and solid and soft. Like a hug. Even just lying on me, even as she desperately tried to get up and away from me, her body felt like a hug.

I need to focus. Now we're covered in dirt and bruises and scratches and pine needles, none of which makes for a good time. I hope she's still having fun. I hope this is worth it.

I realize with a start that I'm still holding Josie's hand. Why am I still holding her hand? I drop it quickly.

"Are you okay?" My voice comes out kind of shaky.

"Yeah." She brushes the dirt off her pants and shirt. "I'm

fine. Totally."

But she doesn't look up at me, doesn't meet my eyes. Is it because it's dark? Or is it because she's mad?

"We're here, I promise." I'm worried she's getting annoyed with my little plan. I sweep my flashlight behind me until the light illuminates what I'm looking for. "There."

We're standing in front of a pile of boulders—big granite formations that dot this part of the mountains. I scramble up a few, pulling myself up with my arms, and then reach behind to help Josie. Not like she needs it. She waves my hand away and launches herself up even quicker than me. Of course.

I stand, lean down, and shove a small boulder out of the way. I point my flashlight down. The beam of light illuminates a small crack in the rocks, just big enough for a person to slip inside.

"We're going in there?" Josie asks from behind me.

"Um. Yeah." I cringe, waiting for her to protest.

But her voice is confident and steady, and her response is quick. "Okay."

I kneel and slide into the pitch black, my feet touching the floor as Josie's feet disappear from view. I inhale the familiar scent—fresh, cool, slightly damp. Then I shine my light up. Above me, Josie squints in the light.

But she doesn't hesitate. In one quick, graceful movement, she slips into the cave next to me. We're standing next to each other in darkness.

I fumble in the backpack and grab a few candles. A couple flicks of my lighter and the cave is illuminated.

It's about the size of a walk-in closet, with just enough

room for me to stand. The top of my hair just barely brushes the top of the rocks. With the candlelight dancing across the walls, it's cozy and beautiful. It feels like another world.

"Wow." Josie's face is flushed from our hike, her mouth open as she takes everything in. She reaches out and brushes the wall with the tips of her fingers. The candlelight casts a shadow behind her that mimics her movements. In the soft, warm light, her eyes glitter. She looks . . . bright. Larger than life in my tiny secret cave. I can't look away.

"What is this?" she asks, her voice curious.

I blink and snap out of my reverie. "I happened across it one day, and I kind of fell in love. So I did a little research. There's an old sign out front. I think a long time ago this trail was used a lot for people to come see these cool rock formations. But at some point, the government or the park system or whoever must have stopped taking care of it. I've never seen another person here." I shrug. "I think it's forgotten."

"Your own secret cave." She looks right at me and smiles—a real, genuine smile—and my heart feels like it's going to burst.

"You like it?" It's a pathetic question, but I can't keep the words from escaping my lips.

She hugs her arms across her chest. "I love it." She sinks down to the floor and crosses her legs. "It feels like we're living in Huck Finn or something."

"Minus the racism." I slide down across from her. The cave floor is smooth and cool. Our knees almost touch. But not quite.

I lean back against the stone wall behind me, and Josie does the same.

"You do a lot of adventuring." Josie's voice is loud in the absolute quiet of the cave. She must feel it too, because her next words come out in almost a whisper. "Here. Jimbo's. That little place where we slept in your truck."

I shrug. "I need to be away sometimes."

"You know, you're weirder than everyone at school thinks you are."

A loud laugh escapes my lips. "What do you mean?"

"You have your own little cave out here in the woods. You are a literal cave man."

She grins at me, and it's infectious; I grin back. "And here you thought I was cool."

"Oh, don't worry. I never thought that."

We laugh, and it echoes off the walls and bounces back at us. When the sound fades, it feels extra quiet in the cave.

"Wanna see something cool?" I ask.

Josie nods. "I always do."

I blow out one of the candles, and she raises her eyebrows. I lean forward to blow out the other one but stop myself.

"Sorry." I lean back.

"What?"

I shake my head. "I don't know. Blowing out the candles . . ." I gesture awkwardly with my hand. "I don't want it to be weird."

"Why? Because it feels like this might be the part where you murder me?" She smiles.

"No, because we're alone. In the dark." I bite my lip.

"Oh." Josie's cheeks turn pink, but she quickly shakes her head. "Don't worry. I know you're not trying to seduce me or anything."

"I never said that."

There's a pause. Josie opens her mouth and then closes it again, and I swear my whole life flashes before my eyes. It's probably just one second, but it's the longest second of my life. Did I get the wrong signals?

Well. It's too late now. *Here goes nothing.*

"Because I think maybe I am. Trying to seduce you." My heart pounds as the words leave my mouth. I can't believe I just said that. I can't believe I just said that to Josie Sedgwick.

"Oh." Josie's face is on fire now. She twists her braid nervously.

"Is it working?" I try to keep my voice light and easy and jokey, and not as if my entire life and happiness and well-being depend on her answer.

Finally, she meets my eyes. The pause is long, excruciatingly long.

And then she finally answers. "Yeah. It is."

CHAPTER TWENTY-FIVE
JOSIE

The look on Mitchell's face—equal parts relieved and happy and even a little anxious—might be the cutest thing I've ever seen. It makes my heart melt and ooze right down my ribcage. It makes an embarrassingly wide smile stretch across my face. It makes my cheeks turn red. It makes me want to kiss him.

Of course, I don't. I've only kissed two boys, ever. One was Jordan Quinn, when we dated for two brief weeks last year. Leah insisted we would be great together, based on the fact we both like Harry Potter. Even after I tried to explain to her *everybody* likes Harry Potter—that she was the weird one for *not* liking Harry Potter—even then, she kept insisting. We went on three dates—two of which were at the mall—and we made out twice, both times in his car. They were very forgettable dates and very forgettable kisses. Turns out there's only so much to be said about Harry Potter, and only so much kissing can fill empty space in the conversation. When he broke up with me to "focus on his studies" (a.k.a. date first chair violin Kristy O'Malley), I was wildly relieved.

The only other boy I've kissed is Mitchell, when we were, like, eleven. And up until a few days ago, I wasn't even sure he remembered. I'm still not totally sure.

All in all, this has not added up to a lot of kissing experience for me. Definitely not as much as Mitchell, I'm sure. I might be a bad kisser. I can't risk it. No matter how happy Mitchell looks. No matter how cute he looks in the candlelight.

Mitchell stares at my face. He stares at my lips. He leans slightly forward, with this kind of blurry look in his eyes, and my heart beats double time. Maybe triple time. Maybe too fast to even tell.

I clear my throat. "So what did you want to show me?"

He blinks and leans back, eyes still dazed. "What?"

I gesture to the candle. "You were blowing out the candles?"

"Oh. Yeah." He leans over and blows on the final candle. The wick sputters, and then the light is gone, and we are in total pitch-blackness.

"You still there?" His voice floats through the darkness.

I laugh. "I don't have a lot of options."

"Right." He shuffles around, and then his knee bumps against mine. "Okay. Just lie down." He pauses. "Sorry. Not in a weird way. I mean—"

"It's fine." Slowly, I lower myself onto the floor and hear Mitchell doing the same. We end up side by side, our shoulders brushing against each other. The sound of Mitchell's breathing is so close to my ear and the warmth radiating from his body is so palpable I have to force myself not to shiver.

"So?" he asks.

I haven't been paying attention. "So . . . what?"

"Look up."

I do. And when I do, I gasp. I can't help it.

"Right?" I can hear the grin in Mitchell's voice. "No light

pollution out here."

Above us, the opening in the top of the cave reveals a perfect starry night sky. The stars don't just dot the sky; they swirl in the sky, they make patterns, they are small and big and bright and soft, all at the same time. The darkness is stuffed with stars, stars crammed in every corner of the great expanse above us. I feel like I could reach up and scoop a handful down and watch them glitter in my palm. I am blown away.

"And I always thought the stars were pretty up at Paintbrush," I say softly.

"They're good there, too. But even the light from the cabin porches at night can mess it up," he says. "Here, there's absolutely no light for miles. And it's a super clear night, too. I checked the forecast before we came."

I picture Mitchell checking the forecast, planning for this night with me, and something swells inside. It makes my heart speed up.

And seconds later, when Mitchell slips his hand over mine, soft and hesitant and careful, I feel like it just might burst.

This feeling, this falling, for Mitchell Morrison of all people, it's so new. I never thought I would be holding hands with Mitchell in a cave. Not in a million years. It's like taking a sip of a glass of water on a hot day, only to realize it's actually sweet tea; it's not what you expected, but it's better. It's what you realize you wanted all along.

CHAPTER TWENTY-SIX
MITCHELL

We are quiet on the ride back. It's well after midnight. I feel wired, adrenaline swirling through my veins. Josie *likes* me. I like Josie, and she likes me back.

But Josie is tired. She's struggling to keep her eyes open. I kind of hope she falls asleep. She looks so cute when she sleeps. But I need to say something first.

"Hey," I say.

She turns toward me, eyes half-closed, smiling. "Hey."

"I want to kiss you." I say it so quickly, it all comes out in one mashed up, made-up nonsense word. *Iwanttokissyou. Eye-wanna-kiss-yew.*

Her eyes flutter as she sits up straighter. "Oh. I—"

"But," I continue quickly. "I want it to be right. I want it to be on your time." I swallow. My heart thumps like crazy in my chest. "I want you to make the first move."

She considers this for a second. "Okay."

"I just wanted you to know. That I want to. Whenever you do."

The truck is quiet again. Too quiet. I'm worried Josie can literally hear my heartbeat, hear the way it's pounding against my ribcage. The way it's practically pounding right out of my chest.

Then, slowly, Josie leans over the console and places her head on my shoulder. Her braid drapes down my back, and her forehead nestles into the crook of my neck.

It can't be comfortable for her. And my arm falls asleep almost immediately. But we stay this way the whole ride home.

It's three in the morning by the time I crawl into my bed. My eyelids are heavy, and a warm contentment spreads through my limbs.

Falling for Josie isn't like other crushes, like kisses I've had with other girls. It's skipping all the hard stuff, the messy stuff, the baggage and backstory and ugly parts. It's like we're halfway there before we've even really begun. It's like slipping on an old sweater, the one hidden in the way back of a forgotten closet. And then remembering that it was always the comfiest.

I wake up with a jolt; one moment sound asleep, and the next wide, wide awake. I'm humming with energy, and my insides are bouncing, and all I can think about is Josie.

Josie, Josie, Josie.

I try to calm myself down. *You're an adult*, I tell myself. *You're not a sixth grader with his first crush. Cool it.*

It doesn't do much. My little pep talks almost never do.

I throw on a white t-shirt and athletic shorts and then walk out to the kitchen. My dad is already dressed and sitting at the table. He has an untouched cup of coffee in front of him, steaming and full. He stares at the wall, his expression empty and blank, borderline catatonic.

But he starts when the floorboards creak beneath me. "Hey, kiddo." He smiles a weak smile.

I want to run outside and hide from this pathetic scene. My feet itch to leave. This isn't my dad. This isn't the same strong guy who taught me how to use a chainsaw and throw a Frisbee and ride a bike. But instead of bolting, I make myself carefully walk to the counter and pour a cup of coffee into my favorite blue ceramic mug. Then I sit down at the table across from him and take a deep breath.

"How's it going, Dad?" I exhale the words.

"Not so great." His voice catches on the last word, and his knuckles whiten as he grips his mug.

Please don't cry, I think. *Please, please, please don't cry.*

"I'm sorry," I say softly. I don't know if I mean that I'm sorry for bringing it up or for what happened with Mom or for not being around the past week. Maybe I mean it all.

He just nods. We let my apology hang in the air between us. Dad stares down into the depths of his coffee mug before taking a deep breath. "Saturday morning, kid." He takes a sip of his coffee and wipes his mouth with the back of his hand. "Think Ned could spare you today? I have some projects I need some help on."

"Yeah, Dad." I nod. "Of course."

I finish my coffee as he putters around the kitchen, rinsing his mug, throwing ingredients for veggie soup into a crock pot, wiping the counter down. It's all so familiar, so normal. For the first time, I let mvself think: *Maybe we'll be all right.*

I spend the whole morning and most of the afternoon helping my dad work on lesson plans for his business class that starts next week. Normally, he co-teaches it with my mom. I'm guessing now he's doing it solo, but I don't ask, and he doesn't offer.

Helping is kind of a stretch, actually. We have all his papers spread out on the front porch, and my dad is dictating changes to me while I write them on his laptop. I'm probably only capturing about thirty percent of what he's actually saying, though. Because most of the time my gaze darts around for Josie.

I see her in the morning, raking the tomato fields across the way. Even from far away I can see she's covered in dirt and her face is bright pink. Josie has a perpetually red face—when it's hot, when she's embarrassed, when she laughs really hard. Her hair is falling out of its braid in big chunks, and the little wisps around her face are plastered to her from sweat. I bet she smells good. That earthy summer smell. I want to go hug her and see. I want to tuck her hair back into its braid. I want to kiss her lips and her salty skin.

What my dad wants is for me to focus. He snaps his fingers in front of my face. "Mitchell. Earth to Mitchell."

I blink up at him. "What?"

"Come join us back on planet earth, dude." He gives me a

playful shove. "Seriously, what's up with you?"

I shake my head and tell him it's nothing, until he leaves me alone again so I can focus and type his words and edit a few spreadsheets. And I'm getting tons of work done, being really productive . . . until I see Josie across the yard later in the afternoon, swinging Ada Macpherson into the air. Ada's delighted five-year-old screech echoes across the yard, accompanied by Josie's loud, happy laugh. Josie doesn't laugh like that a lot. She reserves those laughs for moments of true, total happiness. I want to be able to make her laugh like that.

I'm considering this when the laptop resting on my knees shuts. I look up to find my dad smirking at me.

"Something distracting you, Mitchell?" He raises his eyebrows.

"What?" I open the laptop again. "No. I'm just tired, I guess." I stare intently at the computer screen, then at my dad, then down at my fingers. Anywhere but across the yard.

"Right." My dad sounds amused, but he doesn't push it. "Well, you've been a big help today. Despite your wandering eyes."

"I don't know what you're talking about," I mumble. I close the laptop again and stand up.

My dad checks his watch and sighs. "We better get cleaned up, anyway. Party starts at six."

"Party?" I follow him into the cabin.

"May birthday party?" He opens the crock pot and sniffs his soup. "The party that happens on the last Saturday of every month?"

Shit. I forgot about that. The monthly birthday party. I think tonight we're celebrating Mae and Libby, Joey Macpherson, Eric, and Julie Benson, a.k.a. naked yoga lady. Her partner, Miriam, bakes an awesome lemon cake.

I wasn't going to go, of course. I've been avoiding Paintbrush stuff even more than usual lately. But it's Libby and Mae's birthday. Which means Josie will be going for sure.

Which means that I'll be there too.

CHAPTER TWENTY-SEVEN
JOSIE

I'm surprised when Mitchell walks into the Sanctuary, hands in his pockets, dark hair neatly combed across his forehead. I thought Mitchell swore not to come to another Paintbrush event ever again. And now he's here. And he's here early.

His eyes light up when he sees me, and he makes a beeline right for me. My heart stutters in my chest. I want to run to meet him halfway. I want to throw my arms around his neck and bury my face right under his chin and kiss his collarbone and feel his soft blue flannel under my hands. Ninety percent of me wants to do that.

Ten percent of me wants him to turn around and walk away and let me finish decorating this cake in peace. My brain goes kind of fuzzy around him, and I get nervous. And my heart beats so hard. Most romance novels describe this feeling as romantic and cute. But sometimes it kind of feels like I might throw up.

But he makes it over to me in record time. He's beaming; Mitchell has the most open, readable face I've ever seen. The ninety percent of me sighs with relief and buzzes with happiness. And the other ten percent just sort of evaporates until I can't remember why I ever wanted him to leave.

"Is that lemon cake?" He bounces on his heels. He's standing so close that his chest brushes my denim shirt.

"Yep." I crouch over and carefully squeeze the frosting tube. A small pink flower appears on the cake. "Delicious cake by Miriam. Mediocre frosting decorations by me."

He laughs. "Shut up. It looks amazing." He leans over my shoulder, his breath tickling my neck as he reads. "Happy birthday to Eric, Joey, Julie, and Mibby." He straightens up. "Mibby?"

I close my eyes and try to concentrate. "Mae and Libby. They hate when I call them that. So I thought I'd put it on their cake."

"On their birthday? That's just evil."

I shrug and add a few more frosting flowers. "Technically, their birthday was on May first. We celebrated then, too, and I made them each their own individual cake. Chocolate for Libby, coconut for Mae, just how they like it. So today they can deal with Mibby."

"Sister of the year." Mitchell grins at me.

"At least the best sister of the family. Which is good enough for me."

Mitchell pulls out a chair and sits on it backward, watching me work. "Does Libby have an inferiority complex?"

I snort. "She has a something complex." I look up. "Why?"

"They were both born in May. But Mae's the only one who's got the name to show for it."

"Oh, that." I wipe a smudge of frosting off the table. "My mom didn't know she was having twins. So when Mae popped out, right after midnight on May first, she called her 'my little May baby.' And Mae stuck. But then Libby came a few minutes later. And my mom was so surprised she just picked an old family name."

"So is Josie an old family name, too?"

"Josephine, as in Jo, as in *Little Women*. She wanted to call me Jo. But my dad said it was a boy's name, so he wouldn't let her."

There's silence after this. I don't talk about my dad much. Or ever. Twelve years since I've seen him, and just thinking about him still makes me furious. My mom tells me it's unhealthy to hate someone this long. I think it's unhealthy she *doesn't* hate him.

"Jo." Mitchell leans his chair back on two legs, smirking at me.

"No." I give him a warning look.

"Yep." His chair clatters to the floor, and he gives me an evil grin. "From now on, I'm calling you Jo."

"From now on," I say, "I'm not responding."

He shrugs. "Whatever you say, Jo."

I roll my eyes, but it's hard to be mad at him when he looks so pleased with himself.

I'm putting the last touch on the icing when Myra comes tearing in. Mitchell stands, like an automatic reflex. Myra can do that to a person.

"Josephine. Mitchell." She strides over and puts her arm around both of us in a weird, three-way hug. It would be super awkward if it was anyone but Myra. Today she has flowers in her hair. Let me rephrase that: She has plants in her hair. Flowers would be too normal. A long strand of ivy is woven through her braid, the deep-green leaves contrasting with her soft gray hair.

"New hairstyle?" I ask.

Behind her, Mitchell grins at my question.

"I was out pulling ivy in the forest this morning, and I was just so sad." Myra sighs dramatically, reaching up to touch the shiny green leaves. "It's invasive, of course, so we have to pull it up. Otherwise, it chokes the trees. But that doesn't mean it's not beautiful."

Mitchell nods. "It's just in the wrong place at the wrong time."

Myra bobs her head up and down. "Exactly. So I thought if it can't live here in the forest, I'll give it a new home. Where its beauty can be appreciated."

"In your hair," I clarify.

"In my hair."

"It looks good," I say, and I mean it. If anyone can pull off weaving a giant vine into their hair, it's definitely Myra.

"I'm just glad it's not poison ivy," Mitchell adds.

"Don't get me started on poison ivy." Myra gathers the frosting tubes from around me. Apparently cake-decorating time is over. "Another tragically misunderstood plant."

"Even so. Definitely not a plant you should be putting in your hair." I fix a blue flower and then hand over the last frosting tube.

"I suppose you're right," she concedes. "Well, everyone's waiting." She gestures to the door to the Sanctuary. "Ready?"

I look at Mitchell. He's looking right at me, his dark eyes searching mine.

"Ready," he says.

"Flowers." Ned wrinkles his nose at the plate in my hand, his tone dripping with contempt. You'd think I was trying to hand him a plate of old garbage rather than a piece of chocolate cake.

I sigh. "Is there a problem, Ned?"

"Always with the girly cakes," he grumbles. "Just once I want to see a cake with a gun on it. Or a monster truck. Or a dinosaur."

"Girls like dinosaurs, too, you know." I shift the paper plate from one hand to the other. "And guys can like flowers. Look at Eric." I gesture across the room, where the burly six-foot man is shoveling cake into his mouth while clutching Lucy to his chest. Fork in one hand, baby in the other. He's a pro.

"He's on his third piece," I say. "And it's his birthday. And he clearly doesn't have a problem with flowers."

Ned mumbles something unintelligible that sounds an awful lot like *pansy*. I plant my hand on my hip, about to give him a piece of my mind, when the plate is whisked out of my grasp.

Mitchell takes the plate and shoves it into Ned's chest, forcing the old man to grab hold of it.

"I swear," Mitchell says. "Only you would complain about eating cake."

"I'm just saying," Ned grumbles, picking up his fork. "Things are getting a little soft and mushy around here. Not like in the old days. When Bernie and I would go out and hunt. We'd kill ourselves a deer, and then we'd bring it back and cook it up and serve it to everyone. Now you people are eating tofu and *veggie burgers*"—he spits out these last two words— "and flower cakes."

I roll my eyes. "Next time, Ned, I'll make a cake with a dead deer on it."

"Red icing for the blood and everything," Mitchell adds.

Ned grunts in approval. He jabs his fork into his cake and takes a big bite. "Now that's all I ask," he says with his mouth full.

I walk back to the table to where my own cake is waiting, along with my two sisters, and Mitchell follows. His arm brushes mine, and shivers shoot up my spine.

I plop down on the couch next to Mae, and she hands me my plate. Mitchell takes the seat next to me. Libby sits cross-legged on the floor in front of us, twirling her hair with her fingers.

"Where's your cake, Lib?" I ask.

She shrugs. "Not really hungry."

Mae rolls her eyes at this. "Too many *calories* for supermodel over here."

I pause with my fork halfway to my mouth. "Come on, Libby. It's your birthday party. Eat some damn cake."

Libby leans back on her arms and narrows her eyes at me. Her black jeans hug her legs so tightly it looks like she can barely move, and her red tank top is borderline sheer. She studies her nails and doesn't reply.

"I don't know what your problem is," Mae says around a mouthful of cake. "This is good stuff."

Mae's hair is thrown into a messy ponytail and tied

back with a red bandana. She's wearing black leggings and an oversized white t-shirt that reads *Eat Local* in big black letters. There are cake crumbs all down the front of this shirt, and for some reason this makes me want to lean over and hug her as hard as I can.

She looks like she's a normal fourteen-year-old girl. Libby, with her bright-red lipstick and strategically tousled hair, looks like a vampire who's trying to be sexy.

"It's really good." Mitchell's voice surprises me. I kind of forgot he was here. I turn to him, and he nudges my arm. "And it has some kick-ass decorations, too."

"Oh. My. God." Libby hauls herself to her feet. "I'm just *not* hungry. Sometimes people *aren't hungry*. How many times do I have to tell you guys?"

She stalks away. Mitchell watches her go, his brow furrowed.

"I'm sorry." His voice is a little shaky. "I didn't mean anything by that; I was just saying—"

"Not your fault, dude," Mae says, waving her fork. "She's a crazy person." She stands and holds up her empty plate. "I, for one, am going to enjoy my birthday party. Anyone want seconds?"

Mitchell and I both shake our heads, and Mae wanders away.

"So I see what you mean." Mitchell clears his throat. "About Libby being . . . erratic."

I drop my head in my hands. "She's driving me crazy."

He pats my knee. "She'll come around."

I glance down at where his hand rests on my knee. Mitchell

follows my eyes, but he doesn't move his hand. I lean into him, just slightly, and he inhales sharply.

I'm about to lean my head on his shoulder when a burst of music comes from across the room, followed by a burst of laughter. I sit straight up, and Mitchell does the same.

A string is plucked, high and tinny, and then people start clapping.

"Oh no," Mitchell says.

I smile at him. "You haven't been to a Paintbrush party in a long time, have you?"

He groans. "I forgot about this. I thought maybe everyone had moved past it."

"Oh no. It's actually only gotten worse."

People push the tables and couches in the Sanctuary to the edges of the room. Someone opens the windows, and a cool night breeze floats in. Thank god, because there's at least fifty people in here, and it's already getting hot.

I stand and hold out my hand to Mitchell. "Come on."

He hesitates. "Are you sure you don't want to go on a walk? Or a drive? Or do literally anything else?"

I laugh. But a small part of me, the part of me that loves Paintbrush and the people in it and all the crazy traditions, feels a twinge of hurt at his words. "It's okay if you want to leave."

But I'm staying.

Mitchell studies my face. "Nah." He grins and stands, grabbing my hand. "Let's stay."

CHAPTER TWENTY-EIGHT
MITCHELL

It's ten o'clock, and the birthday party has turned into a full-on country dance. Myra whipped out her tambourine, an older guy named Willy brought out his fiddle, and everything has just gone downhill from there. There's a circle of people clapping in time to the music as Willy wails on his fiddle, the music fast and fun and furious. People keep ducking into the middle to dance, then twirling back out again, only to be replaced by the next person in the circle.

In the corner, Ned and Bernie are perched in their chairs, discreetly sipping from a small flask I can only guess contains their home-brewed moonshine. They're both scowling, but Ned's tapping his foot along to the music. As much as they want to hate this stuff, I can tell they're having fun.

And I'm having fun, which is the biggest surprise of all. I haven't been to a Paintbrush birthday party in a year, at least. I even missed my own last year because I had a swim meet. Not that I was too broken up about it. Every party turns into this, since the day I can remember; a rollicking, crazy dance party, full of hyped-up old people and shrieking kids and line dancing and drinking—by the adults, mostly—and general chaos and craziness. The most recent one I went to was last

March, my mom's birthday month. Myra insisted on teaching everyone an old country line dance, and Ned and Bernie's moonshine went from a small discreet flask to a giant bottle that got passed around until it was drained. The Macpherson kids were playing tag on the dance floor, and my parents left early to *check on something* at the cabin, and it was a total madhouse. It didn't end until 1:00 a.m.

It was kind of fun. But I remember looking around halfway through the night and thinking, *what a shit show*. These parties, they're just too . . . something. Too weird. Too much. *Normal people don't have parties like this*, I thought.

So I decided I was done with them. I made up an excuse every time one came around. I couldn't handle it. I told myself that I'm just not a party person. But the truth is that I couldn't help but wonder: What would someone from school think if they walked in on this scene? And I knew that no matter who it was, they would think Paintbrush was totally and unequivocally bizarre. Like, really fucking weird. And after that thought crossed my mind, I couldn't stop myself from thinking it was weird too.

But here I am. Standing in the circle, clapping my hands as Eric and Wendy twirl in the middle, baby Lucy perched in between them. Lucy giggles, drool spilling out of her mouth, as her dad cradles her to his chest with one arm, his other arm around Wendy's waist. Everyone is laughing at the ridiculous scene in front of us, this three-way jig with a baby. But Eric and Wendy just grin at each other, eyes locked, Wendy's mouth open in a full and genuine laugh. Eric spins her out and then spins her back in, and Wendy twirls right into his chest and tucks herself under his chin. She leans over and kisses Lucy's forehead, and everyone laughs.

They make their way back to the edge of the circle as Julie pulls her partner Miriam into the circle. It's always refreshing to see Julie with her clothes on, rather than doing naked headstands outside in the morning. I can actually look her in the eye this way. Julie and Miriam sashay around the circle, and everyone cheers.

Josie nudges me. I take in her pink face, her shining eyes, her huge smile, and I smile back. I can't help it. She's so obviously, clearly, wildly happy here. And somehow, her happiness overshadows all my feelings of doubt. It's impossible to overanalyze the weirdness of this whole thing when Josie's smiling at me like this.

I step a little closer to her and rub my shoulder against hers. She laughs and shimmies back. I'm so preoccupied trying to come up with another way to casually touch her I don't even notice Julie and Miriam have taken a bow. Not until Myra claps in my face.

"Partner up!" she booms, pushing people together in random combinations. "Partner dance! Everybody grab partners!"

Another Paintbrush tradition. Myra always organizes partner dances. She has a thing for waltzes. Never mind that almost no one else knows how to waltz. She thinks partner dances are a good *bonding experience*, that they *create community*. And also, judging by the shine in her eyes, she's had one or two festive beverages tonight. Myra's a lightweight.

All across the room, people pair off at the same time my

mom walks in, Joe tagging along behind her.

I wait for the anger to hit me, but it doesn't. Just a sharp twinge of annoyance. Ned greets her, then Mrs. Macpherson. Maybe people aren't as mad as I thought.

Someone next to me clears his throat. I turn to see Max Mendez, one half of one of the younger couples here, standing beside me. He taps Josie on the shoulder, and I freeze.

"Miss Josie," he says, smiling, "could I have the honor of this dance?"

I open my mouth to say something—I don't know what—but Josie beats me to it.

"Sorry, Max. Myra already paired me up with Mitchell."

It's not the truth, exactly. But Max just shrugs and clasps his hand over his heart. "Rejection!" He sighs dramatically and winks. "It's okay. I see another partner."

He reaches down and scoops up Ada Macpherson. She squeals delightedly, and they waltz away.

The fiddle begins again across the room. Slower than before, but not exactly a slow song. Like an old-timey waltz.

I look down at Josie. Standing so close to her makes me realize how short she really is. It also makes me nervous.

"You're tiny," I say without thinking. God. What a weird thing to say. My hands are suddenly really sweaty. I try to wipe them on my jeans without being obvious about it.

Josie snorts. "I'm short. I'm not tiny."

I take a small step closer. "You're compact." If I step any closer, I'll be stepping on her feet.

She frowns. "Like a car?"

I shake my head. "Like a fun-size candy bar." I swallow,

hard, and then tentatively reach one hand out and place it on her waist. "One perfect bite."

She laughs, and it relaxes me enough to reach for her hand. "I'm not sure that's a compliment," she says, sliding her hand onto my shoulder. "And please don't bite me."

I grin and raise my eyebrows. "I make no promises."

She blushes, like I knew she would, and I have to bite back a laugh. Every time I make Josie blush, it puts me on even footing again. Makes me feel like I'm an eighteen-year-old who knows his way around girls and not like a stammering, awkward middle schooler with a first crush. Which is how I feel most of the time.

We're dancing. We're dancing here, in the middle of the Sanctuary, surrounded by goofy kids and tipsy adults and everything in between. I never thought I would have fun at Paintbrush again. But here I am. And I know it's because of her warm hand in mine, the way her dark eyelashes flutter as she looks around the room, the way her waist is soft and muscled and perfect under my hand. I want to slide my hand around her back and pull her closer, want her to rest her head on my chest, want to feel her hair under my chin and close my eyes and live here in this moment forever.

But I can't, because people are watching. And because, in a moment of stupid weakness, I told Josie I'd wait for her to make the first move. What was I thinking? If that first move doesn't happen soon, I might actually go crazy.

Josie squeezes my hand in hers. She looks up at me and smiles, and her smile makes my breath catch in my throat. I've seen that smile every day since I can remember. I don't know why, all of a sudden, I have to remind myself to breathe when I see it.

"Hi," she whispers.

"Hi." I tighten my grip on her waist, and she moves her hand from my shoulder, sliding her fingertips slowly, until they rest on the back of my neck. I close my eyes.

When I open them again, she's staring at me, her face so close I can see the flecks of brown in her green eyes. It would be so easy to kiss her. Just a few inches. It would be the easiest thing in the world.

I glance around the room, to make sure no one is watching. Almost everyone is preoccupied. Everyone except my mother, and Josie's mother.

My mom leans in to Layla and whispers something in her ear. Layla's gaze flicks across the room, landing right on Josie and me, and Layla's eyebrows shoot up as she whispers something back. A smug smile spreads across my mom's face in answer.

I remember what they always used to say, when Josie and I were little. When we were sharing graham crackers or wrestling in the grass or squabbling over who got to pick the movie that night. "We'll be related, one day," my mom used to say to Layla.

And Layla would agree. "It's fate."

I know they were kidding, back then and probably even now. I know I shouldn't let their gossip bother me. But the thought of my mom, looking at Josie and me and thinking she had something to do with it—it's too much for me.

I pull back and drop Josie's hand.

Her brow furrows. "Mitchell?"

And I feel so bad. But I can't help it.

"I have to go," I say. And then I stride out of the room and into the summer night.

CHAPTER TWENTY-NINE
JOSIE

I'm left standing in the middle of the dance floor, like I'm a lame girl in an 80s movie. In the beginning of the movie, when she's still sad and pathetic and boyfriend-less.

Mitchell weaves through the dancing crowd, and my stomach sinks. I feel stupid, and I feel stupid for feeling stupid, and I feel stupid for taking it so personally. Doubt creeps into my mind, curling around my thoughts, choking out the good ones from a minute ago, from these past few days, with the scary mean ones—*he's too good for you*, and *you're just a distraction*, and *what are you thinking*.

I shake my head and make my way to the edge of the room. Everyone is still dancing. The fiddle hums through the air, and the dancers are cheerfully stumbling around, and the room echoes with talking and laughing.

I find my mom whispering with Carrie. Joe stands next to them, looking uncomfortable. Good.

Myra moves around the dance floor again, waving her arms. The music changes to a fast-paced, bluegrass rendition of *Happy Birthday*.

"Birthday dance!" Myra shouts, and the pairs of dancers break apart and circle up again. "Birthday people in the middle!"

Mae sheepishly stands in the middle of the circle, goofy Joey Macpherson joining her. Eric is pushed in by a giggling Wendy, and he puts his arm around Julie. Joey starts a ridiculous jig, Julie grabs Mae's hand, and Eric rolls his eyes as they all start to dance.

But of course, Libby's missing. I catch Mae's gaze and raise my eyebrows. She rolls her eyes and points to Mom.

I make my way over to Mom. She's still chatting animatedly with Carrie. I haven't seen her having this much fun in a long time. I would be happy for her, except I'm not Carrie's biggest fan right now. And also, where is Libby?

"Where's Libby?" I scan the room, but there's no sign of her.

Carrie reaches out to squeeze my arm. "Hey, Josie."

I nod at her.

My mom grins up at me. "Hi, honey."

"Hi." I force myself to paste a pleasant expression on my face. "Do you know where she is?"

"Libby?" My mom glances at the crowd. "She went off with some friends, I think. A little while ago."

"She went off with some friends?" I clench my fists. "Mom, it's her own birthday party."

She shakes her head. "You know Libby. Always doing things her own way."

I suck in a breath. "She should have stayed here, Mom. It's late." I'm trying to keep my voice steady, but it's wavering anyway. "Who was she with?"

My mom's cheerful expression falters, and Carrie very subtly backs away a few feet.

My mom blinks up at me. "She's with some friends. They came to pick her up."

"Jesus Christ, Mom." I don't mean to spit the words out like that, but they slice through the air. "She's fourteen years old. She shouldn't be hanging out with kids who can drive already."

She winces. "Josie—"

But I can't stop. "This is unbelievable. Why can't you, just once, tell her no? Tell her she can't do whatever she wants, whenever she wants to do it?"

"I think you're overreacting." My mom stands, reaches a hand out to touch my arm, but I jerk away.

"Someone has to overreact, Mom. Since you won't react at all."

She presses her lips together in a thin line, and I wait. But she doesn't say anything, and this makes me even madder.

I spin around and jog to the door, pushing past Carrie without a word. I jog all the way to our cabin, my feet thumping up the wooden deck. A knot fills my stomach, hard and cold, and for a split-second, I think I'm going to cry.

I pause with my hand on the doorknob and take a deep breath. I squeeze my eyes shut, as tight as I possibly can, and stay like this until the knot loosens and the tightness in my chest dissolves, just a little. Then I let myself push in the door, cross the kitchen, and crawl right into my bed.

It's two in the morning, and I'm still not asleep. Libby got home around an hour ago; she crept in through the front door and then quietly got undressed and slipped under the covers. I thought about saying something to her—*where were you*, or maybe *what were you doing*, or *hey, did you know it's really rude to leave in the middle of your own birthday party*—but the thought of a middle-of-the-night confrontation made me feel like I might throw up. So I pretended I was asleep.

Every time I start to drift off, a new thought sneaks into my head and flashes behind my closed eyelids, messing with my sleep cycle and making my heart pound. I can't stop thinking about tonight—about Libby, about my fight with Mom, about Mitchell ditching me without a word. And I'm mad about all of it, but mostly I'm just . . . sad. Dancing with Mitchell made me sad.

Because when he left me there, standing by myself, I became the kind of girl I always told myself I would never be. The kind of girl who lets a guy make her feel like this. And now, here I am.

And. If this is how it feels when Mitchell leaves me on the dance floor, at a stupid Paintbrush event, how am I going to feel when he leaves for college? We graduate in two weeks. And I have no idea if he's leaving right after, or partway through the summer, or waiting until the fall. But it doesn't really matter. Because he'll be the one leaving, and I'll be the one staying. He'll be the one with the power, the power to say goodbye and end it when he wants, the power to leave and go off and start a new adventure in a new place, with new friends, and new girls. New hot, smart, adventurous college girls. And I'll just be . . . here.

I need to go to sleep. I'm overthinking everything. I roll onto my side and squeeze my eyes shut and will myself to sleep. I will think about sheep and sweet dreams and not about Mitchell. Not about his soft brown hair, or his long, lanky legs, or the goofy way he grins at his own jokes. And definitely not about the way his hand felt on my waist, the way he pressed his fingertips into my back and gently grabbed a handful of my shirt, like he was afraid I'd change my mind and go . . . .

Oh god. This is pathetic. I'm pathetic. I sigh and roll the other way, toward the window. And come face to face with a hand.

The hand knocks on the window, three soft, quick raps. Maybe I'm asleep. Maybe I'm dreaming.

But then it happens again. And when I sit up and peer outside, Mitchell's dark eyes peer back at me.

What's he doing? My stomach sinks at the same time my heart sputters to life, and I slowly swing my legs over and onto the wooden floor. I'm wearing a long t-shirt with Smokey the Bear's face on it and tiny shorts that are hidden below its giant hem. My hair is a mess, too, half of it falling out of its braid and frizzy around my face.

I squint in the darkness for a brush, but I don't see one, and I don't want to wake up Mae and Libby looking for one. So I just smooth my hair with my hands and tiptoe to the front door. This is as good as it's gonna get.

The door creaks a little as I swing it open, and then I'm

padding down the porch in bare feet, across the cool grass and around the side of the cabin. Shit. I'm not wearing a bra, either. I cross my arms over my chest, as tight as I can, and turn the corner.

Mitchell leans against the side of the cabin, wearing gray sweatpants and a white t-shirt. He has bags under his eyes, and his hair is sticking up in a thousand different directions, and he's wearing two different socks. And it's not fair that, despite all that, he still looks good. Like, really good.

He straightens up when he sees me and strides toward me, crossing the distance between us in two quick strides. He stands close, so close I can smell that warm sleepy-smell on him. Like he just got out of bed.

He grins. "Hello."

"Um. Hi?" My voice is sleepy, a little raspy. The night air is chilly, and I shiver and squeeze my arms tighter. I want to be mad at him for abandoning me a few hours ago. But when he smiles like this, it's hard.

"Are you wearing pants?" he whispers.

"What?" I look down. My huge t-shirt hangs halfway down my thighs, covering up my shorts. Very sexy. I scowl at him. "Yes, I'm wearing pants. God."

He shrugs. "Just checking." He inches closer. "Josie."

I look up at him, but then his face is right here, so close, and I have to look down again. "Yeah?"

He shuffles his feet. "I just wanted to . . ."

"Wanted to what?" Even my whisper sounds harsh in the quiet night.

"I couldn't sleep. So I wanted to come over here, so I could . . ."

"So you could what, Mitchell?" I'm starting to get impatient and also worried, because I feel like I know what's on the tip of his tongue. *This isn't working*, he's about to say. *I don't really want to kiss you anymore. I changed my mind. This is a bad idea.*

"I just wanted to do this," he says. And then he steps forward and slides his arms around my waist.

His hug is warm and soft, and his grip is tight, and before I know what I'm doing, my arms are snaking around his neck. Like they have a mind of their own. *Stupid arms.*

He doesn't say anything. I don't say anything. Slowly, carefully, he rubs his chin across the top of my head. I turn and press my forehead into his neck, right underneath his jaw. I feel him inhale, then exhale, slowly, and I tighten my arms around his neck.

He wants me to kiss him, I think. I'm supposed to kiss him, and I want to kiss him, and we're alone, and it's dark, and we should kiss. But I can't seem to move my head. His neck is smooth and warm and soft and perfect. His neck is his best feature. He has the best neck around. I am genuinely worried that it will be physically impossible for me to remove myself from his neck, that he'll have to awkwardly peel me off, that he'll go find Cord tomorrow and say, *Yeah, I thought I liked her, but then I realized she was a weird neck-nuzzler.*

We've been hugging for a solid minute, I think, or maybe ten or twenty, and my arms are going a little numb and his hands are rubbing my lower back in small, soft circles and my eyes are drifting shut. I think that I might be falling asleep.

Slowly, I shift away. His grip tightens for a split second,

like he doesn't want me to go, but then he leans away. The night is cold now that he's not hugging me anymore, and I don't know what to say. Just a few hours ago he left me alone on the dance floor. But then he's leaning in, closer and closer, until our foreheads are almost touching.

This is it, I think. This is when I kiss him.

But he just nudges his forehead against mine and whispers, "Goodnight, Josie."

"Goodnight, Mitchell," I whisper back.

And then he's padding across the grass, his steps silent in his mismatched socks, across the lawn, into the darkness. Gone.

I spend the whole next day, a Sunday, thinking about Mitchell and seeing Mitchell and smiling at Mitchell, but not actually talking to Mitchell. I see him working on something outside with Bernie, hammering away at an old fence. I wave, and Mitchell waves back, and my heart sputters. I see him crossing the lawn while I'm working on the tomatoes, and he smiles, and my heart sputters. I'm on my porch with my calculus textbook in my lap and see him sitting on his porch, and our eyes meet, and my heart sputters.

I'm worried that one of these days my heart is just going to sputter out, and then I'll be dead, and then I'll never be able to hug Mitchell again. And that will be the real tragedy.

With all the sputtering going on, it's probably a good thing I don't actually talk to him all day. At least, that's what I try telling myself. But I also know the reason I'm kind of relieved is that I'm still nervous about kissing him. Nervous he's changed his mind. Nervous I'll be bad at it. Nervous we'll kiss, and then I'll be done, gone, down the rabbit hole of falling for Mitchell. And when he leaves, it'll be that much harder.

I snuggle into my bed at night and try not to think about him. But it's almost like I can feel his presence, real and palpable, all the way from his cabin a couple hundred feet away. Like I have a Mitchell monitor implanted in my brain.

I'd like to say it's annoying, the way my brain won't turn off, the way his face and words and lips bounce around behind my eyelids. But really, I fall asleep with a smile on my face.

CHAPTER THIRTY
MITCHELL

"You told her that you'd wait? For her to make the first move?" Cord's face scrunches up in confusion as he stuffs a chicken nugget in his mouth. "That was stupid, dude."

I sigh as he reaches for another one. "Yeah. That's what I'm saying."

My whole truck smells like grease and french fries and ketchup. Cord and I decided to cash in on our senior privilege today and run out to the nearest drive-thru on our lunch break. The upside of this is that we don't have to eat cafeteria food. The downside is that, between the ten minutes there, five minutes ordering, and ten minutes back, we now have five minutes to actually eat. I basically inhaled my burger and am now watching as Cord singlehandedly eats a family-sized portion of chicken nuggets. A grand total of thirty nuggets— too much for any one human being. It's disgusting but also fascinating. Like a car accident I can't look away from.

"So who cares?" Cord mumbles around a mouthful of chicken nuggets. "It's not like you made some unbreakable promise. Kiss her anyway."

I shake my head. "I don't want to lose her trust. But I'm worried that she'll never kiss me."

"You think she doesn't like you?"

"No, she likes me." I frown. "I think." I run my fingers through my hair and then realize too late that my hair probably smells like french fries now. "She just . . . I don't think she has a lot of confidence in herself. She's . . ." I try to find the word I'm looking for. "Careful. She's careful."

Cord snorts. "So? You're careful, too. You're the most careful guy I know. You've never even had a real girlfriend, for god's sake."

I wipe my greasy fingers on my jeans. "I know that. I just don't think she sees me like that."

"How does she see you?"

"Like the guy who went to a party with a drunk girl falling all over him."

Cord nods at this, taking a noisy slurp of his Coke. "To be fair. You were that guy."

I slump in my seat. "You know, you're not a lot of help today."

I lean forward and rest my head on the steering wheel, only to have a fry tossed at my head. "Hey. No throwing food in my truck."

He shrugs. "Wasn't me."

"Okay, Shaggy." I roll my eyes, reach down, and grab my burger wrapper and grease-stained white bag. "Come on. We're going to be late."

But Cord is still staring at me, chewing his last fry with a smug smile on his face.

I frown. "What?"

"You really like her, don't you?"

I think about shrugging, about rolling my eyes, about punching him in the shoulder and telling him to get out of my truck. But instead, I smile. I can't help it. "Yeah. I do."

Cord grins and shakes his head, popping open his car door. "It's weird, dude. Seeing you like this."

I shrug. It's weird feeling like this.

"But like, good weird," he says.

"Good weird," I repeat.

"It's the best kind of weird to be."

The day rushes by, mostly because I will it to rush by, mostly because all I want to do is be alone with Josie again. I practically sprint out when the bell rings, like I've been doing for the past week. I have many fine qualities, but being casual is not one of them.

I toss my backpack into the backseat and lean against the sunbaked metal of the side of the truck. I scan the crowd emerging from the high school in waves. One minute. Then two. Then three. Still no Josie.

"You know, all that staring is making you look like the school psychopath."

I whip around. And there she is, smiling at me from the other side of the truck.

"You're scaring people," she says.

"Am not." Her hair is in its usual braid over her shoulder, and she wears a plain white t-shirt. I can't see her legs, but I know she's wearing ripped jeans, the ones with grass stains from playing tackle hide-and-seek with the Macphersons. She squints at me in the sunlight.

"So . . ." As soon as her voice trails off, I realize I've been staring at her. Whoops. I have to get it together.

"Ready to go?" I ask.

"Home?"

I shrug. "Wherever you want."

"Home is good, I think."

My heart sinks a little, and I try not to look disappointed. I must do a bad job because she quickly continues. "Not that I don't want to go on an adventure! I just have to study."

I give her a blank look. "Study."

"For finals?" She raises her eyebrows. "Or does the captain of the swim team get exempt from trivial things like end of the year exams?"

"Sadly, no. I have to take them with the rest of the common people."

"You're obnoxious."

I laugh. "No, I'm charming."

I open the driver's door and slide into my seat. A second later, she slides into the passenger's side.

"So don't you have to study too?" she asks as the engine coughs to life.

I turn and squint over my shoulder as I back out of the spot. "I guess." I push the stick into drive, and we turn out of the lot. "If I'm being honest . . ." I sneak a glance at her.

"What?" She looks at me suspiciously.

"I'm doing pretty well in all my classes. I could get a D on all my finals and still make at least a B plus in all of them. Or even an A."

She rolls her eyes. "Well, me too."

"Really?"

She glares at me. "Yes, really. I'm actually pretty smart, you know."

"I know," I say quickly. "It's just that you said you have to study."

"Well, I don't want to lose my spot in the class rank this late in the game." She yanks her seatbelt on. "Aren't you worried about that at all? You're third in the class, right?"

"Right." I'm surprised she knows this.

"So if you slip at all, you won't get to speak at graduation anymore."

"That would be a relief, actually. I'm terrible at public speaking."

She shakes her head. "Says the most popular boy in school."

"First of all, I hate that word. And second of all, remember seventh grade science class?"

"What word?" she asks innocently. "Boy? School?"

"Popular." I glare at her.

"Wait. Seventh grade science . . ." She taps her chin, her eyes scrunched up.

"The life cycle of a frog?" I prompt her.

"Oh my god! The life cycle of a frog!" She bounces in her seat. "I totally forgot! How could I forget? It started out pretty good. But then—"

"But then I got tripped up on the word polliwog."

"Polliwog!" She cracks up. "I remember now. You got to that word, and you just couldn't say it. It was like your tongue got stuck."

I still remember that day vividly, shaking and stuttering in front of my classmates with a beet-red face and brain that had somehow decided to stop working. It was only my second year of public school, and I was still terrified that everyone would think I was the weird hippie kid, still desperately trying to prove myself.

Usually this memory doesn't make me laugh. But with Josie shaking with laughter in the seat next to me, it doesn't seem so bad.

"I was just up there, stuttering away. I couldn't remember how to pronounce it for the life of me."

"Isn't polliwog just another word for tadpole?"

"Yep."

For some reason, this makes her giggle even more. "Then why didn't you just say tadpole?"

"I was an overachiever! I was trying to cover all my bases!"

"And then, you just turned and ran out of the classroom. Just sprinted right out the door."

"I hid in the bathroom till the end of the school day."

"Mr. Reece was so confused."

"I'm pretty sure he still hates me."

She rubs a hand over her face as her laughter subsides. "Oh, please. No one could ever hate you."

It's a throw-away comment, barely even a real compliment. She probably doesn't even realize she said it. But I'm starting to realize that anything nice this girl says to me—every small compliment, every kind word, even every touch on the shoulder—makes a goofy smile spread across my face.

"I'm serious, though." I let my head fall back against the

seat. "I know it was just a stupid middle school project, but ever since then I've hated talking in front of people. There's too much pressure to say something meaningful. At graduation, in front of hundreds of people? I have *no* idea what I'm going to talk about."

She furrows her brow. "But you talk so much. You never stop talking."

"Wow. Thanks."

A pink flush creeps into her cheeks. "No! Not like that. You just . . . I see you at school. And at Paintbrush. You're always talking with other kids or teachers or coaches or Ned or Bernie or Myra or whoever. You always have something to say." She tucks her hair behind her ear. "It makes me jealous. I *never* know what to say. My whole life is just one big awkward pause occasionally interrupted by bits of conversation."

I laugh at this. But she's not laughing. She's intently studying her toes, her bare feet propped on the dashboard as the trees lining the road whiz by outside her window.

I clear my throat. "You're not awkward." I search for the right words. "You just . . . you think."

"I think." She sounds skeptical.

"You're careful with what you say. So everything you say is important. I just chatter away about nothing all the time, but you . . . You don't waste your words." I grip the steering wheel tighter, my knuckles turning white as I try to say what I want to say. "It makes me want to really listen when you talk."

It's quiet in the truck, my words hanging in the air. I carefully, slowly wind my way up the mountain. Taking my time so I can prolong this car ride as long as possible. So I can spend as much time with Josie as possible.

She's still quiet. I hope I didn't say the wrong thing. I'm getting hot, the worry building in my chest.

Just when I'm opening my mouth to say something, anything, to fill the silence, she slides her head onto my shoulder. And then she slides her hand onto my knee, gentle and warm and so totally distracting that I think I might drive right off the road.

"Thanks," she whispers. Her words and breath are warm in my ear, and I close my eyes. Then immediately pop them open again, because *Jesus Christ*, I'm driving a vechile.

"And for the record," she continues, her voice whispery and feather-light, "I'll be mad if you don't study. Because I want you to speak at graduation. Because I think you have lots of good things to say."

My whole body feels fuzzy and warm and buzzing with anticipation, and her whispers make me shiver, and I'm gripping the steering wheel so tightly, like I'm afraid I might burst out of my own skin.

And then we turn the corner, and there's that big empty field, where my truck ran out of gas. Where we spent the night. And I'm not even thinking as I yank the wheel to the right, as the truck rumbles across the grassy terrain, as I pull into the clearing and throw the truck in park and turn to see Josie's face wrinkled in confusion.

CHAPTER THIRTY-ONE
JOSIE

My heart is racing, and my feet are off the dashboard and firmly planted on the ground. I bite my lip. "Mitchell?"

He's staring at me with wide open eyes, deep and brown and shining, glancing from my hair to my lips to my eyes and back. He's scaring me a little.

I try again. "Mitchell, what are you—?"

"Josie, I know I said I would wait for you to make the first move." His leg bounces nervously, a fast *onetwothree, onetwothree*, and he runs his hand through his hair. "But—"

Before he can say anything else, I lean over across the seat and kiss him. Not on the mouth, because I'm still nervous and scared and my heart is thumping a thousand beats per minute. I kiss him right under his jaw, where his skin is soft and smooth.

He closes his eyes, and I feel his sharp intake of breath. I linger for a second, my nose brushing his neck, before pulling away. Because *oh my god*, I should have kissed him on the lips like a normal person. Neck kisses are way too personal. I made it weird. I messed it up.

So I start to pull back. But I don't get very far, because Mitchell slides his hand across the back of my head, warm and gentle, and tilts my head until our lips meet.

I am kissing Mitchell, I think. *This is Mitchell Morrison, and I am Josie Sedgwick, and we are kissing.*

We are really, *really* kissing. His hand is tangled in my hair, and his lips are soft and firm and nice and all over the place, on my mouth and my cheek and my jaw and my nose and then back to my mouth. I smile, because his lips can't seem to keep still, and then his lips land back on mine, and they're smiling too.

I need to take a break, to pull back, to make sure I'm remembering to breathe. But Mitchell tugs on my braid, pulling me back toward him. Tilting his head into my neck. Nuzzling my shoulder with his chin. Softly, carefully, kissing my neck, tiny kisses that land like butterflies from my jaw to my shoulder and back again.

I feel like I'm floating. Like I'm disconnected from my body, like my mind has shut down and my lips are acting of their own accord. And my hands too, because one cups Mitchell's cheek, my thumb rubbing circles on his cheekbone, while the other slips around his neck. He turns slightly, pushes his face into my hand, and kisses my palm. My hand burns.

I could continue this forever, this tugging on hair and sighing and smiling and eyelashes tickling cheeks and hands on shoulders and forgetting to breathe. His skin feels warm, almost feverish, and his hair is messy, and his breathing is a little fast and a little loud, and he is so astoundingly, impossibly, cute.

But he breaks away, kisses the tip of my nose, and then leans his forehead against mine. My eyes flutter open, and his dark eyes stare right into mine, crinkled around the edges.

"Hey," he says.

"Hey." I smile back, my heart thumping, unsure of what to say.

"So." He clears his throat.

"So."

He moves back a few inches, giving me some space. "Good work."

"Good work?" My eyebrows shoot up. "Are you evaluating my performance or something?"

"Nope." He shakes his head, grinning. "Just giving some praise where praise is due."

I press my lips together, but I can't stop myself from smiling. "You're so weird."

"Hey, cut me some slack here. I'm a little distracted." He slumps back against his seat and slowly, dramatically exhales.

"What?"

"It's just . . ." He runs his fingers through his hair. "I've been waiting a long time. For that."

"For what?"

"To kiss you."

Warmth spreads through my face. "Please. We've already kissed."

"Ha!" He sits straight up and points at me. "So you do remember!"

"Our kiss, when we were little?" Now my face is really red. "Of course I remember. It was my first kiss."

"Mine too." His grin widens as he studies my face. "Someone's blushing."

"No, I'm not," I reply automatically. I look determinedly down at my hands.

He leans in close again, so close our noses are practically touching. "Am I making you nervous?" His voice comes out low, almost a whisper.

"God. No." But I don't sound very convincing.

He tilts his face forward. "Because you make me nervous."

Slowly, he trails his nose across my cheek. My eyes drift closed.

"Somehow I really doubt that." I take in a deep breath and let it out slowly.

He kisses my earlobe, and my heart pounds.

"I'm serious," he says. "I would've kissed you a whole week ago. At least. If you didn't make me so nervous."

"Well, I wasn't sure if this was a good idea."

"This?"

"You know. Us."

He pulls back and looks into my eyes. "And?"

"Leah said I should go for it." I grin. "So I did."

He laughs. "Cord said the same thing!"

"Really?" I shake my head. "They're diabolical, those two."

"We have to make sure to never let them meet. They'd destroy us."

"And then the world."

"Exactly."

Our conversation hangs in the air as he looks at me, and I look at him, and then we're kissing again, and I am lost in this moment, even as it etches itself into the marble of my brain.

He pulls away, too soon, and I blink up at him. "What?"

He sighs. "You have to study. Remember?"

"No."

"Well, I remember." He leans across the seat and kisses me on the forehead, and I lean into his kiss. And then he reaches down and turns the key, and the truck shudders to life.

"We're leaving?" I cross my arms. "This is stupid."

He laughs, reaching down and squeezing my knee. "This is great."

He turns around on the grass and pulls the truck back out toward the road. His brow furrows as he checks both ways for traffic, and all of a sudden, I get the impulse to reach out and smooth his forehead, to clear away the frown.

But I don't, because a thought just occurred to me. "So."

He glances toward me. "So."

"I was thinking. Maybe we shouldn't tell anyone about this."

He looks concerned. "Anyone?"

"Anyone at Paintbrush," I clarify.

His expression immediately clears. "Oh, thank god."

I laugh.

"I didn't want to be the one to suggest it," he says. "But the thought of everyone there knowing our business . . ."

"Is horrifying," I finish. "Agreed. So let's just keep this between us for now." I glance at him. "Is that okay?"

Mitchell reaches over and laces his hand through mine. "It's perfect."

CHAPTER THIRTY-TWO
MITCHELL

I am floating. I am happy. I would be skipping right now, if I were the type of guy who skips. I'm not, though—at least not yet—so I just walk across the grass to my cabin and focus on trying to walk in a straight line, like a normal person, and on keeping a goofy grin from taking over my whole face.

It's a Monday evening, after a long day at school, and I'm at Paintbrush, and my family sucks. All I should be thinking about is graduation in two weeks. I should be counting down the seconds until I can throw my stuff in my truck and peel out of the parking lot and never look back.

But I'm not. I'm humming with energy and breathing in the fresh mountain air and feeling so, so much like I'm going to burst out of my skin. But in a good way. In the best way.

I left Josie at her cabin so she could study. To be specific, I left her behind her cabin, where I pulled her into the shadows so I could kiss her again and touch her face and smell her hair one more time, before she laughed and pushed me away and said she had to go.

She's right. I should study. But even if I sit down and crack open a book right now, I know I won't be able to concentrate. The words would swim in front of me, and my mind would spin in cartwheels because *I finally got to kiss Josie Sedgwick*.

And until I get to again, I won't be able to think of anything else.

So I go on a run to get rid of some of the energy burning inside of me. Swimming season ended in March, and I don't plan on swimming in college, so I have to find a way to stay in shape. I run a mile and a half down the mountain and then a mile and a half back up, and it feels good—chest heaving, muscles aching, sweat burning my eyes and matting my hair to my head. It feels cleansing, therapeutic, as my mind clears and my eyes focus on the road, and all I can think of is breathing in, then out. In, then out.

But then I come back and take a shower, and it's still only five. My dad taught in town today, and he's still not back. After a minute of pacing back and forth, I walk into the kitchen, throw open the cabinets, and start grabbing spices.

When my dad walks through the door an hour later, a pot of chili is happily bubbling on the stove and I'm pulling a pan of cornbread muffins out of the oven.

"Mitchell?" He stops just inside the door, sniffs the air, and then slowly, almost suspiciously, makes his way toward the kitchen.

"Hi, Dad." I smile at him as I stir the chili. Partly because I'm happy the chili turned out so great, and partly because I'm excited to devour what I've made. At least two bowls. Maybe three.

He frowns and glances around. "Is . . . is your mom here?"

"No."

"But there's dinner."

"I cooked."

He raises his eyebrows, and I shake my head.

"What? I've cooked before."

"Pancakes. A can of soup." He inches his way to the stove and peers into the pot. "Boxed mac and cheese."

"Fine." I move in front of him, blocking his view of the stove. "Then you don't have to eat it. It'll just be for me."

"No!" He grins at me. "I'm not sure how you did it, but it smells incredible."

"It's just cooking, Dad. No big deal." But the expression that spreads across his face as he sets the table—a little bit tired but mostly genuinely, truly happy—makes me feel really happy. The first time I've felt at home in my own home in weeks.

I almost make it through the whole meal like this. Almost. Until my dad takes his last bite, wipes his mouth, and puts down his fork.

"Excellent meal, Mitchie." He grins at me, and I don't even care that he used my embarrassing old nickname because I'm just happy that he's happy.

"Thanks, Dad." I stand up to clear the plates away, but he stops me.

"Wait a second." He clenches his hands.

I sink back down. "What?"

He exhales, long and slow, and leans forward, resting his forearms on the table. "I know you don't want to hear this."

"Then don't say it." I don't mean for my words to be snappy, but there they are.

"You have to talk to her, Mitchell." He winces, and for a

second I feel bad for him. He doesn't want to be dealing with this any more than I do. "She calls me twice, three times a day. Shows up here at least once a day, but you're never here. She's dying to talk to you. She's desperate."

Blood pounds through my veins, my heart thumping at double speed. "She should have thought of that before she started hooking up with a sixteen-year-old guy who can barely form coherent sentences."

He sighs. "You're being too harsh."

I stand up and grab my plate. "No. I'm not."

"Look, Mitchell, I know you're mad at your mother—"

"No, Dad." I drop my plate back down, and the whole table rattles. "I'm mad at *you*."

He blinks at me. I'm standing, and he's sitting, and from here he looks so tiny. But I keep going.

"You always taught me to stand up for myself. To have self-respect and self-confidence and all that." I'm pacing the kitchen now. "And now here you are, letting her walk all over you."

"It's not that simple."

"You keep saying that. But you're wrong. It *is* that simple. She screwed you over, Dad. She made a choice, and it was a shitty choice, and now she has to face the consequences." I pause and plant my hands on my hips, trying to catch my breath. "Don't let her talk to you. Don't let her come over here. Don't even let her live here." I stop pacing and look him straight in the eye. "Next week, at the meeting? Kick her out of here, Dad." I shake my head. "She doesn't deserve to be here anymore."

"She's your mother, Mitchell." His words are soft, his eyes downcast. "I can't push her out of your life like that."

"I'm leaving, Dad. It's not my life I'm worried about." I grab my plate again. "It's yours."

And with that, I drop my plate in the sink, turn around, and stride right out the door.

CHAPTER THIRTY-THREE
JOSIE

I make up a rule for myself: For every five minutes of studying, I can have one minute to think about Mitchell. I do two Calc problems, hastily sketching derivative graphs and equations into neat solutions in my notebook. I carefully box in the final answers so I can come back and study these problems later.

Then, I move my pen to the margins and let it float over the blank white space, doodling spirals and sunbeams and other nonsense as I let my mind wander to Mitchell. Mitchell and his soft, scruff-free baby face chin. Mitchell and the hard muscles of his back under his worn gray t-shirt. Mitchell and his deep, dark eyes and lazy, easy smile and the way he rubs his palms on his jeans when he's nervous.

Mitchell, Mitchell, Mitchell.

It's not the most productive study system in the world. Because sometimes the studying part turns into the thinking-about-his-cute-nose part. Or the thinking-about-his-hands-in-my-hair part. I'm a little bit worried that I'm confusing my brain. That my final next week will ask: What is the square root of $687i$? And I will answer: Mitchell Morrison's adorably crooked front tooth.

But I guess that's a risk I'm willing to take.

I stop studying after a couple hours to help my mom make dinner.

"You don't have to, sweetie," she tells me as I join her in the kitchen. She's making eggplant parmesan.

I grab a loaf of bread, fresh and crusty and buttery, and start to slice. "I know."

We work in silence for a while, her stirring the pot of sauce and adding spices, me buttering slices of bread and dusting them with fresh garlic. The aluminum foil crackles as I wrap it around the bread, and then I slide the loaf into the oven.

I watch my mom as I work. She's really pretty. I always thought so when I was little, and then I got older and noticed the way guys stare at her when we're out running errands and knew I was right. She doesn't wear any makeup, and her hair is always in a ponytail, and she mostly wears jeans and plain, solid-colored shirts.

But she's young—only thirty-four, just sixteen years older than me—and her skin is clear and smooth, and she's thin and fit and tan from working outside all day. She could date any number of guys—the single men who have come and gone from Paintbrush, the men who try to chat her up at the grocery store or at the farmer's market. Most of them nice, genuine, well-meaning guys.

But she would never. She *has* never, not since my dad. And it makes my jaw clench, makes my chest tighten to think about. Because with all his searing words and punches thrown and drunken rages, he did his best to destroy her. And she let him.

I mean, she's happy now. At least I think she is. She hums quietly as she tastes the sauce and tucks a loose strand of hair behind her ear. She *seems* happy.

But she also seems . . . small. Delicate. Breakable, even. Like she needs someone to stand in between her and the world, to keep her from breaking again.

It's not going to be Mae. It's definitely not going to be Libby. So it's me. As long as I can remember, it's always been me.

My mom switches off the burner. "Ready?"

I slide the bread out of the oven. "Ready."

"Libby! Mae!" she calls over her shoulder as she gathers plates together. "Dinner!"

After a few bustling minutes, silverware is set out, four heaping plates are steaming on the table, and Mae has wandered out of the bedroom and plopped herself in her chair.

"Libby!" my mom calls again as she carries a pitcher of water to the table.

"She's not here," Mae says.

"Oh." My mom pauses, water pitcher hovering above the table. "Where is she?"

Mae shrugs. "I don't know."

I slide into my seat. The cabin is quiet for a moment.

"Well." My mom plasters a too-bright smile across her face, placing the pitcher on the table and dropping into her seat. "She can have leftovers, then. Whenever she gets back."

I bite my lip to keep from talking as she pours three glasses of water.

We dig into our food and talk about school and summer

and Paintbrush until all our plates are scraped clean.

The fourth plate sits cold and untouched at Libby's empty chair. And later, when we're all cleaning up the kitchen, my mom wraps the plate in plastic wrap, making the edges painstakingly smooth, before she slides the whole thing into the fridge with a sad carefulness that makes me cringe.

Even a Libby who is M.I.A. can't ruin my night, I decide, as I pad across the grass. It's nine o'clock, and I have baggy flannel pants on, and there's definitely studying I have to do. Yet here I am, barefoot in the cool grass, tiptoeing around in the dark to find Mitchell. It's a beautiful night, and I'm pushing the disappearing Libby to the back of my mind.

That's what I think, at least, until a mysterious car squeals into the parking lot, pounding heavy metal music echoing from inside and making the windows shake. I bite my lip and sneak a little closer, wondering who it could be, even as the answer sneaks into my head: *Libby.*

I can't exactly make out who's in the car, but from the shuffling and laughing, it sounds like a whole lot more people than that vehicle is legally equipped to hold.

The car comes to a shaky stop, and someone turns the music down.

"Your stop, little lady." A booming male voice drifts across the parking lot, and a chorus of laughter follows.

"I know, I know." Libby's voice this time. "I'm trying to— Jesus, Greg, could you at least pretend to move out of the way—?"

More laughter and then the door closest to me swings open. Libby tumbles out, dressed in a very tiny skirt and a top that I can tell is see-through from all the way over here. I can just barely make out a large guy with a girl perched on his lap in the backseat.

"Watch where you're going, bitch." The big guy grins and pulls the door shut after Libby as the crowd in the car hoots with laughter.

I cringe, and my face floods with heat.

Libby brushes herself off and flips the guy off. She tosses her hair over her shoulder and saunters up to the driver's door, leaning in and planting a kiss right on the driver's lips. I can't tell who it is in the dark, but his outline definitely looks big. And tall. And clearly older than her.

The guy is the one to break the kiss, reaching up and tousling her hair. "See you tomorrow, babe."

"Tomorrow." Libby steps back and waves.

Someone turns the music up again, and the angry screamo singer fills the night air as tires burn their way out of the parking lot.

Libby stares off after the car long after it disappears into the night, arms crossed. Slowly, she turns in the direction of home.

I want to be able to let this go. She was just with some friends. It shouldn't be a big deal.

But I find myself marching up to her as she makes her way home. My bare feet disguise my footsteps, so she doesn't hear me until I speak.

"Libby."

She whirls around at the sound of her name, almost falling off balance. Her expression relaxes when she sees me. And then, a half-second later, it tenses again.

"What are you doing out here?" She crosses her arms over her chest.

"Taking a walk." I'm not really sure what to say. "Who were those people?"

"Oh god. I knew it." She shakes her head. "I *knew* you were about to interrogate me for no reason."

"It's a simple question, Libby. It's not an interrogation." I roll my eyes. "What's the big deal? They're your friends, right?"

"Right," she snaps.

"So why can't you just tell me who they are? I'd tell you if you ever asked who I was hanging out with."

"That's because your answer is always Leah," she sneers.

It's true. Well, now there's Mitchell too, but Libby doesn't need to know that. Even so, her answer still stings. "It's because they're older, isn't it?"

"They're in high school. And soon, I'm going to be in high school. So what's the big deal?"

"You're going to be a freshman. There's a big difference between a senior and a freshman." I take a step closer and sniff the air. "Jesus, Libby. You smell like beer."

"Josie, you are not my mom." She takes a step backward. "Some of the other kids had a few beers. But I didn't. It's not a big deal."

"Some of the other kids? Like the one driving the car?"

"No, not the one driving the car." Her voice becomes more and more shrill as she talks. "I'm not a complete idiot, you know."

"That guy called you a bitch." For some reason, this is what bothers me the most.

"He was *joking*. God."

"If he was really your friend, he wouldn't joke like that."

"Please. People call each other that all the time." She flips her hair over her shoulder and turns around. "I'm done with this."

"Libby." I mean for my voice to come out strict, but it comes out pleading.

She snaps back around. "What?"

I bite my lip. "Could you just promise to try and be careful? Please?"

She rolls her eyes at this. And without an answer, she turns and makes her way to the cabin, leaving me standing alone in the dark.

I start following her but stop, turn, walk a few steps in the opposite direction, and then stop again. My heart is pounding in my ears, and for some stupid reason, my hands are trembling.

Where am I going again? Mitchell. That's right. I'm on my way to see Mitchell.

But I stop again, after just a few steps toward his cabin. My confrontation with Libby has me all worked up. I can't see Mitchell like this. He has enough to worry about without worrying about me.

So I can't go find Mitchell. And I can't go home, because

I might say something I regret. To Libby or to my mom or to both.

So I trudge toward the Sanctuary. There are no lights on, and it looks nice and dark and quiet. I'll be able to be alone.

But of course, I'm not. Because when the door swings open, I see a low fire smoldering in the stone fireplace. And sitting in front of the fire is a person, cross-legged and jabbing at the embers with a long stick. A messy-haired, lanky, broad-shouldered person.

I try to sneak back out, but Mitchell turns at the sound of the creaking door.

"Josie?" He squints in the darkness. "How'd you know I was in here?"

"I didn't." I stand awkwardly by the door in case he wishes I would leave.

But he scoots over and pats the smooth stone floor to his right. I cross the room and settle into the spot next to him, knees pulled up to my chest. We're only an inch apart—maybe even closer—but we're not touching.

He looks at my face. "You okay?"

"Yeah." My reply comes automatically. I glance at him, notice the slump in his shoulders, the way his lips are pressed together. "Are *you* okay?"

"Yeah." But he sounds hesitant.

We sit in silence for a minute. A long minute. It's borderline awkward, the not-talking and the not-touching, after what happened in the truck this afternoon. I think about leaving. But I don't.

Mitchell pushes his stick farther into the flames, until the end finally ignites.

"It's stupid. You know?" He studies the mini-fire as it slowly creeps up the stick.

"What? Playing with fire?"

His lips curve upward. "No. Playing with fire is awesome."

"You know what they say. Those who play with fire . . ."

"Have a great time," he finishes.

I laugh, and he shakes his head. "What I meant was, it's stupid how we humans have this natural compulsion to always be okay. To assure everyone that everything's fine, even when it's not. Like it's a sign of weakness to be upset or something."

I pull the bottom hem of my flannel pants down over my cold toes. "Maybe it all goes back to natural selection. Survival of the fittest."

"Be okay or die?" The corners of his mouth turn up.

I nod. "Exactly."

"Well." He carefully pulls the end of the stick toward his face, and with one quick breath, he blows out the flames. "I think that's stupid."

The fire pops, and then the room is quiet. I sigh.

"It's just this thing." I fidget. "With Libby."

He points at me. "Don't do that."

I frown. "Do what?"

"Don't *just* your problems. *It's* just *this thing with Libby.* Like it's not a big deal." He shakes his head. "If it's a big deal to you, then it's a big deal."

I stare at him, and he stares back, his eyes wide and serious, and my heart melts a little bit. I'm still not used to this Mitchell, the one who's serious and real and not all happy-go-lucky and booming laughter and easy smiles all the time. It still knocks me off balance sometimes.

"Okay." I clear my throat. "I saw her, just a minute ago. Out there." I nod toward the door.

"Libby?"

I reach down next to me, running my fingers over the cool stone floor. "She was in a car stuffed with high school kids, and some were drinking, and I just got upset—"

He clears his throat and raises his eyebrows.

I roll my eyes. "Okay, okay. I *got* upset. Because . . ."

He pokes a burning log with his stick, and sparks fly up. "Because why?"

"I'm not . . . I don't really know. Because she's my little sister and she's growing up too fast, I guess? And my mom isn't looking after her like she should. I mean, I don't even drink and I'm eighteen. She's fourteen. I barely knew what a beer looked like at fourteen. It's like she's moving on fast-forward. Like if I were to leave for a month, I'd come back and she'd have turned into some kind of alcoholic drug-dealer, and I wouldn't even recognize her."

"An alcoholic *and* a drug-dealer?" Mitchell snorts. "That's actually pretty ambitious."

I wince. "I'm rambling. I know."

"No, you're not." He uncrosses his legs, pulling one knee up to his chest. "But . . ."

"But?"

"Sometimes, with family . . . you have to take a step back." He exhales. "And I know that sounds harsh. But sometimes you have to disconnect yourself. Because there's nothing you can do."

"Yeah. Maybe."

But I don't know if he's right or not. I take a deep breath in and then slowly let it out. I glance sideways; his profile is illuminated by the flickering firelight, his dark-brown eyes turned warm and chocolaty, his skin pink and flushed, his lips pressed together in a firm straight line.

"So." I nudge his shoulder. "Your turn."

He snaps his stick in half and tosses the pieces into the flames. "My dad wants me to talk to her." He leans forward and rests his chin on his knee. "And the rational part of me knows I should. But the bigger, angrier part of me can't do it. In a very real and literal way. Like, I cannot get my legs to physically move, or my mouth to speak actual words to her without feeling like I'm going to lose my fucking mind." He pauses. "And then another part of me feels guilty and terrible, like the shitty person I am."

"I feel like that. When I think about my dad, I feel like that."

He glances at me. "Really?"

I nod. "Like I can't ever forgive him. Not in this lifetime. Not in a thousand lifetimes. And like I can't believe my mom can."

"Exactly." Mitchell bites his lip. "The thought of her getting to live here, with him—and my dad, just allowing it—it makes me want to leave and never come back."

The fire in front of us has shrunk into a pile of seething embers, burning with a dull red glow.

Out of nowhere, Mitchell laughs.

"We're a mess, aren't we?" He grins at me.

I can't help it—I lean into him, pressing my shoulder into his, wanting to feel his warmth and his soft sweatshirt, wanting to be a part of that smile.

I shrug. "All the best people are messy."

All of a sudden, his arms are around me, and I am in his lap and leaning against his chest, and all I can hear is the steady thump of his heart.

I feel comfy and warm and safe, and also nervous and clumsy, like the slightest shift in my body weight might hurt him.

I pull away slightly and whisper, "Am I crushing you?"

"Shut up," he whispers back. He tightens his arms around me, and I smile into his chest.

We sit like this for a full minute. Then two. Then three or four or five. I can feel the tension leaving his shoulders, feel his breathing evening out, feel his chin growing heavy on the top of my head. I close my eyes.

"I'll be gone soon," he mumbles, so quiet I can barely hear him. Like he's reassuring himself.

My eyes fly open. My shoulders tense. I don't think he notices. I'm not sure he even knows he spoke out loud.

He nuzzles my hair with his chin and gently nudges my head to the side, his lips landing softly on my hair and then on the corner of my eye.

I want to turn my face up to meet him, to feel his soft hair under my palms.

But. *I'll be gone soon.*

I yank my head back and tumble out of his lap, scraping my knee on the stone floor.

"Josie?" His reaches out to help me, eyes filled with concern.

I scramble to my feet, quickly and not-at-all gracefully. "I'm fine."

He stands so suddenly that he stumbles a little, and his face is dangerously close to mine again.

"Are you okay?" His forehead wrinkles into adorable creases.

"I have to study. I just remembered. About studying." I sound lame, and I know it. I shift from foot to foot.

"Oh. Okay." He kneads his hands together and opens his mouth to say something else, but I cut him off.

"See you tomorrow," I mumble, reaching in and giving him a quick hug.

"Tomorrow," he echoes.

But I'm already turning away, already striding across the dark room. Already out the door.

I cross my arms as I walk back to my cabin, shivering in the now-chilly darkness.

I'll be gone soon. He didn't mean anything by it. And I know that we're nothing serious, nothing official. We're nothing, period. Just messing around, just a distraction from his problems, and from mine. I'm not that crazy girl, the one who gets too attached, who makes something out of nothing. I'm not the girl who lets herself get hurt by a boy.

I'm none of those things. So I'm fine with Mitchell leaving. Totally fine. After all, I always knew he would.

CHAPTER THIRTY-FOUR
MITCHELL

The door swings shut behind Josie as she dashes out of sight. I slowly sit back down, staring blankly at the last few glowing embers in the fireplace.

That was weird. I thought after what happened earlier in my truck, after our heart-to-heart tonight, that Josie would be fine if I kissed her again. I never get that personal with anyone. Not even Cord knows that much about my feelings. And I've been dying, *dying*, to kiss her again. It's all I've thought about, all night long.

But she sprinted out of here like her house was on fire. Or like the Sanctuary was on fire. Or maybe like she was on fire. Whatever was on fire, a rejection like this definitely stings a little bit. Or a lot, actually.

Maybe I'm moving too fast. A girl like Josie—careful and thoughtful and smart—maybe she needs a little bit more time to get used to the idea of her and me. The idea of us.

Or, maybe she decided she doesn't really like me that much. That's a possibility. A horrible possibility, but still.

Well, I refuse to accept that. Until I hear the words *Mitchell Morrison, I don't like you like that* come out of her mouth, I'm going to keep forging ahead. Full steam.

Sighing, I stand up and switch on a lamp. The room glows in the soft light, and I settle myself down on the couch with a notebook in my lap.

It's time to plan my trip, and my summer. Graduation is in two weeks, and then I'm taking off. I just don't know where yet. I applied to a bunch of summer jobs at national parks across the country, but I haven't heard back. I'm supposed to have some answers by next Friday, but I'm nervous. Because whether I get a yes or a bunch of no's, I'm still driving away the day after graduation. No matter what.

I put my pen to the paper and scratch away, writing a list of things I'll need. And then I scratch out a tentative budget.

And then . . . nothing. My pen hovers over the paper, twitching, itching to write, but my mind is a blank white space. I'm trying to picture where I'll go. If it'll be jagged red rocks zooming past my window or frost-tipped mountains or foam-capped waves or swamps or lakes or deserts. Moose with wet muzzles and thick fuzzy antlers, sunbaked alligators, coiled rattlesnakes, a rocky ledge piled with fat and happy seals. If I'll need to pack sweatshirts or swim trunks or both.

I'm trying so hard to picture it, to plan, but I can't. The uncertainty makes it too hard.

And the other hard part? Every time I try to picture myself driving—with both hands on the wheel and into some unknown American landscape—I can't help but picture a pair of bare feet propped up on the dashboard beside me. A battered copy of *Pride and Prejudice* stuffed in the glove compartment. Wisps of soft brown hair tickling my face as they escape from a thick braid. A smiling face leaning out the window. Josie right beside me. Josie everywhere with me.

Shit. This is going to be a problem.

The ride to school this morning isn't awkward, exactly. But it's not great, either. We make small talk and chat about nothing. *We'll take things slow.* I'll give her some space.

Which is why I'm just as surprised as her when, ten minutes from school, the words, "Let's go to the lake," come out of my mouth.

Josie scrunches up her nose. "The lake?"

"Lake Margaret," I say, drumming my fingers on the steering wheel. "Let's go."

"Like after school?"

"Like . . . right now."

"Skip school." Her voice is dubious, and she looks out the window. "I don't know, Mitchell. We're almost there."

"You're right. You're right." I nod. "Stupid idea."

It's quiet for a minute, and then I open my mouth again. "But it's really just review at this point, right? All stuff you already know. And you don't have a single absence this year yet." My voice is picking up speed. I sound like a crazy person. "And the sun is shining, the birds are chirping, not a cloud in the sky . . ."

I gesture grandly out the window, and the truck swerves in all my excitement. Josie laughs and grabs her door handle as I whip the wheel back on track.

"Sorry." But I grin, because now she's grinning. "I'm just a little excited."

She presses her lips together and frowns, and I'm sure she's going to say no. I can already feel the disappointment rising in my chest like a wave.

But then she sighs. "Well, if we're going to go to the lake, I'm gonna need to go back and grab my bathing suit."

Yes! I feel like pumping my fist in the air, honking the horn as loud as I can, screaming into the quiet morning, *Hey everyone! Josie Sedgwick likes me enough to skip school with me!*

But instead, I settle for reaching over and squeezing her knee. "Sure thing."

I turn the truck around, and an hour and a half later, after stealthily snagging our bathing suits and some towels from Paintbrush, after winding our way through the mountains, after a minor battle over the radio, after swinging by a grimy gas station to grab potato chips and trail mix and cold sodas, we're here. We dump our stuff in the sand right next to the quietly lapping lake water and stretch out in the lazy sun. Besides an older couple at the other end of the beach and a woman playing fetch with her slobbery Great Dane, we are entirely alone.

Lake Margaret is big and beautiful, but it gets crazy crowded in the summer. There's always screaming children playing tag on the little beach and sunburnt old men chewing tobacco and very plump ladies stuffed into very tiny swimsuits who blare Top 40 radio at full volume. It's kind of a mess, and I avoid it like the plague. But right now, in the lull before school lets out, before it gets blazingly hot—it's perfect.

"I'm skipping school," Josie says from next to me, like she's amazed by this fact. She's wearing jean shorts and a men's Hawaiian print button-up shirt, and the sunglasses perched on top of her head are a bright-pink thrift store find. She props herself up on her elbows. "I've never skipped school before."

"Nerd." I grin at her. She looks like an obnoxious tourist. A hot obnoxious tourist.

She rolls her eyes. "Right. Like you've skipped so much school."

I shrug. "I'm a man of mystery." But she's right. If I skipped school, I wouldn't be allowed to participate in after-school activities. And since my whole life has revolved around after-school activities, skipping definitely wasn't an option.

She shakes her head. "You're a nerd. Just like me."

"I know." I sigh.

She laughs and flips over onto her stomach. "Well, I always meant to be more of a rebel in high school. So this day is just crossing a number off my high school bucket list."

"And a chance to spend the day with an adorable and charming guy," I add.

"Really? Where is he?" She puts her hand over her eyes and pretends to scan the beach.

I reach over and shove her shoulder. "He should be arriving any moment. Jerk."

She laughs. "Good. He sounds great."

She looks at me, eyes crinkled from smiling, a faint blush on her cheeks, and I lean over and kiss her. It's instinctive, practically. Like I can't help it.

It's just a peck, but the blush on her cheeks deepens.

My heart does a cartwheel across my chest, because her embarrassment is actually adorable, and because kissing her is the best. But also I want her to like kissing me, not to be scared of it.

I sit up. "Speaking of bucket lists." I point across the lake. "See that dock over there?"

She sits up and follows my finger, shielding her eyes from the sun. "The floating one in the middle?"

"Yep." I nod. "I've always wanted to swim out there and dive off."

She scoops up a pile of sand. "Why haven't you?"

"There are always too many people here. I feel like I have to fight my way through the water."

She lets the sand drift through her fingers, gazing across the water. She smacks the last few grains from her hands and hops to her feet.

"So let's go." With one quick motion, she pulls off her shirt and tosses it onto the sand. Her shorts go the same way, and then she's running into the lake.

I stand up and do the same, and do my best not to stare at her. Or at least to only stare at her when she's not looking.

I catch up to Josie, and we wade in together. The late May air might be warm already, but the late May water sure isn't. I stop and shiver, but next to me Josie splashes her way forward and dives right in. She surfaces a few yards away, rubbing her eyes and beaming.

"Is that captain of the swim team really last in the water?" she taunts.

"No way." I point at her. "If you want to play that game,

you have to announce it first. As in, *last one in is a rotten egg.* Or whatever."

She paddles in circles. "How about, last one in the water is incredibly pathetic? Last one in the water is the type of dude who irons his jeans? Last one in the water eats his french fries with a knife and fork?"

"Okay, okay. I get it." I hold up my hands and wade in a little deeper. *Jesus*, it's cold.

"Last one in the water gets sorted into Hufflepuff," Josie continues in a sing-song voice. "Last one in the water has a rolling backpack. Last one in the water—"

"That's it." I launch myself into the water, cutting through the glass surface in perfect diving form.

This. This one perfect moment is why I love swimming. The moment when I'm finally submerged and feel like I can breathe again. The medals and the championships and the teammates—those were all nice too. But this shock to the system, this clarity, this weightlessness—it's why I keep coming back to the water, again and again and again.

It's clear under the surface, and Josie's feet tread water just a few yards in front of me. A few powerful kicks and I'm there, my hand circling her ankles and yanking her down. I hear her muffled screech before she plunges under.

When we come up, she's sputtering and I'm cracking up.

"I can't even be mad." She pushes her wet hair out of her face. "I deserved that."

"Yeah. You did."

She splashes me, sending a spray over both of us. A bead of water drips down her forehead, over her nose and lips, and

I want to kiss that drop of water away.

But if I start, I might not be able to stop, and then we'll both drown.

"So." She nods toward the dock, a good two hundred yards away. "Ready?"

"I was born ready."

She rolls her eyes and starts to swim. "Always so dramatic."

She cuts through the lake in thick, steady strokes, moving surprisingly fast. Of course, if I wanted to, I could really kick myself into high gear and leave her in the proverbial dust. But instead, I keep in pace with her. By the time we reach the floating dock, we're matched almost perfectly, stroke for stroke.

I haul myself up, the dock shaking precariously underneath me. It's not much—really just a square floating piece of worn wood covered in a thin layer of mossy, lakey slime. Who knows who put it out here or when or why. But I love it.

Josie throws one leg over the edge and hoists herself up next to me. We sit cross-legged, right across from each other, knees barely touching, hair dripping.

"There's really not that much room up here, is there?" She leans forward and flicks a tiny fly off the side of the dock.

"This town's not big enough for the both of us?" I make my hand into a gun and point it at her.

She points her own hand gun back. "Exactly."

"So is one of us going to push the other off?" I raise my eyebrows. "Do we have a Titanic situation on our hands here?"

"Yep. And I hate to break it to you, but I'm Rose and you're Jack."

"Um, no way. You're Jack." I make a move to push her off, and she shrieks and grabs my hand to stop me.

"No!" She shakes her head, laughing. "If you push me off, I might never be able to get back on."

"Fine." I pause. "But only if you admit that I'm Rose."

"Fine. But only because of your ladylike good looks and fine manners."

"Don't forget my giant diamond necklace. And the way I like to recline naked on couches while I get my portrait sketched."

"How could I?" She grins, and I grin back, and I realize we are still holding hands.

Slowly, I reach for her other hand. She meets me halfway, weaving our fingers together and clasping tightly. She squeezes both my hands, and that's it—I tug her closer until our foreheads are touching, and then our noses, and then our lips.

She breathes a small sigh as our lips touch, and it makes me want to crash into her and roll around with her on the ground and kiss every inch of her face and her neck and her everything else. Softly, I bite her lip, and she tugs a hand through my hair and grabs a handful, anchoring me in place. She kisses my cheekbones, my neck, my closed eyes, my chin—she is all over the place, she is everywhere, and for once I am not the one making all the moves. And it feels so, so good.

So good, in fact, that I don't realize I'm clutching her a little too close, don't realize that I'm tugging her onto my lap, don't realize that my hand on the curve of her waist is pushing us both off balance—until we're both tumbling into the water.

Later, we're lying on our beach towels, side-by-side, on our stomachs, reading. It's a little bit hard to concentrate with her this close, her damp bathing suit outlining her soft lines and muscled arms and slightly freckled skin. But I'm making it work because I'm finishing up *Pride and Prejudice,* and it's actually really good.

I slap the book closed with a resounding smack. "Are you kidding me?"

Josie jumps, alarmed. "What?"

"She ends up with him?"

"Elizabeth? And Mr. Darcy?" A slow smile creeps across her face. "Well, yeah. They're only the most famous literary couple in the history of literary couples. What did you think would happen?"

"Not that." I shake my head. "He was such a jerk to her. In the beginning. I thought Elizabeth was better than that."

She sits up. "Well, Elizabeth wasn't that nice, either." She wraps her towel around her shoulders. "Besides, he redeemed himself."

I sit up too. "He basically called her ugly. And then she told him he was a dick. How could you get past that?" I stretch out my legs. "Like, how would a relationship ever work, after that?"

She shrugs. "They forgave each other." She pulls on her wet hair, combing it with her fingers. "And they had a history together. Good or bad, that's gotta count for something."

She weaves her hair into a braid, towel draped over her shoulder, face pink in the sun. Her mouth scrunches up a little in concentration, and she focuses on the ground, like she's lost in thought. Like she's really and truly thinking her hardest about Elizabeth and Darcy.

"You should come with me," I blurt out.

Her eyes snap back up to mine as she pulls a hair tie around her braid. "What?"

What am I doing? I pause for a second, take a breath, and realize that, yes, I'm being serious. This is a good idea. This is what I want.

I swallow. "When I leave next week. For the summer. You should come with me."

Her eyes widen, and then her eyebrows furrow, and then she opens her mouth. Then closes it again.

"What are you talking about?" she asks.

My face heats up, and I rub my palms on my thighs. "I'll be traveling for the summer. Road tripping out to whatever national park I get hired at. Seeing the country, hiking around, swimming in every lake and river I can find." I take a deep breath. "And you should come with me."

She bites her lip, and there's a long pause. Actually, it's only like five seconds. But for me, it's excruciating. Real physical pain.

"I don't know, Mitchell." She pulls her knees to her chest, wrapping her arms around her legs. "We don't even know each other that well."

I laugh. "Are you kidding me? Josie, we've known each

other forever. Our whole entire lives."

She cracks a small smile. "I know that." She tugs the towel closer around her. "But being with you like . . . like this"—she gestures back and forth between us—"it's new. You know? It feels like you're a whole new person, practically. Like I've really only known you a week or two."

"Maybe you should kiss me more," I suggest. "Really get to know me."

Her face bursts into flames, and she reaches out and shoves me. I shove her back, and we go toppling over onto the sand.

Our faces are close, and my arm is draped over her stomach. She stares at me, her wide eyes searching my face, and I reach up and rub my thumb over her cheekbone.

Finally, I put my head down on her shoulder. "You don't have to say anything now," I whisper. "Just . . . think about it."

She runs her hand over my damp hair and whispers back. "Okay."

CHAPTER THIRTY-FIVE
JOSIE

When Mitchell and I were little—like really little—we hung out naked a lot. Summers were always hot, and Carrie and my mom would toss us in this little blue plastic pool or let us crawl around in the grass or sit in the Sanctuary eating handfuls of Cheerios—all while we were totally nude. We were young, maybe five, and it was summertime, and clothes were hot and itchy. Plus, when we inevitably smeared dirt or food or mud or juice on ourselves, there were no clothes to wash. Just a toddler to wipe down. So being naked was totally normal. Nothing sexual about it.

Now, Mitchell and I are hanging out all the time with our clothes *on,* and there is everything sexual about it. Not like actual sex or anything. Not even anything particularly juicy or scandalous. Just . . . the way he toys with the hem of my shirt while we're kissing or traces circles on the small of my back. Or the way he sometimes grabs my face with both hands when he kisses me, like he's worried I'll pull away. Or how he makes this low humming sound deep in his throat when I kiss his neck—like he's trying to be quiet, but he just can't. It's not any one big thing, like sex or third base or second base or any other baseball metaphor. It's just a thousand tiny things.

And the tiny things aren't just sexy things. It's also the way his eyes light up when I say his name. And a few nights ago, when we watched a movie, he kept looking at me during the funny parts to make sure I was laughing too. And the way he casually mentions things like my mom's birthday—April fourth—or my least favorite band—Insane Clown Posse—or the time I fell out of a tree and skinned both my knees in third grade—on a dare. The way I've been taking up space in his brain for forever, without even knowing it.

So it's a thousand tiny emotional things, plus the thousand tiny sexy things. Which all adds up to one big . . . something. I think. It's been over a week since we skipped school, a string of days full of kissing and sneaking around and late night talks, and it feels like we're dating. And it's a pretty good feeling.

But we can't be dating. Because Mitchell is leaving. And I'm not going to be the girl who gets left behind. And I'm also not going to be the girl who trails across the country after her boyfriend like a pathetic puppy dog.

I'm not really sure what kind of girl that leaves me to be. Which is what I'm trying to communicate to Leah. It's our last lunch together in the cafeteria. Ever. Tomorrow is finals, and then we have Friday off. And then, graduation.

"I think it's cute," Leah declares. She bites into her gooey chocolate chip cookie. We both got cookies and soda for lunch—last day calls for a celebratory meal.

"Following a boy around is not cute," I reply.

Leah rolls her eyes. "Yes, it is. He likes you. He wants you to come with him. You're not *following* him; you're going *with* him."

"Same thing."

"Nope. It's not."

I take a big bite and let the warm chocolate melt on my tongue. *Yum.* Nine-hundred delicious calories.

I swallow my mouthful. "What's gonna happen when we're hundreds of miles away from home, prancing around Yellowstone or Montana or Florida or wherever, and he decides he's sick of me? Then what?"

Leah stares at me.

I glance down at my shirt, but it's clean. "What? Is there something on my face?"

"What's the matter with you?" she demands. Her bright-red nails click impatiently on the plastic table. "Why would he get sick of you?"

My face heats up. "Oh, please. You know why."

"I absolutely do not."

I gesture down at myself. "I'm not his usual type. You know?" I swallow. "I'm not sexy enough for him."

Leah slams her fist down onto the table, and I jump as all the dishes and silverware shake.

"Unacceptable!" she shouts, and several people look at us.

"What the hell, Leah?" I hiss.

"It's completely unacceptable for you to say things like that about yourself. You are smart. You are kind. And you are way, way sexy." She shakes her head. "Please stop underestimating how hot you are, and just own it."

My face is really burning now. "Oh my god, Leah."

"I'm serious." She points at me. "Mitchell should be thanking God and Buddha and Zeus and anyone else he can think of every second of every day that he gets to kiss you." She picks up her cookie. "And from the sound of it, he probably already is."

I shake my head, but I can't stop myself from smiling. "You know you're ridiculous, right?"

She shrugs and smiles back. "So I've heard."

From across the room comes a shout of "Suck on this, dick-bag!" followed by a chorus of laughter.

Leah sighs and raises her can of soda. "To our esteemed and brilliant peers, on the brink of our graduation."

I raise my can as well. "To the times Principal Jeffers called the football championship sophomore year 'the most important thing to ever be accomplished at this school.'"

"To the time we found not one, not two, but three used condoms on the bathroom floor during the homecoming dance."

"To the time Emma Harris got hit with a tennis ball in gym class and cried."

"To the time Bobby Jenner got his head stuck in a chair and had to go to the emergency room."

We are both grinning now.

"To education at its finest," I say.

Leah smiles. "To you and me."

All of a sudden, I find myself blinking back tears. I swallow the lump in my throat and clink my can against Leah's. "To you and me."

Across the room, people are shuffling around and packing up. I sigh and stand reluctantly. "Only two and a half more hours of this place."

Leah stands and gathers her trash. "It can't go by fast enough."

As I walk past her on my way to the trashcan, she reaches out and smacks my butt.

"Leah!" I glare at her over my shoulder.

"I wouldn't have to do stuff like that if you would just admit that you're sexy," she calls.

I shake my head and keep walking.

"I hate to see you go, but I love to watch you leave," she calls again, even louder.

I laugh all the way to the trashcan.

I'm approaching Mitchell's truck after school when I hear footsteps behind me. Running footsteps. I whip around in time to see a neon blur crash into me.

"Shit! I'm sorry!" The blur backs up a little bit, and now I see that it's Cord. I haven't spoken to him since the night of the party.

Behind him, Mitchell runs up. He reaches out and grabs Cord by the shoulder, pulling him back from me.

"Dude." Mitchell's out of breath. "What the hell?"

Cord is dressed in navy shorts with tiny lobsters printed all over them, along with a neon-green tank top and a blue tie. He leans forward, hands on his knees, chest heaving.

"Um." I look from Cord to Mitchell. "Is everything okay?"

"Yep," they say at the same time.

Mitchell glares at Cord. "Cord was just leaving."

"No, I wasn't." Cord sticks out his hand to me. "I wanted to congratulate you."

I slowly take his outstretched hand. "Congratulate me?"

Cord pumps my hand up and down in the world's most enthusiastic handshake. Mitchell rolls his eyes, and Cord releases my hand and clamps his arm around Mitchell's shoulder. "Many a girl has tried to land this fine specimen of man-meat, but none have succeeded. Young Mitchell was too noble for their childish pursuits."

I bite my lip to keep from laughing, and Mitchell closes his eyes and groans.

"Ohpleasedeargod." It comes out all one word. "Stop. Stop right now."

Cord ignores this. "So, yes. Congratulations are in order." He reaches out his other arm and pulls me in so that the three of us are standing in a sort of huddle that's way too close for comfort. "You are one lucky lady."

My face flushes, and I nod, and Mitchell looks like he wants to die. He untangles himself from Cord's arms and shoves his shoulder. "Jesus, dude. Let the girl breathe."

Cord cheerfully sticks his hands in his pockets. "Sorry, Mitchell. But it had to be said."

"It absolutely did not have to be said." But Mitchell's definitely smiling a little. "And we're heading home."

Cord nods. "As am I."

As Mitchell slides into the front seat, Cord reaches out and touches my arm.

"Yeah?" I'm a little concerned he's going to tackle me again.

He just smiles at me. "In all seriousness, though. Mitchell's a really awesome guy. And if he likes you this much, you must be a really awesome girl."

I shake my head as the truck starts behind me. "I don't know. Sometimes I think he's having some kind of mental breakdown and I'm one of the side effects."

"You're not a side effect." Cord shakes his head, his long hair flopping on his forehead. "The way he talks about you? If anything, you're the cure."

I'm not sure what to say to that. Thankfully, Mitchell leans his head out of the window.

"Josie?" When he sees the two of us still standing there, he groans again. "Oh man. Whatever he's saying to you, I am so sorry."

I laugh, and Cord grins. "Calm down, dude. Just doing a background check for you." He looks me up and down. "Looks like she's clean. So you're welcome." With that he holds up his hand to me. We high-five, and he saunters away.

"I'm sorry." Mitchell watches me as I clamber into the passenger seat. "He gets a little . . . excited, sometimes."

"It's okay." I shake my head. "I was just surprised he knew about you and me, that's all."

Mitchell frowns as he backs out of his spot. "Why wouldn't I tell him about you?"

"I don't know." I shrug. "I guess because . . ."

Because you're leaving in a week. Because sometimes I think you're just using me as a distraction. Because I worry I'm not good enough for you. Because we've known each other for twelve years and been together for less than two weeks, and it still doesn't seem real.

He's looking at me expectantly.

"Because I thought you wanted to keep us a secret," I say.

"Only from people at Paintbrush." He pulls out of the parking lot, and we begin making our way home. "Honestly, we probably shouldn't even be seen together too much at home if we can help it."

I nod. "They're all so nosy. They'll be able to sense something's up."

He grins. "Exactly."

Four hours later, I find myself squished around a tiny table with Mitchell, Myra, and Ned. One of my knees is touching Mitchell's knee. My other knee is pressed into Myra's knee. Across the table, Ned keeps accidentally kicking me—and yelling about sheep.

"Don't try to get me to take any more of your damn sheep, boy." He glares at Mitchell. "I know when I'm being tricked."

Mitchell slumps in frustration. "I'm not trying to trick you. I'm trying to *trade* with you. It's part of the game."

Myra accosted us as soon as we arrived back at Paintbrush this afternoon, roping us into a game of Settlers of Catan to "celebrate the end of life as we know it." I never really thought of the end of high school as "the end of life as I know it," but Myra seems to take it very seriously. She told us the end of high school classes is something to be proud of. And then she guilted us into a board game night with her and Ned.

Now Ned is upset, like he always gets when he plays board

games. And Myra is losing, like always, because she thinks competition is unhealthy and mean-spirited. She's always doing things like giving away her cards for free and letting other players have their way because "it's the kind thing to do." Which doesn't make for a particularly exciting game.

And Mitchell and I are trying not to look at each other or make eye contact or touch each other because we don't want to make Myra or Ned suspicious. All in all, these factors make this one of the least fun board game sessions I've ever had.

Mitchell trades in a few cards and builds a road, and Ned throws up his hands. "That's it! I quit!"

"Ned." Myra frowns at him.

Ned points at Mitchell. "He took all my wood, and now he blocked me, and I won't have it."

"That's how you play the game, Ned," Mitchell says. "I'm not cheating. I'm winning. There's a difference."

Ned crosses his arms. "Likely story." He nods to the board. "Look! He blocked Josie, too." He shakes his head. "It's not polite to block a lady."

I laugh. "I don't want him to go easy on me. I can take it."

"See?" Mitchell raises his eyebrows. "She wouldn't hesitate to block me, I'm sure."

"They have a point," says Myra.

Ned grumbles. "Fine." He picks his cards back up and looks at me. "But only because you remind me of Annie."

We all freeze. Ned hardly ever talks about his wife.

"How does she remind you of Annie?" Myra asks gently. Classic Myra. She would never throw away a chance to talk about someone's feelings.

Ned studies the board as he speaks. "She never wanted me to go easy on her, either. And she sure didn't go easy on me." He looks up. "That's what made it so good, with us. We pushed each other forward."

"That sounds exhausting," Mitchell says.

"Oh, it was. Very exhausting. Very hard." Ned shuffles the cards in his hand. "But all the best things are hard."

"I wish I could have met her," Myra says after a moment.

"You would have liked her. She smiled all the time, and she worked so hard, and she was funny." He swallows before he speaks again, like there's a lump in his throat. "She made me better."

I glance at Mitchell, expecting to find him glancing toward the door, plotting his getaway from all this talk about feelings.

But he's not. He's leaning forward, hanging on to every word. "She sounds great, Ned."

"Yeah, well." He clears his throat. "No use getting all worked up over old things like that." He surveys the board. "Now you all distracted me, and I'll never win the game."

I laugh. "That was our plan all along."

He narrows his eyes at me and opens his mouth, but before he can grumble a retort at me, the door to the Sanctuary bursts open, and Mae comes tearing in.

"Josie." She stops in the middle of the room, her chest heaving, her eyes wild.

"Mae?" I stand up quickly, knocking my cards to the floor. "What is it?"

"Mom just got a call from the hospital." Her eyes water. "It's Libby."

Behind me I hear Myra's muffled gasp, feel Mitchell's hand on my shoulder, feel Ned's eyes boring into my back. But I don't pause to say anything, to ask any questions. I'm already following Mae out the door.

I'm pretty sure my mom hasn't blinked for the past thirty minutes. Not as we piled into Myra's car, Mae and I huddled in the back, Myra gripping the wheel with white knuckles, my mom staring ahead from the passenger seat. Not as the dark granite and faded-yellow lines sped by under our wheels. Not now, as Myra whips around the corner and screeches into a spot in the emergency room parking lot.

Scientifically, I know that this is very unlikely. People have to blink, and thirty minutes is a long time. But I've been staring at her almost the whole time—her face ghostly pale, her hair disheveled, her lips pressed together—and I'm ninety-nine percent sure I'm right.

The neon lights of the ER glow painfully bright in the dark as we scramble out of the vehicle. Even though my mom doesn't have a car, she knows how to drive, and she could have just borrowed Myra's. But Myra took one look at Mom's face and offered to drive us here, down the mountain. Which was definitely a good idea. My mom hasn't spoken a word, either. I think she's in shock.

Mae, on the other hand, can't stop talking. Her chatter has been nonstop since she ran into the Sanctuary and got me, her words filling every particle of space around us. Even now, as the four of us race down a fluorescent hallway, following the ER nurse's directions to Libby's room, Mae can't stop.

"I'm sure it's not a big deal." Her voice sounds too loud in the near-empty hallway. "They're probably making a bigger deal out of this than it actually is."

No one answers her. The slap of our feet on linoleum mingles with the steady beeping and murmurs of conversation from a nearby room.

She keeps going. "Last year my math teacher was in a car accident. Remember? Mrs. Juma? And she said that even though she was totally fine, the ambulance guys still made her go to the ER. Just in case."

She keeps snapping a black hairband on her wrist, each loud *thwack* echoing through the hallway. And through my head. And through Myra's head too, apparently, because the next time Mae reaches for her wrist, Myra leans sideways and grabs Mae's hand. Mae latches on, lacing her pale, smooth fingers through Myra's tanned and wrinkled ones. She looks like a little girl.

"Do you think—?" Mae begins again as we round the corner. But then she stops. And we all stop. Because right in front of us is room 314A. And right inside the open door is Libby.

Myra gasps, my mom clutches her hand to her mouth, and Mae bursts into tears. Me, I don't really know what to do.

A big chunk of Libby's hair is matted with blood—practically the whole left side of her head. A large bruise is blooming on her right cheekbone, right under her eye, and her entire right arm, from wrist to shoulder, is wrapped in a cast.

Her eyes flutter beneath her pale eyelids. When we walk into the room, they slowly open.

"Oh, sweetie." My mom is at the bedside in an instant, blinking furiously, finally, as she fights back tears.

Mae perches on the bottom of the bed, cross-legged and tiny. Myra sits on a chair behind my mom. I stand awkwardly in the middle of the room, somewhere between the bed and the wall.

"We're so glad you're okay," Myra murmurs.

My mom nods. Mae just stares at her twin's face, tears sliding down her cheeks.

I expect Libby's voice to be thin and weak, but it echoes surprisingly loud in the tiny room.

"I'm fine, guys. Really. I promise."

I think she's trying to sound reassuring, but it's not quite working. If anything, she sounds slightly annoyed.

"It was just a little car accident," she continues. "No big deal."

"A little accident?" Mae's voice is scratchy. "Your head is covered in blood."

"Yeah, I could really use a shower," Libby jokes, but nobody laughs. "It looks way worse than it is."

My mom opens her mouth to say something, but a knock interrupts her. We all turn toward the door, where a policeman is poking his head in.

"Is this the room of Miss Elizabeth Sedgwick?"

Libby doesn't answer, so my mom clears her throat. "Yes, it is."

The officer steps inside the doorway, holding a clipboard,

and his eyebrows are knotted together. "And are you her mother?"

My mom nods. Libby stares determinedly at her lap, fiddling with the sheets.

"Ma'am, would you mind stepping into the hallway with me for a moment?"

My mom's gaze flicks to Libby, but Libby doesn't look up. So my mom rises, slowly, and follows the officer out of the room.

We are at the hospital for almost four hours. We wait in the bare waiting room while the officer tells my mom the whole story—Libby was in the passenger seat when the driver, a seventeen-year-old who had way too many beers, ran a stop sign and crashed into another car. The other driver is fine, but his car is totaled. The driver of Libby's car, and the boy and girl in the backseat, all escaped with minor cuts and bruises. I don't know any of the kids; they're all a year younger than me, and my high school is huge. All I know is the driver is now at the police station, the other two kids are at home, and Libby is here in the hospital, hurt much worse than any of them. She is now sporting five stitches in her head, as well as a broken arm and a broken collarbone. And a bad attitude.

I want to feel sorry for her. And I tried, I really did. I watched as she rolled her eyes at my mom when she asked if Libby was in pain. I listened as she gave the police officer snappy answers as he filled out his report. I watched as she refused the hospital food and as she stared off into space when Myra was talking, and when she repeatedly told us all that it's not a big deal. I watched all of this, and I listened to all of this, and I didn't say anything.

But now, my mom is filling out discharge paperwork, and a nurse is instructing her on how to watch for signs of a concussion. And Libby is standing off to the side, texting. She doesn't even say thank you as we walk out of the hospital. She doesn't even glance up.

My chest tightens as we all slide into the car. Mae squishes in the middle seat in the back, me on her left side, Libby on her right. As Myra starts the car, Mae reaches for Libby's hand. But Libby pulls it out of the way, and so Mae's hand hangs awkwardly in the air before settling back in her lap. It's dark in the car, but I can see the hurt flash across her face.

The ride back up to Paintbrush is a quiet one. Myra asks how Libby's doing, and Libby says fine, and that's about the extent of the conversation. I want to ask who the driver was, what she was doing with him, was she drinking too, and what the *hell* was she thinking.

But my mom speaks first. "I'm just happy you're okay." She swivels in her seat and pats Libby on the knee. "Nothing else matters."

I snort. I can't help it. We're still a good fifteen minutes away from Paintbrush, and cars are terrible places for fights. But I can't help it.

Everyone in the car seems content to ignore me. Everyone except for Libby.

She leans forward, glaring at me across Mae. "Is there

something you'd like to say, Josie?" Libby's voice is icy cold.

"I just think it's a little ridiculous to say that nothing else matters, considering you could have killed a person tonight."

Beside me, Mae inhales sharply and Libby rolls her eyes.

"Oh, please. That guy walked away without a single scratch. And besides, it's not like *I* was the one drinking and driving." She crosses her arms.

"You let a drunk driver behind the wheel. That's just as bad."

"Girls—" my mom begins, but Libby cuts her off.

"Josie. Look at me. I'm the one with the broken bones and the cut up head. I'm the victim here. You do not need to lecture me right now."

"Well, apparently I do." My voice shakes, and hot tears burn my eyes. "Because Mom certainly won't. And you're over here acting like the world's most spoiled brat when you could have died and other people could have died."

Libby scoffs, but I keep talking over her, my voice rising. "And since we have a mother who lets you hang out with idiots who drink and drive and who doesn't give a *shit* about where you go and what you do, who apparently doesn't know one single thing about parenting, then yes. I do need to lecture you." A tear escapes from my eye, and I swipe my hand across my face angrily. "And I need to stay home and put my whole life aside, next year, and the year after that, and the year after that, to make sure there's someone around who can keep you from fucking up like this again. Because god knows Mom won't."

There is total silence in the car. My angry words hang in

the air, and for one split-second I wish I could take them back. I expected Libby to snap back at me, or for my mom to say something. But instead it's terribly, horribly quiet.

I let the tears slide down my face as I look out the window. But I make sure to press my lips together so no one can hear me cry.

My mom tucks Libby and Mae into bed when we get home, like they're five years old again. I curl up in the armchair in the living room and listen to their muffled voices, even though I can't tell what they're saying. The three of them stay in there for a good twenty minutes, talking in low murmurs. It feels like I'm excluded from their club.

When my mom finally leaves the bedroom, carefully closing the door behind her, I reflexively pull my blanket up to my chin. My gaze follows her as she moves around the kitchen, placing dirty mugs into the sink and wiping crumbs off the table. Maybe she's going to ignore me.

Maybe I deserve it.

But after a minute, she wipes her hands on her jeans and sighs, a long, slow exhale. She walks over and leans against the wall, arms crossed over her chest, eyes on my face.

I want to say something, but I'm not sure what to say. So I sit. And I wait.

When she speaks, her voice is strong, steady, and clear. "You're smart and independent, Jo. You always have been and always will be. So please don't pretend that this"—she gestures to the closed bedroom door behind her—"is why you're staying."

I look down at my lap.

She continues, "I know I let you three make your own decisions. I know I let you do most of the things you want to do. But it's not because I don't care about you. And you know that." She rubs a hand across her face. "It's because I trust you. When I was in high school, my parents never trusted me. I had a thousand rules—about what I could and couldn't wear or say or do. When I had to be home and who I could hang out with and what clubs I could join and what grades I had to make. All of that. They never trusted me to know what was best for myself. And because of that, I never learned to think for myself, and I hated them, and I ended up doing every single thing they told me I couldn't do. And as you know, that got me into some trouble." She pauses for a moment, and the slightest hint of smile appears on her face. "A good bit of trouble, actually."

She's talking about getting pregnant with me when she was only a junior in high school. I want to say something, but I have a feeling she's not finished.

She sighs again, and this time, her voice is tired. "So don't think I don't care about where you go or worry about where you are. I worry all the time. But I leave you guys free to make your own choices. And if that means making mistakes now and then—well, good. Because that's how you learn."

She straightens up from the wall and walks toward me. She leans down and kisses me on the head, and she smells like fresh mint and soap, and I have to hold my breath to stop myself from crying again.

"You need to go to bed, sweetie. You've got finals in the morning."

I nod, and she walks toward her bedroom. At the doorway, she turns around again.

"And, Jo? I know you love your sisters, and I love that you watch out for them. But I know you, and I know that you didn't choose Paintbrush over college because of them."

I swallow the lump in my throat. "Then why did I?"

"I think maybe you're not quite ready to leave." She smiles, her small smile. "And that's okay."

She disappears into her bedroom, and I quietly sneak into my room and climb into my bed. I burrow under my quilt and listen to the soft breathing of my sisters, and I think about what my mom said.

Is she right? Am I just looking for an excuse to stay at Paintbrush? I think about the people here—Myra's long messy braids and bossy voice, the grumpy grumblings of Ned and Bernie, the adorable Macpherson kids, the gurgling laugh of baby Lucy, my mom and sisters. I think about the beautiful mountains and my favorite hiking trails and the sunny days I spend farming and reading and selling at the farmer's markets in town.

And then I think about college, somewhere distant and different, a generic green campus swarming with smiling students. Where I could read books and learn new things and, for once in my life, get a taste of something new.

And then I think about Mitchell. *Mitchell.* I haven't thought about him since I dashed out of the Sanctuary. And I haven't texted him because my phone is dead.

I hope he's not worried. I hope he knows I'm okay.

CHAPTER THIRTY-SIX
MITCHELL

I'm pacing. I've *been* pacing. After Josie sprinted out the door and out of sight, I didn't know what else to do. I've already walked the entire perimeter of Paintbrush, around the cabins and the common building and the outer fields. I walked it barefoot, the grass cool beneath my feet. I walked the whole thing once, then twice. Now I'm on my third lap. I keep my phone clutched in my hand, and I check my messages approximately every thirty seconds.

But Josie never calls.

I'm hit with a tiny twinge of annoyance. It's been three whole hours, at least. Josie could have let me know what was going on. After all, she is my girlfriend.

She is my girlfriend, right? I guess we've never quite talked about it. These past few weeks, we just kind of . . . fell into our relationship. It didn't feel quite like starting something new. It felt like opening something up again, something great. So I didn't feel like I needed to officially ask her to be my girlfriend or anything. I felt like she just kind of was.

Now I'm worrying that my girlfriend doesn't think she's my girlfriend. And I'm worrying about Libby and about Josie's family. And in the very back of my mind is my final tomorrow morning, which I have studied very, very little for. Needless to say, I'm not in the best of moods.

Which is why this is a very, very bad time for Joe Jagger to try to talk to me. Yet here he is, in all his disgusting fake-surfer boy glory, blond dreads bouncing up and down as he makes his way across the grass. Right toward me.

I quickly turn to make my escape, but Joe calls after me. "Mitchell! Dude!"

I reluctantly turn to see that he's now jogging, a stupid cheerful grin on his face, like a brain-damaged puppy. I can already feel my fists clenching.

He skids to a stop in front of me. "Saw you pacing around out here, bro."

He looks expectantly at me. He seems to think this statement merits some kind of answer. I just cross my arms.

He continues, undeterred, "Well, I thought since you're up, and I'm up, this might be a good time for us to chat."

"It's really, really not."

"Dude." He raises his palms in the air in a shrug. "We gotta talk this out sometime, you know."

My pulse accelerates, my heartbeat pounding in my ears. "No, I don't know. And I have to go."

"Mitch." His goofy California drawl now has an edge to it. "Just one minute of your time. I swear."

"It's Mitchell." I shake my head. "And I can't. Sorry."

"I know it would make your Mom really happy if she thought—"

"Please, *please*, don't talk to me about my mom. I do not need you to tell me what would or wouldn't make my mom happy." I stare at him, straight in the eyes. "Seriously. Drop it."

I turn to go, but I only take one step before Joe grabs my upper arm, his grip tight and forceful.

So I turn around and punch him.

My fist lands right on his nose with a satisfying crunch, and Joe falls to his knees. I've never punched someone before, and I honestly didn't know it would hurt this much. My hand is throbbing. But looking at Joe—hunched over on the ground and sputtering, blood dripping from his nose onto his stupid white linen shorts—it's totally worth it.

I don't see my mom running until she's already reached us. She gasps, kneeling next to Joe to inspect his face.

"Oh god. Honey." She pushes his hair out of his eyes, and I feel like I'm going to throw up.

"Mitchell." She looks up at me. "I was watching from our cabin"—she gestures behind her—"and I couldn't believe it." For the first time since her dinner announcement, she looks angry at me. Really and actually angry. "What the hell were you thinking?"

My mom rubs Joe's back while he gingerly raises his hand to his face. He prods at his nose and screeches in pain, and I wince. There really is a lot of blood.

I take a step backward. "I'm sorry." I struggle with the words. "I just couldn't . . . I'm having a bad night."

And with that, I turn around and sprint away.

After another hour of pacing around in the back field, cradling my hand against my chest, I decide I need to go home. As the front porch creaks under my feet, I cross my fingers that my dad is asleep.

But no such luck. He's waiting for me just inside the door. And from the look on his face, I can tell he's been on the phone with my mom.

"Mitchell. Morrison." He points to a kitchen chair, and obediently, I sit.

He reaches into the freezer, grabs a package of frozen vegetables, and then tosses it onto the table. The peas land with a splintering thud and skid toward me, leaving a wet streak across the wood.

I gingerly lay the frozen bag across my knuckles. The damp cold stings my swollen hand, and I shudder. My dad sits across from me, slowly and deliberately folding his hands. Finally, he stands, crossing his arms over his chest.

"Have you ever seen me hit someone, Mitchell?"

I sigh.

"I didn't quite catch that," he snaps.

My dad never snaps. He must really be mad.

"No," I answer reluctantly.

"Have you ever seen your mother hit someone?"

"No."

"Have you ever seen anyone here at Paintbrush hit another

person? Or talk about hitting another person?" He's pacing now. "Or engaged in any type of violence of any kind, in any way, shape, or form?"

"No." The ice is still stinging, but at least my knuckles are feeling a little bit better.

"So why, Mitchell, did your mother just call to inform me that you punched Joe Jagger in the face?" His face is flushed, and his voice is quiet and a little scary. "Why would you think that was a good idea?"

I lean forward, all the way, until my forehead touches the table. "I don't know, Dad." My voice is muffled as I speak directly into the scratched wood. "It wasn't a good idea, and I'm sorry."

The room is silent. I lift my head to look at him and find him blinking at me. Clearly, he did not expect me to apologize.

Finally, he sinks into the chair across from me. "What happened, exactly?"

So I tell him. About Libby in the hospital, about how I've been pacing around the last few hours, and about the way Joe grabbed my arm. I even tell my dad about me and Josie. I know we promised not to tell anyone, but I can't seem to make my mouth stop talking.

When I'm done, my dad stares at me. I realize that this is the most I've spoken to him in the past few weeks, and a pang of guilt hits me. I've probably shocked him into silence with the sound of my voice.

"Well." He sits back down, rubbing his hand over his scruffy beard. "You're going to have to apologize."

"I know."

"To Joe. And to your mom."

"I know."

"But right now," he continues, "it sounds like you really just need to go to bed."

"But Josie might call." I hold up my phone.

In one swift motion, he leans across the table and snatches the phone from my hand.

"If something were really wrong, she would have called by now. No news is good news and all that." He walks over and places my phone on the counter. "Go to bed. I'll keep your phone out here, on loud. So you can hear if she calls, but you can't keep checking it like a madman."

"Dad—"

"Nope. You need to sleep." He points toward my room. "So go sleep."

I get up and slink off to my room. I'm too tired to fight him.

I'm about to close my bedroom door when I hear his voice again. "Mitchell?"

I crack the door open. "Yeah?"

"Do you really think you broke his nose?"

"I don't know." I consider this. "But it was definitely bleeding a lot."

He presses his lips together, and I know he's trying to suppress a smile. "Must have been quite a sight."

I grin. "It really was."

He shakes his head, and I close the door. Even though I'm still worried about Josie and mad at Joe and cradling my throbbing hand, I'm still smiling a little as I fall asleep.

I toss and turn for most of the night, and I'm up so early in the morning I don't know what to do with myself. I'm buzzing with nervous energy. When I check my phone, I find a text from Josie that reads: *Everything okay. See you in the morning.* Which is good news, but not super informative.

I find myself killing time out in my truck, sipping on coffee and skimming through my chemistry textbook. I'm not really absorbing much, though. Mostly I'm staring out the windshield, watching the sky get lighter and waiting for Josie to appear.

When I finally see her, walking toward me in the morning light, banana in hand, wearing rolled up jeans and an old red flannel, I scramble out of the car. I can't help it. I jog toward her, and when she sees me jogging, she breaks into a grin and starts jogging too. When we reach each other, she drops her backpack on the ground and wraps her arms around me, burying her face in my neck. I hug her so tight that I lift her off the ground, and she laughs.

"Hi," she says.

I put her back down on solid ground and then pull away to look at her. "Hi."

She looks around quickly and then reaches her hand up behind my head, pulling my mouth down to hers. She threads her fingers through my hair, and I wrap my arms around her waist and lift her up in the air.

Josie is so careful, normally, so contained, her movements tidy and slow. This morning she is all hands and lips and smiles, and my heart feels like it might burst out of my chest.

When I put her back on solid ground her face is slightly

pink, and I have to resist the urge to press my face against hers, cheek to cheek, just so I can feel that warmth.

"Sorry," she says.

"For what?"

"For mauling you just now."

I grab her backpack off the ground. "Don't ever be sorry for that."

She starts toward the truck, and I fall into step beside her. "I missed you." She shakes her head. "Which is stupid, because I just saw you yesterday. But it felt like a long time."

"I know." I reach for her hand and squeeze it. "I divide my time into two now: Josie-time and Not-Josie time. Every Josie-time second goes by crazy fast. At the speed of sound. Or the speed of light. Whichever's faster."

"The speed of light. 299,792,458 meters per second."

"That one. Nerd." I grin, and she shoves my shoulder. "But every Not-Josie-time second goes by so, so slowly. An entire infinity in every second."

She grabs her backpack from me as we climb into the cab. "You're such a poet, Mitchell Morrison." She raises her eyebrows. "Even if your science could use a little brushing up."

She fills me in on the way to school—Libby's accident and her injuries and her trip to the hospital last night. Josie says she argued with her mom, too, but when I ask what about, she avoids the question.

I don't want to leave her to go to class. Even though she's chatting and laughing and smiling, there's a layer of unease underneath it all. She seems nervous, a little on-edge. Like there's something she's avoiding talking to me about.

It doesn't hit me until halfway through my third and last final. I'm conjugating the word for to try *en Francais*—essayer. *Essaie, essaies, essaie, essayons, essayez, essaient*—when it hits me: the meeting is tonight.

Myra's specially mandated community meeting. Where my dad gets to decide whether or not my mom can stay. Where the fate of my mom's relationship with Joe is decided. I can't believe I almost forgot.

I have a hard time concentrating on the rest of the exam. *Qu'est-ce que ta nourriture favori?* What is your favorite food?

I can't imagine my dad will let them stay. There's no way. Not after last night's debacle. Not after the way Joe grabbed me. Not after the way my mom has acted this past month.

I scrawl something quickly. My handwriting is practically unintelligible. *Ma nourriture favori est les légumes.* My favorite food is vegetables. One thousand percent not true, and I'm not even sure I spelled legumes right.

But I stand and shuffle my papers together, heaving my backpack onto my shoulder. I gingerly place my exam onto Madame Renee's desk.

"*Tu est fini?*" She raises her eyebrows.

I nod. "*Oui.*"

"Well, then." She shrugs. "*Bonne chance*, Mitchell."

"Thanks," I mutter lamely in English. I am already halfway out the door.

Josie keeps asking me questions. Normally, this wouldn't bother me. But it's really getting in the way of me kissing her.

"You haven't heard anything back yet?" Her back is pressed against the truck's window, her legs stretched out on the wide backseat. I am leaning over her, hands on her knees, lips pressed against her neck.

"Not yet." I slide my mouth up to her ear.

"Not even a no? None of the national parks emailed you back yet at all?"

"Not even a no." I gently bite her earlobe, and her eyes flutter closed.

I kiss my way up her jaw, and her hands slide up my arms. But just when I'm about to reach her mouth . . .

"So what are you going to do? If you don't get into any of the programs?"

I sigh and slump forward, pressing my forehead into her shoulder. "Josie . . ."

"Sorry." She laughs quietly, and her shoulder shakes beneath me. "I know this isn't what you had in mind when you parked the truck here."

"No. It's not." I sit back up. "This is make-out meadow. Where we had our first kiss."

"Second kiss," she reminds me.

"First *real* kiss. It's a place for kissing." I raise my eyebrows. "And any other fun and illicit activities you can think of. Not twenty questions."

"Always so dramatic." She rolls her eyes right back at me. "I've asked, like, five questions. Maybe. And you haven't answered any of them."

Her eyes sparkle, her hair is a little bit tangled where I've been running my hands through it, and the collar of her shirt is pulled all the way to one side. She looks messy and flushed and beautiful.

I sigh. "What will I do if I don't get a job somewhere else this summer?"

She nods.

"I don't know." I run my fingers through my hair. "I haven't thought about it much." I pause. "I guess I might stay at Paintbrush."

Her eyebrows shoot up. "Really?"

I can't help but hear the glimmer of hope in her voice, and it makes my heart happy. "Yeah." I squeeze her leg. "After my dad kicks my mom out tonight . . . things won't be so bad. And I'll get to be with you."

"*If* your dad kicks your mom out."

I shake my head. "He will. He has to."

But I'm not actually as confident as I sound. Just thinking about tonight makes me nervous, makes my heart pound and my fists clench. So I lean in again, to kiss Josie's lips and maybe her hair, and to lose myself in her. So I don't have to think about anything that isn't her.

She puts her finger to my lips. "One more question."

My shoulder sag, but she continues. "Are you going to the meeting tonight?"

"Yeah." I hadn't really considered it, but once the word leaves my mouth, I know it's true. I need to be there tonight. I need to make sure my dad makes the right decision. "I'll be there."

"Really?"

"Really." I lean in again. "Now can I ask you a question?"

"Yeah?"

I am inches away from her face. Up close, I notice she has a spattering of golden flecks in her green eyes. Almost like freckles. "Can I kiss you now?"

She tilts her head in mock concentration. "I don't know, I might have a few more—"

But that's all she gets out before I press my lips to hers again. I push my hand into her hair, and her hand sneaks under my flannel, gripping the small of my back. And just like that, everything I'm worried about evaporates away, spiraling into tiny particles and drifting off into nothingness. Like magic. Kissing Josie is like real and actual magic.

The Meeting Place is even louder than usual tonight. All through community dinner, the table is filled with buzzing and gossip and whispering. Some people are trying to pretend they aren't talking about what's going to happen at the meeting after dinner. Lots of others don't even bother, loudly stating their opinion. I hear my mom's name and my dad's name thrown around the whole night, whispers of "John" and "Carrie" and "Joe." Even a "Mitchell" or two thrown in there.

I sit all the way at the end of the table, eating a giant helping of parsley mashed potatoes and avoiding all conversation and eye contact. Josie sits a few seats down, occasionally glancing at me. She's sitting next to Libby, whose arm is in a sling, helping cut up her chicken. Libby keeps rolling her eyes.

My dad is sitting next to Myra at the head of the table. They spend the whole meal huddled together, talking in hushed tones and nodding seriously. And somewhere in the middle, my mom sits next to Joe. From where I'm sitting, it seems that Joe is talking a mile a minute to the people around him, shoveling food in his mouth with a voraciousness that can only be described as alarming. My mom hasn't touched her food, and she hasn't opened her mouth once.

Never have the people of Paintbrush eaten so quickly or cleaned up the meal so efficiently. By the time Myra stands to make her announcement, everyone is back in their seats, places cleaned, looking up with expectant expressions. All except my dad, who's staring determinedly at his lap. And my mom, who looks like she might throw up.

"Well." Myra looks around the table. "As most of you know, tonight is a special meeting."

She looks anxious, which is unusual for Myra, and I feel bad for her. Nights like this are not what Paintbrush is all about.

"I am saddened that we have a situation on our hands like this," she continues. "As you all know, Paintbrush is a community. We pride ourselves on our commitment to the environment, on purposeful and practical living, and above all else, on our mutual respect and support." She swallows, hard, and then continues. "So when one of our members begins to feel threatened, or uncomfortable by another member, or members, it is time to examine the situation and to remedy it."

Around the table come nods and murmurs of assent. With every passing second, my heart beats faster and faster. I try to make eye contact with my dad still sitting at the head of the table, but he won't look at me. He won't look at anyone.

"It is unfortunate," Myra continues, "when a situation becomes so precarious that we are forced to consider suspension from the community." Her eyes are glistening, and her voice is wavering slightly. "In fact, it's never happened here before. But tonight, we will hear from both Carrie and John. We will listen carefully, with open hearts and minds. Then I will open the floor for input from any one of you who feels that they have a significant and helpful thought to contribute." She gestures at my dad. "And finally, it will be up to John to decide the final verdict."

She gazes out over the forty or so wide-eyed and tense faces gazing back at her from the long wooden table. "If anyone finds fault with this plan, please say so now."

Silence falls across the room, and Myra nods. "Okay. Then, Carrie, go ahead."

My mom stands, her hands shaking, and Joe places one protective hand on the small of her back. She searches the table, looking from face to face, until finally her eyes settle on me. Instinctively, I look down.

"What I did was wrong." For a woman whose hands are shaking, her voice is surprisingly strong. "It was wrong because it hurt John, and it hurt Mitchell, and it hurt the community."

Several people turn to look at me. I ignore them.

"But it was still the right move for me." The shaking lessens as she continues, and her voice gets stronger and louder. "I fell in love with Joe, and I can't apologize for that. And Paintbrush is my home"—she gestures to Joe—"is *our* home. And if we could be forgiven, and accepted here, then we would love to stay."

A tear runs down her face, but her chin juts up in the air. She is not backing down. That familiar anger claws at my chest, and I stare at the table in front of me. When I stare at the table, I can be as angry as I want. When I look at my mom's tear-stained face, I come dangerously close to feeling sorry for her.

No one says anything to reply to my mom. She sits down, Joe rubbing her back. I can see a bruise on his face from here, and I can't help but feel slightly smug.

At a nod from Myra, my dad stands, slowly and purposefully. My heart pounds in my chest, so hard I can feel my pulse behind my eyes and through my fingertips. I press my palms into my knees and stare at his face. He stares back, straight into my eyes, and I will him to make the right decision.

Tell her no, Dad. Tell her no.

His eyes never leave my face. "I'm not going to make this into a long ordeal, and I'm not going to give some big explanation. Carrie and Joe are as much a part of this community as I am." He takes a breath. "They are welcome to stay."

My heart drops like a stone, sinking into the pit of my stomach with an actual burst of pain. Like I've been drop-kicked in the chest. My dad's eyes bore into mine as whispers and murmurs break out across the table. His expression is resolute, but his lip trembles slightly. He knows I'm upset.

I break the eye contact. I can't look at him. I can't look at anyone.

"Settle down." Myra stands, her voice booming across the room. "Now. Does anyone have anything they need to say? Anything useful?" she adds sternly.

Most people shake their heads. Hot anger grips my chest. No one's going to say anything. My mother destroyed my family, and no one's going to tell her what she deserves to hear.

"I respect John's decision," Ned says gruffly.

"Seconded," says Bernie.

There are mumbles of assent. Myra lets her gaze sweep the table one more time before nodding. "Okay. Then that's that. Carrie and Joe can stay. Meeting dismissed."

I stand. I know my mom is about to make a beeline for me, and probably my dad, and Josie too.

So I turn and stride to the door, slipping out into the night.

CHAPTER THIRTY-SEVEN
JOSIE

When I finally find Mitchell, he is cross-legged, resting against the old toolshed out by the back field. He leans his head against the worn wood, eyes closed, mouth set in a firm line.

"Hey." I nudge his foot with mine.

"Hey." He doesn't look up. He doesn't even open his eyes.

I think about settling in next to him or kneeling in front of him or pulling him into me and wrapping my arms around him. But his vibe isn't just sad. The air around us is . . . uneasy. Tense. I have no idea what he's feeling. Like he's an old firecracker I found in the garage, and I'm waiting to see if it's still active. If he's about to explode in a fiery mess or just fizzle out.

I cross my arms over my chest and stand awkwardly next to him. And wait.

Finally, his eyes open. But he's still not looking at me. He's staring off into the dark.

"I'm so sick of being angry all the time." He rubs his eyes with a balled up fist.

"At your mom?" I shift from one foot to the other, rubbing my arms to keep goose bumps from rising in the chilly air.

"At her. At my dad. At Joe." His hands find the grass below him, and he yanks up a big clump. "At this whole stupid place."

His jab at Paintbrush stings. Like always. I bite my lip and try to think of the right thing to say.

"And at myself," he continues. "I'm always mad at myself." He tosses his handful of grass to the ground and reaches down to grab another clump. "Sometimes, I'm even mad at you."

"Me?" My voice comes out shaky and weak, and it makes me cringe.

He looks up at me, finally, his eyes wide open. "I've been ready to leave here for months. Years. I was going to get the fuck out of here. That's always been the plan." He rubs his palms on his jeans. "But now, there's you."

"I've always been here. There's always been me."

"Well, now you're . . . different." He drums his fingers on his knees. "And I let myself get attached to you, and that made me attached to this place again." He clenches his fist. "And that sucks."

His words hit me hard, like a punch to the stomach. Like the air gets knocked right out of me. It takes me a few seconds to respond. "Wow. Thanks."

"Wait, no." He sighs, frustrated. "That came out wrong. *You* don't suck. I'm glad I'm with you."

"It really doesn't sound like it." I'm fighting back tears, which is so embarrassing. I hope he can't hear it in my voice.

"Josie. You know what I mean."

"Yeah. I do." My hands are trembling. I tuck them into my pockets so he can't see. "We can't do this anymore, Mitchell."

His head snaps up, eyes wide in surprise. "What do you

mean?"

I shake my head. "We can't be together."

All of a sudden he's standing, just inches in front of me, reaching for me. "Josie, no. That's not what I meant."

His hands skim my arms, but I step back out of his reach. "It's what *I* meant. You hate this place."

"Well, yeah." He shrugs. "But that doesn't matter. We can leave here, like we talked about. You can come with me this summer, we can travel around the country, we can—"

"Mitchell." I cut him off, my voice louder than I intended. He's not listening. "I like it here."

His eyes widen. "I know you like Paintbrush, but you can't expect to stay here and garden tomatoes forever—"

"Why not?" My heart is racing. "Why can't I stay here forever? I like it here. I *love* it here. These people are my family, and this place is my home." I blink, trying to clear the tears already forming. "And that's why we can't work. Because you hate this place so much." I swallow, hard. "How could you ever be with someone who loves it?"

"That's not true." But his response is half-hearted, and we both know it.

His eyes are shiny, his expression shocked, and it takes every ounce of self-control for me to not reach out for him, to press my head into his chest and tell him that we'll be okay.

But that would be wrong. Because we won't be okay. He's leaving, and I'm staying, and that's that. And if I'm being honest with myself—really and brutally and horribly honest— we probably weren't even a thing. Not even a real relationship. After all, Mitchell never called me his girlfriend. He was just using me as a distraction from his problems.

And I let him. Like the stupid girl I promised myself I'd never be.

Mitchell's lip is trembling, and I have to go. If he cries, I'll cry. And I've been humiliated enough by this conversation.

"This is just a stupid fight." His voice is shaky. "I'm just upset. Let's forget the last five minutes ever happened." He takes a step closer to me. "We can figure all this out."

"I'm sorry about what happened tonight, Mitchell." I close my eyes. "But I have to go."

And before he can say another word, I turn around and run away.

CHAPTER THIRTY-EIGHT
MITCHELL

I jump into the truck and slam the door. I slam it hard and loud, and it feels so good that I swing it back open just so I can slam it again.

Then I drive. I drive a few minutes away and stop. Maybe I should go after her.

So I turn around and drive back to Paintbrush. I pull up and then get out of my truck. And then I picture myself begging for her to reconsider, and I picture her rejecting me. Again. I kick my tire, and I get back in, and I slam the door again.

I don't realize I'm crying until I show up on Cord's porch. I send him a text, and seconds later he swings open his wide white door to find me standing under the dim porch light, swiping at my eyes.

"Shit." He reaches out, grabs my shoulder, and pulls me inside.

Cord doesn't make fun of me for crying or for caring this much about a girl. It's not awkward when we hug or when I cry onto his shoulder, and he doesn't even get mad when I push his gross little white dogs off the bed so I can sit down. He listens to everything I say, and he gets me a glass of water when my throat gets raspy, and he gets me extra blankets for my bed in the guest room. And when I ask if I can sleep on the futon in his room instead, he doesn't ask why or get all weird. He just nods and pulls it into the bed position and asks if I need any extra pillows.

When I go to college, I'm really gonna miss this guy.

I thought the feeling of another person in the room with me, the soft snores coming from Cord's bed, would make me feel better. I thought maybe it'd be easier for me to drift off. But no. Here I am, completely fucking exhausted and totally unable to sleep. I'm not even angry any more. I don't have any anger left in me. I just feel . . . empty. My mom chose Joe over me. Tonight, my dad chose my mom over me. And Josie chose . . . herself over me? That doesn't feel right. She chose something over me. Maybe she just chose everything over me.

The point is, she didn't choose me.

I feel hollow and heavy, like my chest is empty but my bones are made of lead. I want to sink further and further into the futon, want to burrow into Cord's ridiculous down pillows and sleep for a million years and never wake up. Because when I wake up, I have to deal with the fact that I really don't have a place to go. After tonight, I know it for sure: Paintbrush is not my home.

"Cord?" I whisper.

"Yeah?" His pillows muffle his bleary voice.

"Can you tell me something? To distract me?" I sit up and punch my pillow into place, trying to settle down.

Cord rolls over to face me. "I'm working for my dad's company this summer."

"Seriously?" I crack a smile. "Wait. That means you're going to have to wear—"

"A suit," he grumbles. "Don't remind me. And get this: They drug test twice a month."

"No," I gasp.

"Yep. No smoking the whole summer."

"Did you get forced into this by your parents?"

"Nope. I signed up for this torture by choice." His voice is fading again, sleep catching back up to him. "I need the money. And I figured it couldn't hurt for me to chill out a little bit, you know?"

"Cord Cofax, real estate mogul. Has a nice ring to it."

The only answer I get is a snore. But the image of Cord in a suit, like a real-life adult, is all the distraction I need.

I don't know when I finally fall asleep. But I do know that when I wake up, it's past noon, Cord is making pancakes in the kitchen, and I have a pounding headache. And when I check my phone, I have an email. From Canyonlands National Park.

And it's a yes.

I actually have two emails from Canyonlands, but that's beside the point. The point is: I officially know where I'm going to be this summer. And it's officially far away from here.

I need to tell Josie. I need to talk to her and see where we stand. So I spend the entire afternoon looking for her—

knocking on her cabin door, searching around the grounds, even asking about her. But she's impossible to find. When Libby opens the cabin door, she just glares at me—her black eye making her look even scarier than usual—and tells me Josie's "out." When I find Maddie Macpherson reading underneath a tree, she tells me Josie was out gardening this morning but hasn't seen her since. When I ask Ned if he's seen Josie, he raises an eyebrow and asks me why it's any of my business. Basically, no one even pretends to be helpful.

After four hours of searching, I end up wandering into the Sanctuary. Myra's in here, sitting cross-legged on the floor. She is surrounded by scraps of paper and ribbons and glue and scissors and glitter and stickers. It looks like a craft bomb went off.

She looks up when I enter and screeches. "Stop!"

I freeze. "What?"

She picks up a nearby newspaper and throws it over whatever it is she's doing. She carefully spreads the pages out so that her craft project is completely covered.

"Do you need me to leave?" I'm half-hoping the answer is yes. I'm not in the mood to get roped into a crazy Myra plan.

"No, no, no. Just a graduation surprise." She motions for me to come in. "Have a seat."

I walk into the center of the room. "I didn't really come in to sit, actually. I was just wondering if you've seen Josie around?"

"I saw her this morning, but not since." She peers at me, studying my face, and then stands up. Actually, it's more like she jumps up. For a seventy-year-old lady, she sure moves fast.

"Sit." She points to the couch, and her voice tells me she's not messing around. "I'll be right back."

When she emerges from the kitchen a minute later, she's carrying two steaming mugs. She places one in front of me and settles back down on the floor.

I sniff my mug suspiciously. "What is this?"

"Tea. Drink it."

"What kind of tea?" Myra's always trying to feed me weird shit from the forest, so I've become very suspicious of anything she tries to serve me.

"The good kind," she says impatiently. "Just try it."

I take a sip, and it actually tastes good. Like lemons and mint and also maybe lavender. The warm liquid heats up my chest, seeping into my bones. Sighing, I sink into the couch. "Thanks, Myra."

She watches my face as I drink, her eyebrows knit together. She's wearing a huge knit blanket-scarf type thing, even though it's actually pretty warm out. Myra's always cold.

"How are you doing, Mitchell?" she asks.

"I'm okay."

She narrows her eyes. "How are you *really* doing, Mitchell?"

She's known me since I was five. Which means she can see right through my fake smile. I close my eyes. "I don't know."

"You're still angry with your mom." She says it like a statement, not a question.

"Yeah."

"Me too."

My eyes fly open. "What?"

"I'm mad at Carrie, too." Her voice is matter-of-fact. "We all love your dad. He's great. Watching her hurt him like that? It upset me, too."

I try to absorb this. "I don't understand. This is your place, Myra. You started Paintbrush. You could kick her right out in a heartbeat. Joe, too."

"First of all, Paintbrush is not just *my* place. It's *our* place. We all have equal ownership in this community."

"Yeah, yeah," I say.

She glares at me.

"Second of all." She pauses to take a sip of her tea. Myra's always good for some dramatic effect. "Do you know why this is called the Indian Paintbrush Community Village?"

"After the wildflower. Indian Paintbrush."

"Well, yes. But why did I name it after that particular wildflower?"

"Because it's pretty?" I have no idea what she's getting at.

"It is pretty," she agrees. "I love when the red blooms cover the mountains in the spring. They're not just pretty, though. The Native Americans used to eat the flowers. They helped to strengthen the immune system and make their hair shiny." She shrugs. "Plus, I'm pretty sure it just tasted good."

"Oh." I don't know what else to say. Sometimes, Myra's tangents don't make any sense. Actually, most of the time.

"So I decided to eat it." She smiles. "Turns out it was poison."

"*Poison?*"

"Yep." She beams at me. "I was vomiting for days."

"But you just said the Native Americans ate it."

"Apparently they only ate the flower. The roots, as it turns out, are very toxic."

"Jesus, Myra." I think for a second. "So why would you name your community after something that poisoned you? That's like naming your first-born child after some guy that bullied you in high school."

"Just because the roots poisoned me doesn't mean the flower isn't beautiful. And delicious. It may have bad parts—"

"Uh, yeah. Like the *poison*."

She nods. "Like the poison. But that doesn't mean it's all bad. It's still a good flower and a good plant, important to its native environment and ecology. It's just not perfect."

"Oh god. I feel an analogy coming on."

She grins. "I don't know what you're talking about." She stands back up, stretching her legs. "But that's why I chose the name. People aren't perfect. Places aren't perfect. Everyone has flaws. But one flaw—or one mistake—doesn't mean you should write off that person forever."

"Or that plant," I say.

"Exactly." She pats me on the shoulder. "Just think about it, Mitchell."

"I'll try."

She grabs my empty mug and heads back toward the kitchen. I slump over sideways until my face is squished into the couch cushions. In my pocket is my phone, the email from Canyonlands pulled up, burning a hole in my pocket. Two days until graduation, and I have a lot of decisions to make.

Oh, and a speech to write.

CHAPTER THIRTY-NINE
JOSIE

I'm exhausted. I want to crawl into my bed and sleep for an entire year, or maybe even two. I'm exhausted from avoiding Mitchell, from ducking around corners and hiding behind people and sneaking around Paintbrush, like I'm a ridiculous bumbling spy from an old timey movie.

I'm exhausted from helping Libby, who is in a lot of pain from her collarbone and arm. *Helping* is a pretty loose term; it's more *doing whatever stupid task Libby orders me to do because I feel bad about fighting with her after she got in a car accident.* Yesterday, I made her homemade vegetable soup because she insisted she was getting a cold and just *needed* homemade soup to "strengthen her immune system." And then she insisted I paint her toenails pink because she can't do it herself. I have no idea why her toenails need to be strawberry sugar considering she's basically confined to the house for the next month or two. But I feel guilty, so I did it. I even did a topcoat.

I'm exhausted from weeding because I've been working like crazy on the tomato beds to keep my mind off things. I pulled weeds for four entire hours yesterday, and now my arms and shoulders feel like they're on fire.

I'm also exhausted from crying because, you know, Mitchell. And I'm exhausted from being angry at Mitchell. And I'm exhausted from fighting the urge to apologize to Mitchell. Basically, I'm exhausted from all things Mitchell.

We broke up—or ended it, or whatever it was—on Thursday. Now it's Saturday, and graduation is tomorrow. Leah and I are supposed to sit together—the whole Sedgwick/ Seely thing—but I'm not going. I texted her that I'm not going. Mitchell will be giving his speech, and my whole family will be there in a big happy celebratory mood, and I won't be able to handle all the pretend-happy. So instead I'm going to be pretend-sick.

However, Leah's response to my text was an immediate *I'm coming over*. So now I'm forced to sit out on my porch in the cheerful sunshine and await her arrival instead of lying on my bed in the dark and feeling sorry for myself, like I want to.

It takes her exactly twenty minutes to show up, which means she probably broke every speed limit on the way over. She marches her way across the lawn, her wedge sandals and edgy black dress looking super out of place against the worn rustic cabins. I prepare myself for the inevitable verbal attack.

"Hi, Leah," I say.

She reaches out and punches me in the arm, hard, and I yelp.

"Jesus Christ, are you kidding me?" I grab my throbbing arm. This girl is way stronger than she looks.

"No." She glares at me. "I'm not." She lowers her fist and crosses her arms. "Josephine Sedgwick. What is the matter with you?"

I sigh. "I'm not going, Leah, and you can't convince me."

"Maybe I can't convince you, but I can drag you. Kicking and screaming, if I have to. This is your high school graduation. You only get one of these."

"Graduations are overrated. And besides, you're not strong enough to drag me."

"Oh, really?" She raises her fist for another blow, and I hold my arms above my head.

"No! Stop!" I plead.

She lowers her fist with a sigh and sits beside me on the porch, wrapping her arm around my shoulder. "What's going on?"

My lip starts to tremble, so I bite it. And I squeeze my eyes shut. I will not cry over this anymore. I will not cry over a boy.

"Mitchell and I are over."

"Oh, Josie." She wraps her other arm around me and squeezes me into a hug. "What happened?"

"I don't really know." I lay my head on her shoulder. "He said he gets mad at me sometimes. But I'm pretty sure I broke up with him."

Tears well in my eyes. One spills out and snakes its way down my cheek. I cover my face with my hands and groan. "Crying over a boy. It's so embarrassing."

Leah frowns. "Why is it embarrassing?"

"Just . . ." I shake my head. "Letting myself get all worked up over a guy. It's dumb."

"It is so not dumb." She grabs my hand. "It's love. Love is the most important thing in the world. It would be stupid to *not* get worked up over it."

"I don't think we were in love."

"Maybe you weren't *in* love. Not yet, anyway. But you love Mitchell. And he loves you. You guys have loved each other your whole lives practically."

She's right. You can't grow up with someone the way we did and *not* love them.

"Crying over a boy is nothing to be embarrassed of. God, Josie. You need to cut yourself some slack once in a while."

I nod against her shoulder, but I don't trust myself to speak, so we sit in silence for a few minutes.

"Thanks, Leah," I finally say.

"Don't thank me," she says. "Just come to graduation tomorrow. It won't feel right graduating high school without you there." She squeezes my shoulders. "Besides, it's our chance to celebrate leaving the nightmare that is North Mountain High."

"I wouldn't call it a nightmare so much as a hellhole."

"A torture chamber."

"A snake pit."

"So you're coming?"

I reach down and grab her hand. "I'll be there."

Dinner is quiet. It's been quiet the past few days. Despite Libby's initial snappy attitude, she seems to have sunk into a sadness. Maybe it's being kept home from school or being in constant pain, but she clearly feels bad.

It's not until we're all almost finished with our vegetable

soup that Libby speaks.

"Brad broke up with me." She doesn't look up as she says this. She just spears a piece of chicken and takes a bite.

"Brad?" asks Mae.

"You have a boyfriend?" asks my mom. "I would have hoped you'd tell me if you had a boyfriend."

I think of Mitchell, and a pang of guilt hits me.

"He was the one driving the car," Libby says quietly.

My mom freezes, fork in midair. "Oh."

"Well, I'm not sorry about it," Mae says around a mouthful of mashed potatoes.

"Mae." My mom flashes her a warning look.

"What? He almost killed her!"

"You could try to have a little sensitivity."

"He texted me and told me it was over." Libby's voice is a shaky whisper. She still won't look up.

"He *texted* you?" Mae snorts. "What an asshole."

"Mae," my mom warns again, but Libby shakes her head.

"It's okay. She's right. He is an asshole."

Mae leans forward, arms resting on the table. "If I were you, I'd never forgive him."

My mom sighs. "That's not a very productive way of thinking."

"Really?" I put my fork down. "You think she should forgive him?"

"Well, I certainly don't think she should get back together with him." My mom dabs her mouth with her napkin. "But you have to forgive at some point."

Mae points at my mom. "I disagree."

I nod. "Me too."

But Libby's gaze is on my mom. "Did you ever forgive Dad? For what he did to you?"

I glance at Mae; she widens her eyes back. We almost never talk about Dad and what happened when we were little.

"Yes." My mom pushes her plate away and folds her hands in front of her. "I did."

"How can you, though?" The words come spilling from my mouth. "He *hit* you. He tried to *destroy* you. How can you forgive him? That's like letting him win."

She speaks slowly, like every word is a careful choice. "I would never return to your father. What he did was wrong; there's no doubt about it. But forgiving doesn't mean I'm weak." She focuses on me. "It means I *didn't* let him destroy me. It means I *did* win." Her voice is earnest and clear. "Keeping all that anger bottled up inside me? Holding a grudge for the rest of my life? Now *that* would have destroyed me."

We all stare at her. No one is eating. Mae and Libby just blink, processing all this. Me, I'm reconsidering everything. I never thought of my mom as strong before, especially not these last few years. Now I'm ashamed I ever thought she was weak.

"Besides. I could never fully regret my relationship with your father." My mom studies each of our faces, her lips tugged up at the corners. "Now I have all of you."

At this, Libby bursts into tears.

I'm not kidding. Loud, messy, heaving sobs. Mae and I stare, open-mouthed, as our sister gets up and throws her arms—well, her one good arm—around my mom's neck. I haven't seen Libby display this much emotion in years. I wasn't even sure if she was capable of tears anymore.

"I'm so sorry, Mom." Her voice cracks. "I'm so, so sorry."

My mom wraps her arms around Libby, rubbing her back in circles. "It's okay, sweetie. Mistakes are a part of life. We just have to learn from them."

Libby nods, sniffling. Mae and I exchange glances.

Libby pulls back when her crying subsides. "Even though I missed the last few days of school, am I allowed to go to Josie's graduation tomorrow?"

Now I'm really surprised. I would have thought Libby would jump at the chance to get out of going to my graduation ceremony. It's out in the hot sun, on the football field, and everyone is forced to sit for hours while they call every single name. All six hundred of them.

"It's okay, Libby," I say quickly. "You don't have to go."

She blinks at me. "But I want to go."

My heart melts a little at this.

Mae chimes in. "You're our big sister. Of course we're gonna be there."

I don't know what to say to this, so I just smile. I smile, so I won't tear up instead.

My mom disentangles herself from Libby and stands, picking up dirty dishes. "And Libby, honey, I don't think you'll have to worry about seeing Brad there. I don't think many juniors attend the ceremony."

"Are you kidding me?" Libby wipes her eyes with her free hand, her voice filled with venom. "I hope he's there. I hope he sees me and my beat-up face and broken arm, and I hope it makes him feel like shit."

Mae cracks up at this, and my mom shakes her head. And for once, I really admire Libby. Because while she's parading her injuries around hoping to see a certain boy, I'll be slinking around avoiding another boy entirely.

Graduation day is *hot*. It's not even eighty degrees out, but the harsh sun shining on the football field makes it feel like one hundred. We're all drenched with sweat in our black vinyl robes, practically melting in the heat.

Tiny beads of sweat drip down my neck. I'm glad I didn't wear much makeup. I'm wearing a red-and-white checked sundress with a scoop neck and a twirly skirt. It's nicer than I ever dress, and it's the type of dress that calls for makeup, but it would have melted right off. Of course, Leah is sitting next to me, wearing pounds of perfectly applied makeup and a teeny-tiny white lacy dress with five-inch heels. She's perched on the edge of her seat, and I don't see a drop of sweat on her. Figures.

Principal Jeffers is droning on up on stage, about community and school spirit and who knows what else. I'm not really paying attention. I haven't really been paying attention the whole ceremony. Because Mitchell is sitting up on stage in his cap and gown, his brown hair brushed to the side for once. He looks gorgeous. Can guys be gorgeous? Well, he is. Gorgeous and smiling and polished. And gorgeous.

It hasn't been too hard so far, because he's been up on

stage, and I've been tucked back here on this white plastic chair. We're too far away to even make eye contact, which is great, because I've been able to stare at him freely for the last hour straight.

But when Principal Jeffers introduces Mitchell, my heart starts pounding and my leg starts bouncing. Leah grabs my knee to make me be still and gives me a look that clearly says *pull it together*.

Mitchell takes the podium like he's been giving speeches all his life. Like speaking in front of over two thousand people is no big deal. Like he does it all the time. I can see that familiar lazy grin, the easy posture and relaxed shoulders. He looks like the Mitchell from a month ago, before his mom left his dad. Before I knew he was more than just that carefree smile. When our whole relationship was based on car rides to and from school. Before we held hands, before we slept overnight in his truck, before we made out in backseats and discovered secret caves. Before we were us.

"My name is Mitchell Morrison, and I'm honored to have the opportunity to speak to you all this evening."

He stops to clear his throat, and I realize I'm leaning forward in my chair, mesmerized. It's only been two days since I last heard his voice, but it feels like an eternity.

"I'm going to keep this short, and I'm going to keep this sweet." His gaze sweeps over the stadium. "I know what a good graduation speech is supposed to be. It's supposed to be *follow your dreams* and *find your passion* and *you can do anything you set your mind to*, with a few *congratulations* and *we did it*s sprinkled in." A murmur of laughter ripples through the audience. "But I know all that, and I suspect you all know that as well. So instead of thinking about the places you'll go, take a moment to think about the place you've been." He pauses. "Take a moment to think about home."

My heart catches in my throat. This does not sound like the Mitchell I know. This doesn't sound like the Mitchell from two days ago.

"We are all going on to exciting futures and new opportunities, moving on to the proverbial bigger and better things. But with that in mind, remember that the only reason we're prepared to move on is because of the place we came from. Our families, our friends, our hometowns—these are the things that made us who we are today." His voice softens. "These are the things we can never forget."

"So let's take a moment, right now, and appreciate the people who made you who you are today. The people who are your home." He grips the sides of the podium. "The people who have *painted* on the canvas of your life."

A loud whistle comes from somewhere in the crowd at this, piercing and solitary and familiar. *Ned.* Of course he came. And of course he whistled at an inappropriate time.

"So if I leave you with any one profound thought, let it be this: No matter where you go, never forget where you came from."

He looks up, and for one split second I swear he's staring straight at me.

"Never forget your home."

There is a long pause, and then he smiles and nods. "Thank you."

Loud applause fills the stadium, and somewhere up front a group of football players starts chanting, "Mitchell! Mitchell! Mitchell!"

As Principal Jeffers takes the microphone again, urging everyone to settle down, I let out a long, slow breath. Leah nudges me, concern in her eyes, and I find her hand and squeeze it. *I'm okay.*

The next few speeches fly by, and before I know it, roll is being called. All the speakers and administrators gather onstage as the A's start lining up.

Abel. Adorno. Aggy. Alvarez. Each one crosses the stage, shaking hands with the long line. *This is going to take forever.*

And then the next thought comes tumbling on the heels of the first: Oh, god. I'm about to shake Mitchell's hand.

CHAPTER FORTY
MITCHELL

I pulled off my speech okay, which was my second biggest task of the day. Now comes the first biggest: facing Josie for the first time since we ended things.

And not just facing her. Shaking her hand in front of a stadium of thousands and trying to act like a normal person about it. Shaking her hand, not hugging her or kissing her or asking her what went wrong or begging for her back or telling her that I'm leaving tomorrow.

Just shaking her hand.

Hundreds of students go by before her, but it all passes in a blur—hundreds of handshakes, a couple of jocks slapping my back, a few girls I know reaching out and giving me a quick hug, Cord hugging me so tight that he practically strangles me. It must take forever, but it feels like a minute passes. Maybe even less.

And then, all of a sudden, she's here. Her hair is out of its usual braid and tumbling around her shoulders, and she must be wearing heels because she comes up to my chin instead of just my chest. Her eyes meet mine, she bites her lip, and she looks so beautiful and lovely, and all I want to do is kiss her.

But I've been rejected by Josie enough the past few days;

I'm not sure risking another rejection is a good idea, especially not so publicly. And besides, we only have a few seconds. So I settle for a handshake. But when her small hand is clasped in mine, I can't help it; I hold on a beat longer than necessary and slowly, deliberately, rub my thumb over her palm. And the way her eyes widen, the way a small smile tugs at her mouth, the way she blushes? It's better than any kiss. And it gives me a tiny, tiny glimmer of hope.

The rest of the ceremony passes in a blur. The line of students finally ends, and the whole class begins the procession out. I'm one of the first to leave. As I walk past the stadium seats, I hear a particularly loud wolf whistle. A bunch of screams. A few familiar voices. I look up, and there they are—Myra, Ned, Bernie, the MacPhersons, my mom and dad, Josie's family and a bunch of other Paintbrush people—whooping and whistling and clapping and cheering and making a hugely embarrassing scene in general. They're the loudest people in the stadium. They stick out like a sore thumb. They're obnoxious and crazy and out of their minds.

And for once, I don't mind at all.

CHAPTER FORTY-ONE
JOSIE

Paintbrush looks amazing. All the tables have been dragged outside and covered in lacy tablecloths and are now sagging under the weight of tons of food. There is icy lemonade and sweet tea served with lemons in mason jars, bouquets of daffodils everywhere, and of course, a bonfire roaring off to the side. Ned and Bernie love any excuse to light things on fire.

The best part is the lights—delicate strands that blink like fireflies wrapped around every tree trunk and branch on the property. There are even strands of lights strung from roof to roof, crisscrossing all over and creating a glowing canopy that illuminates the yard under the dark night sky. It looks perfect, like from a movie or a magazine or a fairytale. It's beautiful.

And it's all for us. For Mitchell and me. The last time someone graduated from high school at Paintbrush was five years ago, or maybe even six, when the Willson twins lived here. But they were homeschooled by their parents and had only been members for two years. I was in middle school, but I remember that party, and it was nothing like this. Everyone just ate some cake in the Sanctuary. But Mitchell and me, we're the originals. The first kids at Paintbrush. So tonight is special.

Leah touches my arm. "Hey. I have to get going."

"Already?"

"I know. But my mom baked me a strawberry cake, and if I'm not there when she cuts it, my brothers will devour it all within seconds." Her eyes gleam. "And you know how I feel about strawberry cake."

"You'd kill your own family for some strawberry cake."

"Exactly. And I don't think murder is an appropriate way to celebrate my graduation." She peers around at the crowd. "No Mitchell?"

I wave my hand. "He's around. But I'll be fine."

Leah grabs my hand and squeezes. "Promise?"

I squeeze back. "Promise."

I've already decided that trying to avoid Mitchell tonight would really just be a waste of time. It's our party. People will notice if we're weird, and then things will be awkward. Besides, something about the way he smiled at me at graduation, the way he touched my hand . . . It gave me hope somehow. Maybe he's decided to stay this summer. Maybe the things I said to him were wrong.

"Hey, guess what?" She drops my hand, voice eager.

"What?" I'm wary. Leah's guessing games can be dangerous.

"Myra just hired the first ever agricultural intern for Paintbrush."

"Agricultural intern?" I squint at her. "How do you know?"

"Because it's me." She curtsies.

I double over in laughter, and she shoves me.

"I know, I know. Picturing me up here farming is

ridiculous." She grins. "And Myra's said she's paying me in fresh produce and warm hugs. Whatever that means."

"It means exactly what you think it means." I recover myself and throw an arm around Leah. "I can't wait to witness this."

"Hey, when I apply to those fancy New York schools in a couple years, they'll see I'm well-rounded."

"Get ready to get dirty, Leah."

She glances down at her pristine white dress and sighs. "I'll try."

By nine, lots of people are already tipsy. Even though the party's been going on for less than two hours. There's a big semi-circle of chairs on the lawn, and for the past half hour people have been toasting to Mitchell and me. The toasts have ranged from cute, like Maddie brandishing a champagne glass full of sweet tea; to very long and sappy, like Myra tearing up as she described each year of our life in detail; to ridiculous, like Ned, ranting about his own high school years; to stern, like Bernie telling us to "not screw it all up." After everyone settled down, Myra gave us each these huge homemade scrapbooks full of embarrassing baby pictures, awkward middle school pictures, and every goofy picture in between. But overall, it's been fun.

My mom has been watching happily the whole time. She's more chatty and cheerful than I've seen her in forever. It makes me happy to know that I've made her happy. Watching her smile makes me smile.

The toast-making crowd breaks up, and I make my way over to her. But I've only taken a few steps when she's intercepted by Carrie. I stop and watch, hidden by the crowd milling around.

Mitchell's mom has tears streaming down her face as she ducks in close to my mom. They whisper together before my mom pulls Carrie in for a hug. They wrap their arms around each other, and Carrie's shoulders are shaking. It's kind of heartbreaking.

I turn around and immediately make eye contact with Mitchell. I step back, startled, as he makes his way toward me. I don't know what to expect. But as he gets closer, the corners of his mouth tug up into a smile, and his face relaxes. Relief washes over me in a wave.

But then he glances past me, focusing on something behind me, and his jaw tenses and his smile falls. I know what he's looking at and I wince, scanning his face. I can't tell if he's sad or mad or just surprised. But before I can make up my mind, he spins on his heel and walks off in the other direction.

I end up talking to Wendy and Eric and playing with baby Lucy, so I lose track of Mitchell for a while. It isn't until I hear a loud clanging that I look up to see Myra banging her fork against an empty mason jar, Mitchell standing sheepishly beside her. Mitchell's dad is there too, his hand placed proudly on Mitchell's shoulder. For some reason I can't quite place, I get a sharp, sinking feeling.

"Attention! Attention!" Myra screeches.

Beside her, Mitchell winces.

The buzz dies down, if only a little bit. Lucy coos happily in my lap, her tiny hands grasping at my hair. She seems determined to stuff some of it in her mouth.

"Our graduate has an announcement to make," Myra continues. "He didn't want to make a big fuss. But I said what are graduation parties good for, if not for making a big fuss?"

She nudges Mitchell, who looks like he's trying very hard not to roll his eyes.

He steps forward and runs a hand through his hair. Even from way back here, I can see that his face is red. "So . . . yeah. Turns out that I got a job for the summer."

My back stiffens.

Myra nudges him again. This time he really does roll his eyes. But he also smiles.

"Okay, okay. I got a job at Canyonlands National Park. With their youth service corps." He clears his throat. "And I leave tomorrow."

His dad beams with pride as he throws his arm around Mitchell's shoulder. Someone starts applauding, and then everyone follows suit. The crowd breaks up, people moving to shake Mitchell's hand and clap him on the back, and the hum and buzz of the party starts up again.

I stay where I am and stare at Mitchell through the crowd. I don't realize Lucy is squirming on my lap, kicking her little feet unhappily, until she lets out a wail.

"Sorry." I'm not really sure who I'm talking to. I pass Lucy off to Eric.

"Good for him!" Wendy exclaims.

She bounds off to congratulate him, and Eric moves toward the food table with Lucy. And I'm left sitting in the grass, stunned.

I shouldn't be stunned. I should have known this was coming. I *did* know this was coming. But I guess it didn't hit me until right now. Mitchell—the Mitchell I grew up with, the Mitchell who was my first playmate, my first friend, my first classmate, my first kiss, my first everything, my Mitchell—is leaving. And I'm staying here.

Adrenaline floods my veins, and I inexplicably get the urge to run, to sprint, away from the party and this place. I stand, head pounding, just in time to see Carrie striding to her cabin, head down, shoulders slumped. For the first time in this whole debacle, I feel really sorry for her. I know what she's going through. She's getting left behind too.

I smooth my dress. Suddenly I don't feel very pretty in my red dress, and I don't feel like this party is a fairytale. I just feel lost. I start to make my way toward the food table but stop. I'm not hungry. I scan the crowd for Libby and Mae, but they're sitting cross-legged on the grass, knees touching, laughing and talking. It's been a long time since I've seen Libby laughing like this. I don't want to interrupt.

Just when I've decided to sneak back to my cabin, I see him. Mitchell. He steps right in front of me, a few feet away. I meet his gaze and hold it. And then he jerks his head slightly toward the side and strides off into the night, slipping out into the dark, off into the field behind the Sanctuary.

I wait one minute and then follow him.

He's leaning against a tree, a big sprawling oak, his hair glinting in the moonlight. He's staring up at the sky, but when I come around the corner, he straightens up and shoves his hands in his pockets. He looks so tiny next to that giant oak, like he's five again, like he's the little boy I met the first day I moved into Paintbrush, the boy with skinned knees and dirt-streaked hands and a big, sloppy grin on his face. My Mitchell.

But then he steps toward me, and I see the broad slope of his shoulders, his perfectly messy hair, the way his button-down shirt skims the flat plane of his chest. He's still Mitchell, but he's different now. And I'm not so sure he's my Mitchell anymore.

I go to tuck my hands into my pocket but then realize I'm wearing a dress. I settle for crossing my arms.

"Congratulations." I mean it sincerely, but my voice comes out strangled.

He doesn't respond, doesn't say thank you. He just runs a hand through his hair. "I have something to tell you. Something to show you, actually."

"Okay," I say slowly.

"Something you might not like."

I hesitate. But one look at his face, sad and expectant all at once, and I give in. "Okay."

He pulls his phone out of his pocket, scrolls through something on the screen, squinting in the bright light. He finds what he's looking for and holds the phone out to me.

It's warm in my palm, and there's an email pulled up on

the screen.

Dear Josephine Sedgwick,

Congratulations! You have been accepted into the Youth Service Corps at Canyonlands National Park.

My heartbeat speeds up, until I can feel my pulse pounding in my head, in my fingertips. I skim the rest of the email. Then I hand the phone back to him.

Mitchell's face is wary.

"You applied for me?" My voice is even, emotionless. Probably because I don't know what I'm feeling.

He pockets the phone. "Yeah."

"Without asking me?"

"Yeah."

"Mitchell." I close my eyes. "Is it really so hard for you to accept that I want to be here, at Paintbrush? That my place is here?"

"I just wanted to give you an opportunity. That's all."

"I don't need an opportunity, Mitch—"

"What are you so scared of, Josie?" He steps closer to me, his jaw clenched.

"Me?" I step closer too. "What are *you* so scared of, Mitchell? You won't even try to talk to your mom."

He glares at me. "That's a totally different thing, and you know it."

"Maybe I'm scared of leaving, but you're scared of staying. You're scared to forgive her, for some stupid reason."

He doesn't say anything, so I continue. "I don't know if you think it'll make you weak or too attached or what. But I know you're scared, and I think it sucks."

"Well, I think it sucks that you broke up with me. I think that really, really sucks." He practically spits the words out.

"Please." My face heats up. "We weren't even really together."

He stares at me. "What are you talking about?"

I shrug. "I could tell. That you were with me because you needed *someone*. Not because you needed *me*."

"How could you think that?" He takes another step closer, and now we're just inches from each other. "Do you think I would go through the trouble of sending out two applications for every job I applied to if I didn't need *you*?" He looks up at the sky and runs his hands over his face. "God, Josie. After everything we've done together and been through together. Of course I need you. Of course I *want* you."

His words hit me hard, right in the chest, so much that I take a step backward. But he's there, stepping forward after me, filling the space between us. He reaches out toward my waist but seems to think better of it and lets his hand fall back to his side.

"You make my life better." His words are low and fast, almost a whisper. "And you're right. Maybe I am scared. But the thing that scares me the most is being without you."

I broke up with him because I was scared of getting hurt, because I was scared of being another stupid girl crying over a boy. But this knowledge—that he's scared of being hurt, too— it somehow makes things a whole lot less scary.

He's watching me, his eyes focused on my face, and I can't help it. I step into him, sliding my arms around his neck, and then his hands are wrapped around my waist and his face is buried in my hair, and he's hugging me so hard that I'm vaguely worried I might have bruises in the morning. And also vaguely aware that I don't care.

I slide my face up to his and push our foreheads together. His breathing is fast and shallow, and his eyes are squeezed shut, and his grip on my waist is like iron. And I'm realizing that in my effort to avoid getting hurt, I didn't even consider the fact that he might get hurt as well.

"Mitchell." Our lips are grazing, almost but not quite touching, and my voice is the faintest of whispers. "What if I do go?"

"Go where?" His eyes are heavy, his voice low.

"To Canyonlands. With you." I take a breath. "What will happen after that? With us?"

He shrugs under my arms. "You can't plan your whole life, Josie." His nose traces a circle on my cheekbone. "You just have to take a chance."

I have more questions, more thoughts whirling around in my head, more decisions to make. But I lean up on my tiptoes and kiss him, deep and purposefully and serious. I kiss him with everything in me, and I try not to think about how it feels like we're saying goodbye.

CHAPTER FORTY-TWO
MITCHELL

I get up early on purpose in order to avoid some kind of ridiculous goodbye scene. But of course, it doesn't work. As I lug my overstuffed duffel bag out of the house, I see a bleary-eyed Myra on the lawn by my truck, accompanied by Ned, Bernie, Wendy and Lucy, Layla and Mae and Libby—and my mom.

I look over my shoulder and eye my dad. "Seriously?"

"What?" He tries to give me an innocent shrug, palms facing toward the sky, and then stuffs his hands in his pockets. "I had to tell Myra. And then I guess word kind of spread."

At least it's too early for Julie's naked yoga.

I try to summon up that old annoyance, that frustration with how ridiculously nosy and over the top and inescapably involved everyone is at Paintbrush. But I can't. Walking toward this crowd of people, up at the crack of dawn to come and see me off, braving the early morning chill and sacrificing sleep to say goodbye . . . There's not a single twinge of annoyance in me. I'm just happy.

Except for the fact there's no Josie.

It was a long shot, getting her to come with me. I knew that. And yet . . . I had kind of hoped. At the very least, I had hoped for a goodbye. I had hoped that one final kiss wouldn't have to last me the whole summer. Or even worse, my whole life.

"Took you long enough to show up," Ned grumbles, but he's grinning.

Wendy smiles at me. "We wanted to make sure we didn't miss you."

Everyone is gazing at me, happy and expectant, and I feel a lump in my throat I didn't expect. "Thanks, guys."

While my dad tosses my bags into my truck, I go around and give hugs. One-armed squeezes with lots of back-slapping for Bernie and Ned—"man hugs" as they call them. A hug for Wendy, and a kiss on the forehead for baby Lucy. And then a long, long hug with Myra. She doesn't say anything—not *be safe* or *good luck* or even *may you find peace* or any other typical Myra saying. But the way she hugs me, the way she wipes her eyes when she thinks I'm not looking—it's enough.

I'm a little surprised when I reach Layla and Mae and Libby. "You guys didn't have to come out this early," I say.

"Well, we kind of did," says Mae.

I frown. "What?"

They are all three smiling; Layla looks quiet and reserved, like she has a secret, but Libby and Mae can't stop fidgeting and giggling.

"Um—" I start. But before I can get the words out, I look behind them and see Josie trudging across the lawn.

She has a huge backpack on, and she's struggling with the suitcase in her hand. I stare at her. It seems too good to be true.

"Is—?" I clear my throat. "Is she going on a trip?"

"You tell us," Mae says. She smirks, and I take a second to process her words.

And then I'm running.

I'm already halfway to Josie when she finally looks up. She stops in her tracks as I barrel toward her. But then a wide smile splits her face, and she drops her suitcase as I come to a screeching halt in front of her.

"Good morning." I am bouncing. I can't help it. I can't stand still.

"*Great* morning, actually." She grabs the handles of her enormous backpack, and she looks so adorable that I want to pick her up.

"Going somewhere?" I raise my eyebrows.

I expect a snappy retort of some kind. But instead, she just nods. "Yeah. I am."

"I have to warn you. There aren't any tomatoes to be grown out in the deserts of Utah."

I'm half joking, but I also need to be honest with her. I need her to be one hundred percent sure. I need her to be all in.

"I know." She shifts from foot to foot. "But there are cactuses."

"Cacti."

"Whatever. Either way, those spiny little guys are pretty cool." Her eyes sparkle. "And I think a summer like this will look pretty great on my college applications next year."

I can feel how goofy my smile is, but I can't help it. "So I know we were trying to keep this"—I gesture between us—"a secret from everyone at Paintbrush. But I think, given the circumstances—"

She leans forward and kisses me, her hands on either side of my face, and I kiss her right back. My heart is bursting, and

I kiss her with every ounce of energy and happiness I have in my body.

A loud wolf-whistle pierces the air, and we break apart.

Mae yells "Gross!" across the lawn.

Josie takes a step back and looks down, embarrassed. But I'm too happy to be embarrassed.

I grab her suitcase, and we make our way over to the crowd. Everyone is sporting grins and raised eyebrows, but no one looks all that surprised. They just look happy. Except for my mom, who looks partially overjoyed and partially like she's about to cry.

While Josie's making the rounds I just made, I walk over to my mom. She hugs her arms, bracing herself, like maybe I've come over here to yell at her, and that makes me feel terrible.

"I have a favor to ask of you," I say.

Her lip trembles, her eyes misty. "What do you need, honey?"

I scuff the toe of my shoe in the dirt and shove my hands deep into my pocket. "When I get back here, at the end of the summer, I have a lot of stuff that needs to be moved up to my college dorm."

She stares at me, eyes wide and confused.

"So," I continue. "It's gonna be a long car trip. At least thirteen hours on the road. It might even take two days."

Slowly, she nods.

"Would you mind driving with me up there?" I smile at her, for the first time in weeks, and a knot unravels in my chest. "I could really use your help."

Her eyes are shiny with tears. "Of course, Mitchell. Of course I'll help you."

"Thanks, Mom," I say. And then I reach out and pull her into a hug.

Both of us are teary by the time I let go. I give everyone one final squeeze, including my dad. And then I look at Josie.

"Well, here we go."

I slide into the driver's seat, and she slides into the passenger side. I twist the key, and with a loud screech, my truck miraculously starts. We wave to everyone, back out of the space, drive to the exit of the parking lot, and I put my blinker on to make the turn onto the road.

And then I stop.

"What?" Josie looks at me. Her feet are already perched up on the dashboard, her window already rolled all the way down, the sun shining right through windshield.

"You're sure you want to leave?" I ask.

"I'm not *leaving* leaving." She pauses. "Just . . . taking a break."

I consider this. "A break."

"Besides." She gestures around us—to the neat rows of cabins behind us, to the long open road and tall green pines ahead of us, to the mountains that stretch out to our left and right. "I don't think you can ever really leave this place."

We gaze out the windshield. She taps her fingers on the dashboard, my knee jiggles up and down, and beneath us, my truck hums, eager to push forward.

Finally, she reaches down and laces her warm hand through mine.

"Ready?" She smiles at me.

I take a deep breath. "Ready."

And we drive.

ACKNOWLEDGEMENTS

Writing my first book has been a weird and wonderful process, and I'm so grateful to all the people who helped me along the way. Thank you to:

Jim and Jessie Bucchin, the most spectacular parents in all the land. Having two people who believe wholeheartedly in everything I do, who support every decision I make no matter how crazy it may be, who are proud of every single one of my accomplishments, big and small—there are really no words to describe just how lucky I am. Just know that this book is a product of the insane amount of love and support you guys have given me. Thank you, thank you, thank you.

Dan and Liza, for being my best friends and my partners in crime. You are my original adventure buddies, and every new adventure I go on (both real and fictional) is inspired by you two.

Ann Amidon and Helen Bucchin, for always being my two biggest fans.

Jeff Csatari and Maryann Coca-Leffler, for their invaluable publishing advice.

My Carolina family, for letting me borrow your state. I know I'll always be the damn Yankee, but you guys made me fall in love with the mountains that inspired me to write this book.

My amazing editor, Krystal Wade, for Stephen King and for fearlessly slaying my adverbs. I'm so grateful for the time and energy you spent shaping my book. I thank you, and Josie and Mitchell thank you.

The entire team at Blaze Publishing, for giving Paintbrush a chance. My book would not be what it is without your hard work and dedication.

David C. Amidon, Jr., for teaching me everything about everything. I miss you.

And finally, Sean Anderson. To say you are patient with me would be the understatement of the century. I could write another entire novel about the ways in which you are amazing, but instead I'll just say: I couldn't do any of it without you.

ABOUT THE AUTHOR

Hannah Bucchin has spent her life falling in love with beautiful places, both real and fictional. She grew up in charming Bethlehem, PA, went to college in sunny Chapel Hill, NC, spent a summer studying wildlife in Tanzania, volunteered on organic farms across New Zealand, and hiked all over Acadia National Park in Maine. When not writing, reading, or adventuring, she likes to daydream about the dog she'll adopt someday, listen to music from the sixties, and exchange ridiculous texts with her parents and siblings. Paintbrush is her first novel.

THANK YOU FOR READING

Now that you've finished reading this book, we'd like to ask you to take a moment to leave a review. You never know how a few sentences might help other readers—and the author! And, as always, Blaze Publishing appreciates your time and support.

www.blazepub.com

CHECK OUT OTHER BOOKS FROM BLAZE

After a financial collapse devastates the United States, the new government imposes a tax on the nation's most valuable resource—the children.

Surrendered at age ten—after her parents could no longer afford her exorbitant fees—Vee Delancourt has spent six hard years at the Mills, alongside her twin, Oliver. With just a year to freedom, they do what they can to stay off the Master's radar. But when Vee discovers unspeakable things happening to the younger girls in service, she has no choice but to take a stand—a decision that lands her on the run and outside the fence for the first time since the System robbed her of her liberty.

Vee knows the Master will stop at nothing to prove he holds ultimate authority over the Surrendered. But when he makes a threat that goes beyond what even she considers possible, she accepts the aid of an unlikely group of allies. Problem is, with opposing factions gunning for the one thing that might save them all, Vee must find a way to turn oppression and desperation into hope and determination—or risk failing all the children and the brother she left behind.

Glori Rigby

because i love you

Sometimes, love is sacrifice.

Eight weeks after sixteen-year-old Andie Hamilton gives her virginity to her best friend, "the stick" says she's pregnant.

Her friends treat her like she's carrying the plague, her classmates torture and ridicule her, and the boy she thought loved her doesn't even care. Afraid to experience the next seven months alone, she turns to her ex-boyfriend, Neil Donaghue, a dark-haired, blue-eyed player. With him, she finds comfort and the support she desperately needs to make the hardest decision of her life: whether or not to keep the baby.

Then a tragic accident leads Andie to discover Neil's keeping a secret that could dramatically alter their lives, and she's forced to make a choice. But after hearing her son's heartbeat for the first time, she doesn't know how she'll ever be able to let go.

AUDREY GREY
SHADOW FALL

The asteroid hurtling toward the earth will kill billions.

The Emperor and his Gold Court will be safe in their space station, watching from the stars. The Silvers will be protected underground. But the Bronzes must fight it out at the Shadow Trials for the few remaining spots left on the space station.

When an enigmatic benefactor hands Maia Graystone a spot in the Trials, she won't just get a chance at salvation for her and her baby brother, Max: She gets to confront the mother who abandoned her in prison, the mad Emperor who murdered her father, and the Gold prince who once loved her. But it's the dark bastard prince she's partnered with that will make her question everything, including her own heart. With the asteroid racing closer every day, Maia must trust someone to survive. The question is who?

$16.00
1/18

CPSIA information can be obtained
at www.ICGtesting.com
Printed in the USA
LVOW11s0454110717
540912LV00001B/1/P